CANDY

AND

BETRAYAL

OF
CANDY
AND
BETRAYAL

A Wicked and Twisted Tale

J. L. JACKOLA

tivshe

Copyright © 2023 by J. L. Jackola

Library of Congress Control Number 2023918462

Paperback ISBN 978-1-960784-30-8
Hardback ISBN 978-1-960784-31-5
Electronic ISBN 978-1-960784-29-2

Distributed by Tivshe Publishing
Printed in the United States of America

Cover design by Dark Queen Designs
Map design by WorldWyrm

Visit www.jljackola.com

Also by J. L. Jackola

AUTHOR'S NOTE

Welcome to the world of witches and candy houses.

Of Candy and Betrayal is a spicy dark fairytale retelling of Hansel and Gretel that is intended for mature readers. It contains situations that may not be comfortable for some readers, including stepbrother romance, why choose, mmc with toxic tendencies, explicit sexual situations, language, violence, and death.

Hold on to your peppermints and lollipops because the breadcrumbs are about to drop, and this is one path you'll want to follow to the end!

J. L.

For those who find the bad boys exhilarating.

CHAPTER ONE

HUNTER

The woods were too dark, and I didn't like how the trees loomed above us like long, spindly monsters. My stepsister, Gemma, was a few steps behind me, her hand linked tightly in mine.

"Move, Gemma," I told her, jerking her along.

My father stopped and glanced around, so I paused my steps, causing Gemma to smack into my back. "What the hell, Gemma?" I scolded, my nerves on edge.

"Shut up, Hunter. You stopped without warning," she snapped back. She was trying to be brave, but I could hear the nervous quiver in her voice. She was only thirteen, after all. Six years my junior. Her mother had married my father, and now I was stuck with a stepsister. A whiny, annoying stepsister I wished hadn't been part of the arrangement. Although none of the arrangement had been anything I'd wanted. My mother had died five years before. An accident, my father had told me. But I knew better. The fall that had killed her hadn't been from her clumsy footing. Now, two wives later, my father had done it again.

Gemma's mother was dead, another victim of my father's deranged obsession. The girl only thought her mother was sick in bed and we were collecting herbs, but I knew the truth. I had seen her mother and what my father had done to her.

"Gemma, go that direction. Hunter and I will look this way," my father said, taking the first steps toward what I suspected would be my last straw.

"Out there?" she asked, her voice a mere whisper.

"Yes, now get going. Your mother is sick, and we need the herbs. This forest is the only one where they grow."

"But it's dark, and I can't see."

"Take Hunter's torch. Hunter can share mine."

He ripped the torch from my hand and shoved it into Gemma's. She looked at him, then at me. Her eyes pleaded, terror etched on her face. No one entered these woods at night. My father was smart. He'd taken us miles from town in the wagon to a forest where even the bravest didn't enter. The locals said it was the home of witches and fairy tale beasts that would shred your body to feast on your soul.

The look in Gemma's eyes killed me. I found her annoying, but I didn't want her to die out here.

"Father—"

He jerked my hand from hers and pushed her forward.

"Go, Gemma. Your mother needs you to be brave."

Her big brown eyes glanced at mine again, the torchlight leaving her strawberry hair so dark it almost looked black.

"Hunter?" she said my name with desperation.

I almost gave in, almost grabbed her hand and ran with her, but my father took my arm, pulling me in the other direction. She stood there, staring at us as we walked away, and I never took my eyes from her. Something about the terror in her eyes screamed at my conscience.

"Come on, son." My father hurried me along, the distance growing between us and Gemma.

Her bottom lip trembled before she turned away, the forest swallowing her up, the torchlight dimming with every step.

I stared until I could no longer see her, and the moment she disappeared from sight, I knew I couldn't do what he wanted. My father may have been a murderer, and I may have looked the other way because I'd always been too young to do anything, but I would not be an accomplice to Gemma's death. No matter how much she aggravated me.

"Let me go." I ripped my arm from his hold and backed away.

"Hunter, what are you doing?" My father's face was a haze of fury.

"I won't be a part of this anymore. She won't survive—"

"That's the point. We don't need that brat."

"Enough, Father. I'm going to find her." His eyes narrowed in a lethal glare. "You can't keep killing, and I won't stand by—" He punched me, knocking me to the ground. Blood spurted from the split in my lip.

"You're a weak, pathetic excuse for a son. You want to be the righteous one? Stand up for that slut's spawn? Go right ahead. But don't return, or I'll kill you, too, if you can ever find your way out of the forest."

He turned his back on me and stormed away. Fear seeped into every part of me as the light from his torch faded, leaving me with only a sliver of moonlight. My father had left me, throwing me away, just as he had Gemma. And I was his son. It proved that he thought nothing of anyone but himself. His need to kill, to hurt, was one he chose over all else. I'd seen it as we'd moved from town to town—the women he'd take, women who disappeared far too fast. I never knew what became of them. I'd only seen the bodies of the ones he'd married, like my mother, like Gemma's. But I'd experienced the sting of his belt, the beat of his fists when he couldn't take pleasure from another victim. I'd sheltered Gemma from it for the year she'd been with us, but it would have only been a matter of time before my protection failed.

I stared at the path he'd taken before bringing myself to my feet and turning in the direction Gemma had gone. The darkness of the forest was almost impenetrable, but I used the sliver of moonlight to guide my way, following the trail she left. On and on, I walked, not finding her until I heard weeping. My feet hit a puddle, my boot sinking to my calf, and I almost lost my balance.

"Gemma?" I whispered, unsure of what was out there with me—witches, goblins, or any other vile form of beast.

"Hunter?" She sounded so small and frightened.

I followed the sound of her voice and found her in the dark, curled at the foot of a tree.

"Where's your torch?" I asked, kneeling in front of her.

"I dropped it when I stepped into the water. It's gone." She wiped her nose on the sleeve of her cape.

"We'll use the moon. Come on." I offered her my hand. It hung in the air until she tentatively took it, and I brought her up. She leaned into me, clinging to me, her body shaking. "I'm sorry. My father's an asshole."

"I know. Thank you for coming back for me."

"Don't thank me yet. I have no idea how to get us out of here." And I didn't. I'd gotten turned around, not remembering the direction I'd taken, and I had no sense of which way led us from the forest.

"Then let's just walk. It must end at some point." She sounded so sure and brave that I didn't want to tell her it was called the Endless Forest for a reason. It had no end. At least none that anyone had ever recorded.

I took her hand, and we walked further. I chatted with her, trying to take her mind from the grave situation we were in until we stepped out into an open space, the full moon bright above us. Witches fed on the full moon, bleeding their victims dry. Or so I'd always heard.

"Look," Gemma said in a hush.

I followed her finger, seeing a small cottage across the way.

Something about the way it glittered in the moonlight gave me chills, and I pulled her closer to me.

"I don't think that's someplace we want to go."

"It's a house, a pretty house. How can it be bad?"

It can have a nasty witch who will eat you, I wanted to say but refrained, not wanting to frighten her.

"Well, well. Look what we have here."

I turned to the voice, finding a boy close to my age standing behind us.

"Hi!" Gemma said, unaware of the hairs that were standing on my neck.

"Hi, yourself. It's a little late for a stroll in the forest, isn't it?" he asked, moving closer.

I yanked Gemma back, not liking how his eyes glimmered with hunger when he looked at her. There wasn't anything I liked about him. His entire persona made me apprehensive. From his messy gray hair with black streaks to the mismatched eyes, one blue, one gray. Even down to the black button-down shirt he wore with bands of silver down the sleeves and the belt of leather that looked like it was from some kind of reptile skin. Its scaled texture had a luminescent glow to it that didn't sit right in my eyes.

"We're lost—"

"No, we're not," I blurted, cutting Gemma off. "My father is waiting for us on the other side of this open space."

"Is he really?" he said, looking back at where I'd gestured. "Strange, I didn't sense anyone there. I only sensed you."

He wore a cocky grin, as if to dare me to come up with another excuse for him to leave us alone.

"Hunter, we—"

"Gemma," I hissed.

"Gemma? What a pretty name."

He stepped closer to her, and I shoved her behind me.

"Ouch," she complained, pushing against my hand. I

wondered what had happened to the frightened girl I'd rescued only minutes before. She was becoming the annoying one I despised, and I was about to hand her over to the witch, or whatever he was, just to shut her up.

"We're just passing through," I tried again.

"Is that right?" His eyes flicked to the small cottage, and I glanced over, seeing that the door had cracked open. A hand emerged, wrinkled with long, pointed nails. Swallowing my fear, I backed Gemma up a few more steps. "My mother is preparing dinner, and she'd love to have company."

"Dinner?"

"For fuck's sake, Gemma. Will you shut up!" I was one second from tossing her into the guy's arms and running.

"That's not a very nice thing to say to your sister," he said, his voice dropping so that every word was like a snake slithering over my skin.

"She's not my sister," I grumbled.

He raised a brow, that grin turning sly.

"She's a bit young for you, isn't she?"

"She's my stepsister, and gross." Even the thought turned my stomach. She was still a child.

Gemma punched my back and tried to move, but I kept her in place. No matter how strong she thought she was, I was bigger and stronger.

"Shame. She'll be a pretty thing in a few more years." He sniffed the air. "A very pretty thing. Maybe I'll convince Mother to keep her for me."

My fist reacted before my brain did, and I punched him squarely, sending him to the ground. Turning quickly, I grabbed Gemma by the shoulders.

"Run, don't look back. Don't stop. Do not come back here. Run as fast as you can until you find your way out of this forest."

"Hunter—"

"Now, Gemma!"

I heard the boy moving behind me. My punch had left him dazed, but it was wearing off. The door to the cottage opened wider, and my heart pounded.

"Run," I snarled and shoved Gemma.

She stumbled away, confusion and hurt on her face.

"That was a risky move. A brave one, but a risky one," he said.

I couldn't do any more to protect her. What happened now was in her own hands. I turned back to the witch's son. His face was etched with anger, the grimace on his mouth accentuated by the blood dripping from his nose and running over his lips.

"I'm not the most level-headed guy," I said.

"Clearly." His eyes moved to the cottage again.

I heard the door open wider with a slow creak and dared to look over. Another boy, who looked the spitting image of this one but with no black streaks in his gray hair, stepped from the house.

"Fetch her and bring her back," the haggard voice of the witch said from within the darkness of the cottage.

"No!" I yelled, turning toward where I'd pushed Gemma away. She wasn't there. She'd run, just like I'd told her to. I lurched toward the cottage to stop the second boy who followed Gemma's path. Pain hammered me, spiraling through my body and latching onto every one of my muscles so that I collapsed in agony. From where I lay, I watched as a pair of weathered bare feet drew closer to me.

"He's a feisty one. Bring him. When your brother brings the girl back, we'll let this one watch as we feast on her skinny bones."

I couldn't talk, but my scream echoed through my head as the boy dragged me to the cottage.

"Can't we keep her? She's young, but she's pretty, and in a few years, she'll be the right age for me to have fun with her."

"And what will your brother say if I give you the girl?"

"He gets plenty of girls. This one can be mine."

I was screaming at them in my mind, but my words remained locked behind whatever spell the witch had put on me.

"I'll think on it. I don't like the idea of feeding her for all those years."

My body bumped roughly against the entrance to the cottage as he pulled me inside.

"I'll feed her," he answered excitedly. "She can be my pet. How old do you think she is?"

Too young! I screamed in my mind, praying the other boy didn't find her.

"Eh, maybe thirteen. She may already be of breeding age."

I struggled against the spell, trying to kick and move, but to no avail. The need to protect Gemma was stronger than I would have thought with as irritating as I found her to be. The idea of this boy touching her in any way sent a flush of red-hot heat through me. She may not have been my sister, but I would still protect her from this monster and his family.

He tossed me into a cage, locking the door as he squatted down to look at me. "Is she of breeding age?" he asked me. "Think of how much she'll scream if I steal her virginity now."

He continued to leer at me, and I could see his sick mind thinking about it. Gods, she was just a girl. What I would have given to bash his head into the cage bars until nothing was left but pulp.

"Oh, you can't talk, can you?" He waved his hand, and the spell released.

I lunged at the bars before he could react and grabbed his throat through them. His eyes widened, a hint of fear behind them.

"You fucking touch her, and I'll make your death insufferable."

His mother cackled. "Oh, but he's got fire, Ernan. He's going to be delicious."

I squeezed his neck tighter, enjoying how he was struggling to break away, his eyes bulging. My fingers began to ache, my control of them slipping as they peeled away from his skin on their own.

He broke away, landing on the floor and rubbing his neck. The penetrating stare he gave me was one that almost burned my skin.

The door to the cottage opened, and my eyes darted around the other boy as he strode inside. Gemma wasn't with him, and I held my breath, hoping he hadn't killed her.

"Where is she?" his brother snarled.

"I couldn't find her. I lost her trail."

Relief flooded me, and I released the breath I'd been holding. She'd gotten away. She'd listened to me, and now she was safe. My future, however, was not as hopeful.

"You what?" my captor roared, leaping from the ground and tackling his brother.

They fought, and I stared in disbelief as magic shot around the room as fast as their fists were moving.

"Enough!" the witch roared, pulling them apart with her power. "This one will be food enough for a week. We will cook him tomorrow. Tonight, we celebrate the full moon. The others are attending the moon ritual, and we're expected to be there."

"But the girl was mine," he whined.

"Now she belongs to the wolves. There will be other girls. There always are. Now get ready."

She walked over to the cage where I sat, still rubbing my hands to bring life back to my fingers. Her withered skin hung in long strips on her face, her beady black eyes barely visible amid the flesh. She had a few locks of gray hair left on her head, but even those hung precariously from her balding scalp. Her long fingers wrapped around the bars as she leaned closer to me.

"Did you know the semen of young men brings youth back in witches?" She squatted down as I stared slack-jawed at her, my stomach knotting at the thought. "It's been a long time since I've had one, and you look like you could bring me unspeakable pleasure. I plan to ride you until my beauty returns, which might take all night. Think dirty thoughts while I'm gone, so you're nice and hard for me."

I gagged, the thought revolting in so many ways.

"When I'm done with you, we feast."

She walked away as the bile filled my throat. The thought of even touching her was stomach churning, but to think of fucking her was horrifying. I wasn't innocent. I'd fooled around enough with the local girls to know what I was doing, but there was nothing I wanted to do to this witch. Nothing but burn her.

THE WITCH and her sons were gone most of the night. During that time, I tested every bar on the cage, every inch of the floor, every space above me, attempting to find a way to freedom. There was none. My future held a night of traumatizing sex with a moldy witch and death. I wasn't sure which I dreaded more, the sex or the dying. The dying sounded more enjoyable the longer I thought about it.

After hours of trying to escape, I flopped back, apologizing to my dick, which was about to get violated in unspeakable ways. Shuddering at the thought, I took solace that Gemma had escaped, although the comment about wolves had me worried. She was weak and stupid; I wasn't so sure she could survive a night in these woods.

The door to the cottage opened, and my heart thudded uncontrollably. I could have sworn my dick shriveled. But it wasn't the witch who entered; it was the second gray-haired boy, the one who had failed to find Gemma.

He hurried over to me, fiddling with the lock.

"My mother is dead. She was bragging about how she had you and would use you to reclaim her youth. Another witch killed her. Ernan doesn't know yet. He was off with a young witch when it happened. It won't be pretty when he finds out."

"Why are you telling me all this? So I can look forward to some other old crone fucking me?"

"No, the witches are fighting for rights to you. I snuck away, but they won't be far behind me once they decide who gets you."

"That's something to look forward to."

The lock opened, and I gaped at him.

"Go. Your sister is safe. I couldn't hurt her. She's too pretty, and I know what my brother would do to her."

"She's safe?" I wasn't sure if I could believe what he was telling me, and I had a nagging suspicion in the back of my mind that I shouldn't trust him.

"Yes, I led her to the edge of the forest. She's gone, and they won't find her. My brother is an ass, and he would have hurt her."

"Wait, you're good?" I asked, still unsure.

He scrunched his face. "Don't call me that. I'm not good. I'm a witch's son. I won't ever be good, but I won't kill children. My mother does that, and I'm glad she's dead. Now go before my brother returns or the witches find you. Don't return to this forest, or I'll let you die next time if I don't kill you myself."

He stood, his face set in a deep frown, his arms crossed over his chest. There was something about him that seemed different from his brother. I didn't know what it was, but it gave me a mistrustful feeling I couldn't shake. I wasn't about to stand and discuss it with him, however, so I ran, fleeing the cottage and never looking back. Putting the nightmare behind me, I ran the rest of the night until the pink of dawn shone in tiny slivers through the trees. I burst through the tree line, leaving the Endless Forest and its nightmares behind.

CHAPTER TWO

HUNTER

FIFTEEN YEARS LATER

The inn was busy, but I stayed in the corner in the shadows, an observer to the goings-on around me. It was amazing what you could find out when you listened. Like how the governor had a room where he stored his most precious items. A room that always had two guards posted on the other side of the door and was unreachable because it was on the highest level of his home. And it was a room I was planning to enter this very evening.

I tossed a few coins on the table just as the tavern wench approached me.

"That all you're planning to have this eve, sir?"

"That's it for now," I replied, returning her flirting eyes with a coy grin. "But I might be hungry again later tonight."

She raised a brow, her blue eyes playful. I'd enjoyed a quick romp with her the night before and was looking forward to another one. She'd made the most delightful squeals as I'd pounded her from behind.

"I look forward to that," she said, brushing past me to collect her coin. I looked back as she leaned over the table, remembering how I'd hiked her skirts up and picturing doing it over the table instead of the bed this time.

"Damn," I muttered, turning away and adjusting my hard-on with the subtle move of my hand.

I'd take her once more before I made my way from this town and on to the next. I was to meet my buyer on the following eve in Spindara, and I'd need to leave before dawn. I'd yet to meet him, receiving the instructions and a hefty deposit by messenger. Instructions that made it clear I needed to complete my job this eve and meet him the next day. There'd be just enough time for a bit of pleasure before I left. First, I needed to finish the job the buyer hired me for, and that involved a visit to the governor's.

Making my way out of the tavern, I drew my collar up, keeping my head low. The street was busy, lined with vendors selling their goods at the annual Festival of the Harvest. It was an event that made this the perfect night for what I needed to do. I slipped by a few people, my brisk steps pausing when a flash of strawberry hair caught my eye. It was darker than I remembered, but my hair had darkened with time so hers may have. Taking a chance, I detoured from my intended route and followed the long locks, the owner of whom I couldn't quite catch. It took a few minutes before I could grab her arm and turn her to me. My heart thumped with expectation, my hope brimming, then faltering as a middle-aged woman with green eyes scowled at me.

"How dare you!" her husband said as she snatched her arm back.

"I'm sorry. I meant no harm. You looked like...like someone I once knew. I thought perchance you were her."

"Well, you can see that she's not," he snapped.

I made a courteous bow and hastily disappeared into the

crowd before they could start a commotion. Making my way to an alley, I leaned against the stone wall. My heart was racing, just as it did each time. The incident had heightened my nerves, leaving my hands shaking. It was always like this when I thought I found her. Fifteen years had passed, yet I still looked for Gemma in every woman I saw, each one with strawberry hair or brown eyes. I should have given up hope of finding her, but I hadn't. I'd become obsessed, my search spreading through the world until there wasn't a corner of it I hadn't been.

Guilt and curiosity drove me. The guilt was ever present. Guilt that I'd left her in the woods alone, that I'd let my father take her there in the first place. I swiped my hand down my face. This was not the time for memories or guilt. I had a job to do, and I needed to focus on that job. Steeling myself, I moved from the alley and made my way to the governor's home. It was an ostentatious building, three stories high and towering over the rest of the town.

I hid in the shadows, moving to the back of the home then scaling the wall until I reached the small window of the room. There was a tiny way in and out that was just large enough for me to slide through. But it was on the slanted roof over the room, making it more difficult to access. Fortunately, this wasn't the first place I'd robbed. Although I preferred more exciting jobs like killing beasts or even people, stealing had its advantages. It was less messy, and no one got hurt. Don't get me wrong, I didn't kill without remorse, and the more violent jobs I took needed valid reasons behind the kill. My first had been the hardest, but after cutting my father down before he murdered his newest wife, the rest were easy.

I scaled my way to the window, using my tools to open it. There was just enough room to move through it, so I let my rope down, securing it before sliding down cautiously. The small stream of moonlight from the window was the only light, and that was sporadic as the evening was a cloudy one. It was enough to guide me to what I was looking for, however. In the center of the room sat the large opal stone—the seeing stone. The only one of its kind, once thought to have belonged to a witch. For something so precious, one would think the Governor would be more protective of it.

I stayed in the shadows of the room, making my way closer. As I closed in, I spotted movement across from me. A figure in white was slowly weaving in and out of the other treasures stored in the room, unaware of my presence. There was another thief in the room. I pulled my knife out as the figure drew closer to the stone, but I almost dropped it upon discovering that the thief was wearing a nightdress. A female?

I snuck closer, rounding behind her as she neared the stone. There was no way I was losing the stone to a female, especially one dressed the way she was. She didn't even look like a thief. I couldn't see any details of her, other than the nightdress and long locks that were strewn down her back. Their color was too hard to decipher. As she reached for the stone, I snuck up on her, drawing one hand over her mouth, the other bringing my knife to her throat.

"Scream and I slit your throat," I said.

She stilled, and I ran through my options. We were both in a room where we weren't supposed to be. If she screamed, she'd draw attention to herself. I was considering dropping my hand when she elbowed me, knocking the knife from my hand and lunging for it as it fell.

"Fuck," I muttered, lurching for it at the same time. She rolled to her back as she hit the ground, her hand reaching over her head for the knife, but not before I landed on top of her and pinned her hands.

"You're not taking my stone," she said.

I wanted to say something back, but even in the darkness, her beauty enthralled me. She was exquisite—her features soft, her full lips forming just the right pout, and thick eyelashes that framed dark eyes. Her body was naked below the nightdress, her curves pressing against mine and causing a reaction I didn't need in this situation.

She stared at me, her eyes growing wider in my silence. "Hunter?"

My name broke my trance, and I jerked back, losing my grip on her hands.

"It's really you, isn't it?" She moved to rise, but my senses returned, and I held her down, hovering over her to put some distance between our bodies. There was something familiar about her eyes, which were large and doe-like.

"How do you know my name?" I growled, worry nudging me. This woman knew me, yet no one in this town knew me, aside from the tavern wench I'd slept with and even she didn't know my name. I didn't have time for this; my window for taking the stone was dwindling fast. The guards did regular rounds once every hour to ensure the room was secure.

"Have you forgotten me? Is that why you never came for me? So quick to leave me in the forest?"

Her words hit me like the swift kick of a horse. "Gemma?" It couldn't be her, though. I'd searched everywhere for her. And this gorgeous woman couldn't be the annoying brat I remembered.

"Yes."

I continued to stare at her, unable to believe that this was the same girl. It had been fifteen years. I'd changed since then, no longer the young man I'd been the day I'd lost her in the woods. Why wouldn't she have changed? But change was an understatement. She had blossomed in a way that made my pants uncomfortable. Even in the dark, I could see it, my body reacting to her in ways it shouldn't now that I knew who she was.

"Are you going to continue to gawk at me or let me up?"

I'd rather have kissed her pouty lips, but that wasn't an appropriate response or thought, so I released her. Rising, I held my hand out to her, averting my eyes from the way the thin material of her nightdress clung to her breasts.

"What are you doing here? And in that?" I asked.

She pulled her long hair from her face, exposing her slender neck. "I'm getting something."

"Getting something? In the middle of the night, in that?"

"Yes. What are you doing here?"

"Don't redirect my question. Why are you in a nightdress in the Governor's home?"

Her stance changed, her shoulders lifting, further accentuating the swell of her breasts below the material. "I needed a way in." I scrunched my brows at her answer. "Don't give me that look. It's better than the way you got in here."

I laughed because there was no way it was easier. "You're fucking the Governor so you can steal..." I glanced around, my eyes falling to the stone. "...the seeing stone."

"Maybe."

I moved closer to her, irritated, for some illogical reason, that she was using her body to gain access to the stone.

"Don't judge my ways," she hissed. "You left me to fend for myself after you and your father dumped me in the Endless Forest."

"I didn't dump you. I went back for you and almost got eaten by a witch!"

"But you didn't and when you were free, you didn't even bother—"

There was a rattle at the door, both our heads swiveling to it.

"Dammit." I took her arm and dragged her to the rope. "Can you climb?"

"What?"

"Can you climb?"

"In this thing?" she asked, her eyes darting behind me toward the door.

I pulled my knife out and ripped the bottom of her nightdress, trying not to stare at the creamy skin below. The door opened and I could hear the guards talking. Thankfully, they were deep in debate and hadn't entered the room yet. "Climb, Gemma."

She didn't hesitate to hop on the rope, moving surprisingly fast. Most women didn't have the upper body strength, and I'd worried I'd have to put her on my back and climb. But she made it up with ease. I glanced back at the stone. The first guard had entered. My time was up, but there was no way I wasn't collecting my pay for this job.

"Halt!" the guards commanded, spying me.

I made my way up the rope and was through the window as they continued to yell for me to stop. They were only halfway up when I gained my footing on the roof and released the rope, sending them falling with a bone crunching thud.

"Ouch," Gemma said, and I turned to her, my anger rolling from me in waves.

"I just lost a lot of money because of you."

"Are you going to leave me again?" she asked, her smart-ass tone grating on my nerves.

"Shut up and follow me. Stay low, stick to the shadows."

"I know what I'm doing," she retorted. I couldn't help but notice how her brown eyes were a light amber in the moonlight.

"Sleeping with the Governor isn't the same as escaping in the night."

"Fuck you."

Gladly, I thought before I chastised myself for it. She was my stepsister, and she was still just as annoying as she'd been all those years ago. I grabbed her hand, hating how perfectly it fit in mine, and dragged her behind me.

She surprised me again, scaling her way down the wall and following me as I skirted the crowds. When enough distance lay between us and the Governor's home, I stole a cape from a group of drunk men and threw it at her. "Put this on. They'll be searching for the Governor's concubine in her nightdress."

"I wasn't a concubine."

"It sounded better than whore." I didn't know why I was so angry at the thought of the man touching her, or of her having sex with him. There was no reason I should have cared, but it bothered me.

She yanked my hand, pushing me against a wall and getting right in my face. Again, my body reacted to her closeness, the way her eyes shimmered in the darkness, and her strawberry blonde locks caught the sparkle of moonlight. The way her breath smelled like honeysuckle. She faltered for a moment, as if fighting the same reaction.

"I am not a whore. And even if I was, you're not my brother, so you have no right to judge anything I do. You left me that day. Left me to fend for myself and that's what I've done. No matter how demeaning or difficult, I've survived. But I am no whore."

I wanted to grasp her neck and pull her lips to mine, to feel her panting breaths against me. She was right. I wasn't her brother. And her words validated my body's response to her. As wrong as my mind was making it, there was nothing wrong with it.

"Then why were you sleeping with the Governor? I've seen the guy. He's not someone I'd imagine made you come often."

She pursed her lips, leaning into me, bringing her mouth to my ear. She was too close, and sparks pulsed through my body as she pressed against it. "It takes just the right man to make me come. Not many are up to breaking me," she whispered.

Gods, what were we both doing? Flirting while the Governor's guards chased us down, flirting when we were the only family we had left, even if we weren't really family. I couldn't help but play along. I was too far past the point of return. "I beg to differ. I'd imagine you break quite easily with the right man. And I'd imagine it's a beautiful sight."

Her breasts heaved against me as she took short, ragged breaths. "It's glorious," she breathed, "especially with the right man inside of me."

I balled my fists, fighting the urge to slam her against the wall that was pressing at my back and pound her into it until she was screaming my name.

"You've changed, Hunter." She moved from my ear, her cheek grazing mine deliberately slow. "Your ego has grown and so has your cock." Her lips were so close, all I had to do was turn my head the fraction of an inch and her mouth would be mine to claim. "Do you make the girls come, or do you just take what you want?"

With a laugh, I replied, "It depends on the girl."

"And what would you do to break a girl like me?"

The jump in my pants was painful, and I felt her smile against my face. My thoughts were dirty. The idea of sinking my tongue into her soaked pussy was one that had me throbbing. But this game was dangerous, and I suspected she knew what she was doing. That somehow she'd taken charge, testing just how far I would go. She had me so worked up that I'd go all the way at this point...if we weren't being hunted.

I grabbed her waist, turning us and thrusting her against the wall so hard she gasped. Excitement played in her eyes, enhancing her beauty. And now that we were under the full moon, I could see that she was stunning.

"I could break you easily, Gemma."

"How?" she breathed.

How? It was a question I didn't want to answer because I knew every way I could make her crumble. Every way I could elicit cries from her that would destroy me. That would make her body tremble so uncontrollably she would coax the release from my body. I needed to stop this. It wasn't right, no matter how I tried to convince myself it was. She was family.

"How, Hunter?"

I squeezed her waist, loving that her mouth fell open in response, her body pushing into mine. I could only imagine how wet she was and how she'd feel as I slid into her. Leaning closer to her so our bodies were flush, I worked my hands up her waist. Stopping just far enough to discern the weight of her firm tits, I restrained myself from doing what I really wanted to do to her.

I moved my face against hers, just like she'd done to mine, until my mouth was against her ear. "I'd suck those taut nipples as I sank my fingers into that wetness I know is soaking you right now." She inhaled sharply, the sound calling to my dick like she had a leash on it. "I'd torment your swollen clit while I continued to plunge my fingers into you, my tongue and teeth owning your nipples until you were so close you'd be begging to come. But I wouldn't let you. I'd remove my fingers, licking each one clean before I sank my tongue into your soaked pussy and tasted that sweet nectar until you were writhing in desperation and screaming my name. Only then would I let you come. And that would only be the first time. Because I'd want to have you clamping down on me as I'm thrusting into you. To have you fall apart around me so intensely that you milk every drop of cum from me as I fill you like I guarantee no one has ever filled you."

Her breaths were so short, her legs squeezing together so tight that I wondered if she'd come for me right there. I drew my face back, my thumbs brushing below her breasts, wishing I was under the material so I could caress her soft skin. Her face was flush, her pupils dilated, and every heave of her chest left me aching.

"Too bad we're family, Gemma. Because I guarantee you've never come for anyone the way you will for me."

Will...I'd said will as if it was inevitable. And maybe it was. We'd only just reunited. In fact, it couldn't have been more than an hour since we had and we were this turned on, this needy for each other. I knew it should have disturbed me, but it didn't. I forced my hands down her waist and not over her breasts like I'd wanted.

"We're not family," she rasped.

"But we are. We're the closest thing to family either of us has. Your mother is dead, killed by my father and my father is dead, killed by my hand. There's no one left but us."

I backed up and removed my hands. She looked as if she might fall, teetering a bit before she caught her balance.

"You good?" I asked, giving her a smirk.

She scowled, those lips pouting perfectly again so that I couldn't help but wonder how they'd feel wrapped around my dick. I wiped my hand down my face and turned from her.

"Are you good?" she asked. "That bulge in your pants looks mighty uncomfortable."

"Shut up and put the cape on."

"Think you can walk when you're that hard?"

She was playing with fire, and it annoyed me. "Think you can walk with your arousal dripping down your legs?"

I heard her huff as I scanned the crowd. Guards had filtered out and were searching the crowd. I'd need to get her to the inn fast. They might not recognize me, but they would know her. She'd been the Governor's guest, and she was the only one wearing a white nightdress. I reached back, meaning to take her hand, landing on her thigh instead. She inhaled sharply, but I didn't turn around, knowing if I did, I'd lose my resolve to keep this to dirty play. She stepped closer, my hand slipping. If I wasn't crouching, I'd have been fine, but the move sent my hand between her thighs, the clothing the only thing keeping my fingers from where they were itching to be. As it was, her arousal bled into the material, my fingers twitching at the touch.

"Is it dripping?" she asked with a humorous tone. She knew she was. Damn, she was going to be a handful. But then again, she always had been.

I pulled my hand away, rubbing the dampness over my finger-tips and longing to bring them to my mouth.

"Stay in the shadows. There are guards everywhere searching

for you. Keep the cape close to you and do not let your legs or your clothing show."

"Fine." I could hear the disappointment in her voice, and it killed me. She really thought I'd continue. It made me wonder how close she'd been to coming, a thought that did not help relieve the tightness in my pants.

Standing, I put my hand out more strategically this time and dragged her behind me. She was sharp, quick to step back when she was visible, keeping up with me and staying in the shadows with me. When I knew we had to cross the road to get to the inn, I stopped her, pulling her in next to me and wrapping an arm around her. "Don't do anything stupid. Pretend we're a couple attending the celebration."

"After that foreplay earlier, that might not be too far off," she mumbled as we walked.

"You're my stepsister, Gemma." I wasn't certain if I was trying to convince her or me with my words.

"Which means nothing, Hunter. You want me."

"Any man would want you. Apparently, any man has had you."

I heard the hiss through her teeth, her elbow meeting my ribcage with a sharp blow that made my teeth clench.

"Any man but you," she said.

"That's a shame because you really need to come, and it seems like you haven't had a good orgasm in years." What was I doing?

"And you don't want to give me one?"

I wanted to scream. How had we gotten back to this point? The only benefit was that we looked like a normal couple, going unnoticed as we reached the inn.

I stopped her, yanking her against me. "I can promise you, it wouldn't be just one." Letting her go, I walked into the inn, enjoying the small cry that slipped from her.

The tavern was busy, packed with people who had filtered in from the outdoor events. No one took notice of us. No one but the tavern wench who made her way to me as I headed toward where the rooms were.

Her eyes dropped when she noticed Gemma, who thankfully still had her hood drawn.

"You have company?" she asked, a hint of disappointment in her voice.

"Unexpected," I answered gruffly, giving her an apologetic look. I would have enjoyed taking her again to get Gemma from my mind, but I didn't think Gemma would like me going at it in front of her. The image of both women entered my mind, and I shook it away, even more disturbed by the way my pants tightened.

"I wouldn't mind joining you and your friend," she said, my dick springing forward so hard I nearly fell over.

"But his friend would," Gemma said, dropping her hood.

The tavern wench's face dropped. "I see." Damn, I'd gone from one guaranteed fuck to two and now to none. All because of Gemma. My annoyance with her was slowly returning.

"It's not what you think," I said, grabbing her arm. I probably should have gotten her name the night before, but I'd been too horny. And I wasn't sure why I felt bad that she appeared hurt about Gemma. She'd been a fling, and I was leaving town the next day. "She's my stepsister."

She looked between us, her brows creasing.

"I'm serious."

"He is," Gemma said. "If you two want to fuck, I can stay downstairs. There are a few cute drunken men in here who might be worth spreading my legs for."

A stab of jealousy raked through me.

"No, you won't, and neither will I." The tavern wench furrowed her brows at my words, and I felt the need to explain further. "She's running from her husband. That's why I came here, to find her. She slept with both his brothers and now he's trying to kill her for her adultery."

I could sense Gemma seething beside me, but I didn't look at her. "Do you have any clothes she could wear? I had to sneak her from the house in her nightclothes and that's not something a respectable woman like her should wear."

She looked at Gemma with pity. "Sure, I can fetch something. Should I bring it to your room?"

"Yes. And don't mention to anyone that she's here. I need to keep her hidden from him until I can leave with her in the morning."

She scurried off with a few glances back as I led Gemma to my room.

"You made me out to look like a whore!" Gemma yelled as soon as I closed the door.

"You cost me another good fuck. Besides, you were whoring yourself when I found you."

There was fire in her eyes, and I was glad I was across the room from her, or it may have burned me.

"You cost me the seeing stone," she said, her jaw taut with tension.

"The same stone you cost me." I noticed she'd advanced a few steps toward me, and I'd done the same.

"That was my stone. I worked hard to get into that room."

"Can you work hard on your back?" The squint of her eyes made them darken. I moved a step closer, intent on antagonizing her more. "I guess you can if you're spreading far enough."

"Why you—" She lunged for me, but I grabbed her fist, twisting her arm behind her back and bringing her body flush against mine before she could react.

"I what?" I was having a hard time not imagining her with those legs spread below me now that I had her body pressed to mine.

"You're an ass. Just like you were when we were young."

"Well, you're just as annoying and obnoxious as you were

when we were young." But I still wanted to kiss her, to take that pouting bottom lip between my teeth and bite it.

She drew a ragged breath, the fury fading from her eyes. We were too close again, that attraction increasing with every raise of our voices and every step closer we'd gotten. A knock at the door interrupted what would have been my mouth devouring hers and I pushed her away. Fuck, I was so hard it was awkward. Gemma was getting to me every minute I spent with her.

The tavern wench was at the door. Her big blue eyes took me in and only then did I realize my breathing was just as ragged as Gemma's was.

"I found a dress and some boots. I think they're the right size. Sometimes guests leave things when they depart."

I took the clothes, thanking her, but she lingered. Damn, she wanted more, and I should have seen it the prior night. I wasn't interested in more. Not with her, not with anyone.

"Are you sure..." she trailed off.

"She wants to know if you want to fuck her again, Hunt," Gemma teased, using the old nickname she'd given me when we were young. "You might as well alleviate that frustration somewhere."

I gave her a dirty look, noticing how flushed her cheeks were. My dick strained, but not in reaction to the tavern wench. It wanted Gemma.

"Thank you for the commentary," I retorted. Turning back to the girl, I said, "Thank you for the clothes. We'll be leaving in the morning, so why don't you find a nice boy from your town to entertain? The barkeep's son couldn't take his eyes off you last night." And he hadn't been happy when I'd gone to my room with a mug of ale in one hand and his girl in the other.

She blushed, then dropped her eyes before hurrying off.

"You're such a heartbreaker. Isn't she a little young for you?"

I closed the door and threw the clothes at Gemma. Crossing

my arms, I leaned against the door. "You're a little young for me, but that didn't stop you from flirting with me."

"I wasn't flirting with you." She lifted the dress, looking from it to me. "You expect me to wear this?"

"What's wrong with it?"

"Besides the fact that this woman's tits are about two sizes smaller than mine, it's a dress."

"You're wearing a dress now."

She picked up what remained of the bottom of her nightdress, revealing more skin on her thighs and setting my heart racing. "This is a nightdress, and an ugly matronly one at that."

"Didn't stop you from getting laid."

Glaring at me, she stormed over to my pack and began rummaging through it. I went to protest, but she took one of my tunics out and proceeded to lift her nightdress over her head as if I weren't there. My jaw dropped, my eyes perusing the body below. She hadn't been lying. She did have an ample chest, one I wouldn't mind suckling for the rest of the night. There wasn't a stitch on her body, and I couldn't keep my eyes from devouring each curve, each dip, each swell until my shirt blocked my view.

"You're sleeping on the floor," she said, throwing the dress on the floor and pulling back the blankets on the bed. I still couldn't take my eyes off her. The way she looked in my shirt was too sexy, and it had me flustered. She was tall, so the bottom came up to her mid-thigh and I no longer needed to imagine what was above those thighs. I could imagine nestling between them, however, and that was trouble.

"I'm not sleeping on the floor. This is my room. Why don't you go back and take the Governor's bed? I'm sure his wife would appreciate that."

"She would. In fact, she enjoyed it when I slept with them."

My jaw dropped again as she turned her back to me, pulling the covers to her chin. Gods, the man had them both? I should have taken her earlier offer to bring the tavern wench in with us.

Although, I wasn't quite sure I'd dole out equal pleasure. I wanted to touch her, and only her, no matter how tempting the tavern wench's tight body was. I'd had it and I was certain from what I'd just seen that Gemma was just as tight.

"You're not taking my bed. You're lucky I let you tag along. I could have left you there with the guards to explain why you were in that room." I lifted my shirt over my head, knowing I'd torment her with my bare chest against her back. And I was planning to get as close to her as I could, no matter how much it killed me. Crawling into the bed, I heard her inhale, followed by several strained breaths. I leaned over her. "How did you get in that room, anyway? I had the only alternate access."

She leaned into me, her hair soft against my chest, and I cursed my terrible choice of going shirtless.

"No, you didn't. The Governor has a secret entrance from his study. I followed him one day. He likes to go in and jerk off to one of the nude paintings he stores in there."

I grimaced at the thought. "He had you and his wife, yet you still had to give himself a hand job?"

"You're not counting the maids he takes. He has impressive stamina. I guess from your reaction you don't."

She peeked over at me, a devious smile on her face.

"My stamina is fine," I griped.

I snatched the blanket and laid on my back, hating how close she was. Hating that I wanted her, that I couldn't control my body or my thoughts around her, that not touching her right now was the hardest thing I'd done since the day I'd left her in the woods.

CHAPTER THREE

GEMMA

Hunter. My mind couldn't grasp that he was there. That he was alive. That he was so incredibly sexy. I'd almost leaped into his arms in excitement that he was alive, but his body on top of mine had me too stimulated to react normally.

I'd had a crush on him when we were younger. He was older, and I found his broodiness attractive. That and the mop of brown curls on his head and those heartbreaker green eyes. But now? Now he was irresistible. Muscles that rippled under his shirt, a jawline that could bring any girl to her knees, and that deep baritone that sent butterflies through my nether region. He'd had me so wet when we'd been outside, my back flush to the stone wall as he whispered his dirty words to me, things I could tell he wanted to do to me. The gigantic bulge that pressed on my pelvis was evidence of it. And I could tell it was formidable enough to bring me a climax like I hadn't had in ages...maybe ever.

I shuddered as he asked me questions, laying so close to me, his thick arms behind his head while he stared up at the ceiling. I peeked over at him, checking out the defined chest that was covered only partially by the blanket we shared. He'd pressed his chest against my back earlier, and I hadn't been able to resist leaning into it. The combined feel of it and the erection protruding from below his pants threatened to send me over the edge. He wanted me, but he was holding himself back. And maybe that was a good thing. We'd been brother and sister for a year, although we'd never really been close. He'd kept me at a distance, and I'd followed him around, keeping hidden so I could watch him. We'd been siblings, but not really. Blood didn't bond us, we were no relation, and there had never been love between us. Our parents had forced us to become a family, one his father had ripped apart within a brief time span.

I'd ventured back to the town of my youth, the one Hunter and his father had shown up in one day, likely on the run from another town where his father had enacted his crimes. I'd been intent on killing my stepfather, but he was already dead, murdered years before by a stranger who had fled in the middle of the night. Hunter. I hadn't known then, had thought Hunter was dead, thought there was no chance he was alive. Even though I'd searched for him in any man with a mop of brown waves on his head.

And now, here he was, lying next to me. The two of us sharing a bed, acting like the attraction that was penetrating the air in the same way I wanted him to penetrate me, didn't exist.

"So you've been traveling the realms all these years by your-self?" he asked, as if it was unbelievable that a female could do such a thing.

"I'm not some frail flower. Your father left me in the woods. I escaped a witch who I thought had eaten my stepbrother and survived the Endless Forest. I used that to my advantage, built myself a reputation—"

"For sleeping with men?" I could hear the humor in his voice, but I still turned and elbowed him.

He grabbed my arm, and my body instinctively rolled into his. The bottom of the shirt I was wearing lifted so that my bare leg rubbed against his pants, and I moved it unintentionally, the heat between my legs growing.

"I don't sleep around for money. Only when it's necessary for the job." I lifted myself and hovered over him, seeing his eye flick to the open neck of the shirt where I knew my breasts were hanging seductively. He'd already seen my body, but his eyes were still ravenous. I wanted him to kiss me, to pull me to him and raise me over his hardness as it filled me. I swallowed, shoving the thought away. He was wrestling with his attraction to me and the tie that bound us, that damned link between our parents that made us something. Even though it really was nothing, especially after all this time. It had fractured, scattering in pieces to the wind the day he'd turned his back on me in the Endless Forest. I jerked free of his hold and dropped to my back, trying to catch my breath without it being obvious that he had such an effect on me. "I have a reputation...and not that kind. I've made a name for myself, and people hire me for different jobs."

I hadn't been proud of the things I'd done when circumstance had first led me to do them, but I'd found a mentor who had helped me discover the strength in myself. Helped me become the woman I was today: strong, independent, fearless, and someone to be feared. He'd been a lover who had taught me the ways of my body, how to use it to my advantage, and how a man should please me. He'd been that for me until he wasn't, and we'd parted ways, his past and mine too convoluted for us to be anything more than lovers.

"And what kind of name have you made for yourself?" he asked, and I heard the doubt in his voice.

I peered over at him. "The Ginger mean anything to you?" I asked with a raise of a brow, knowing he'd recognize it. He was stealing the seeing stone, which meant he was just as embedded in the underbelly of society as I was.

He turned toward me, and I couldn't help staring at his muscular chest. "The Ginger? The notorious Ginger?"

I nodded with a proud smile. I'd worked hard for that nickname to become a title to fear.

"You're The Ginger?" His eyes were large, then his brow furrowed. "Do you have any idea how much I hate you? It's a competition to get the good jobs from you. And...wait, those jobs are—"

"Murder, beast wrangling, thieving."

His mouth opened and closed a few times before he said, "No, you can't be."

"Try me."

"Last cold season, there was a job in Moreling. The king wanted something from Iceliar. What was it?"

I looked up at the ceiling, remembering that job in that blasted northern region of Iceliar. "He wanted the ring of the beast. A damn gaudy thing if you ask me, and the troll who coveted it was a nasty wanker. It took me three days to figure out how to down him, and then I ended up drowning him when he chased me over a frozen river. Ugly fucker, too. The governor job was much more rewarding."

"You're The Ginger? Fuck me—"

"I would have—"

"Shut up, Gemma. Seriously, I had that job. It was mine, and then...dammit, you seduced the king, didn't you?"

I couldn't help but laugh. "That one was worth it. That man knows a thing or two about pleasing a woman."

"Oh, good gods. Do you ever keep your legs closed?"

"Keep it up, and they'll remain closed for you." I was pushing it, but I wanted him so badly my clit was aching.

He growled, a sound that caused my legs to tighten. "You cost me a year's worth of income for that stunt."

Forgetting about the dampness that was spreading between my legs, I thought about what he'd said. "Wait, you're *The* Hunter. Shit, you couldn't even come up with a clever name? You use your own name for an alias?"

"Like Ginger is a stretch with your hair."

"You didn't know who I was," I snapped.

"And you didn't know who I was."

He flopped on his back and remained quiet. All these years, I'd searched for him, and he'd been right with me almost every step of the way. The Ginger and The Hunter were rivals. We were at the top of our fields, the elite of the thieves and the monster slayers. If I didn't get the job, he did, and vice versa. And all this time, I'd never known.

"You were out there this entire time. Right under my nose," he muttered.

"Within steps of you each time," I returned in a hushed voice. I wasn't certain what else to say, so I rolled to my side. "Goodnight, Hunter."

He was quiet before I heard him say with a sigh, "Night, Gem."

THERE WAS a hand on my breast. It was large and warm, and I liked the way it felt as it encased me. There was a chest against my back, just as warm, but solid like a mountain that was there to stop the world from getting to me. Opening my eyes, I blinked at the soft stream of early dawn that was flooding through the window. Hunter. It was his hand that had somehow slid up my shirt and engulfed my breast. My nipple rose at the thought, and he hugged me tighter. His chest rose and fell with his breaths, and a distinctly large bulge formed against my ass. His hand flexed, squeezing my breast, and the heat between my legs rose, arousal seeping from me. He moved his hand down my body, and I bit back my moan, hearing the soft snores that were still coming from him. I didn't want to wake him. What he was doing to me in his dream felt too good. He squeezed my hip, his length bucking against me as his fingers grazed my thigh. They were dipping precariously close to where I knew once he went, he wasn't returning because I wouldn't let him.

Get up, Gemma.

Begrudgingly, I took his hand and moved it from me, careful not to wake him. Then I slowly climbed from the bed, wishing I could have stayed there longer. I looked down at him, watching as he rolled to his stomach. He stretched out, his enormous form filling the bed, his back strong and muscular. I wanted to reach my fingers down and touch every ridge, every groove that formed him.

Making my way across the small room, I snatched the dress from the floor and changed out of his shirt, taking a moment to sniff his scent that still clung to the material. The dress fit but the bust was snug, and if he'd thought I was a whore before, this dress didn't help the image. My tits were almost falling out it was so obscene.

"That's criminal," I heard him say. I looked up to see his green eyes evaluating me, lingering on my cleavage. He was sitting up, rubbing his eyes like a small boy might. But he was no boy. Every part of Hunter was a man.

"It is, isn't it? It'll have to do." I brushed my fingers through my hair and weaved it into a braid, tying it off with a small piece of fabric I'd taken from the hem of the dress. When I peered back up, he was still looking at me. His expression was one I couldn't read, but his eyes were full of wonder, as if he was seeing me for the first time. "Did I leave a strand out?" I asked, patting around on my head.

"No, you look...fine." I met his eyes, unable to hide my

surprise because I knew from his demeanor what he wanted to say. "You've really bloomed, Gemma."

The heat rose in my cheeks and I looked away, unsure of how to respond.

"I need to go," I said, blowing his comment off and moving to the door.

He was out of bed, his hand slamming the door closed before I could even take another breath.

"Where do you think you're going?"

My lips tightened. I didn't answer to anyone, especially a man. "I have a job to finish. Unless you're going to get the seeing stone for me?"

"Now why would I go and do a thing like that when I'm being paid to retrieve it?"

I crossed my arms, staring him down, trying to ignore how close he and his bare chest were to me.

"You're not leaving this room until I say we leave. There is a town full of guards who are hunting for you right now. You played your cards and used your feminine wiles to get into that room, but you let your guard down, and now they know you tried to steal the stone."

"I didn't let my guard down. You got in my way."

"You don't think they would have realized you were the thief once it went missing?"

"I came highly recommended to the governor and his wife. They would never have even thought that I had anything to do with it."

"Highly recommended? How does that work? Here's my favorite slut. Enjoy her for a while?"

I smacked him, the force stinging my ears as much as I knew it had stung his face.

He slammed me against the door, his arms caging me, his body pinning mine. If he was trying to deter me with these positions, it wasn't working. I would have stirred his ire all day if it meant he was touching me, no matter how rough the touches were.

"Smack me again, and I will hand you to the guards and watch them hang you," he snarled, his green eyes dark.

"No, you won't because then you wouldn't get a taste of me." I enjoyed playing with him, the way his expressions reflected his desires. How his grip tightened on my arms, his jaw clenching.

"Who says I wouldn't take that taste first?"

I couldn't stop the hitch in my breath and hated the curve of his lips at my reaction.

"Who hired you to steal the stone?" he asked, changing the subject too soon.

Shit, now that was something I didn't want to tell him. "It's confidential."

He raised a brow, not releasing his hold on me.

"I can't give the name of the buyer, Hunter. You should know that."

"I don't give a fuck. You're in an awful rush to get that stone. A smart thief would stay low and strike when things calm down, not walk right into the wolf's den."

"I need that stone."

His eyes squinted as he studied me. "Tell me who and why you're so desperate to put your neck on the line for it."

"The witch's son."

He reeled back, releasing my arms. "What?"

"I never stopped looking for you," I admitted. "It took me years, but I found my way back to the forest. I searched for it for years, but I'd run so far from it that its location alluded me. When I finally discovered it, I found the cabin run-down and empty. My only chance of finding out what happened to you was gone. I don't know how long I sat there and cried, cursing myself for not being brave enough to go back that night. Cursing you for letting your father send me into those woods in the first place."

OF CANDY AND BETRAYAL

"I didn't have a choice."

"No? You couldn't have stopped him? Couldn't have stood up to him?"

"No," he said through gritted teeth. "I went back for you, Gemma."

"After you sent me away, turning your back on me. Just like you did every day. Wanting nothing to do with me. You acted like I was a plague, and all I ever wanted was to be near you, to have some attention from you."

"I couldn't give you attention. I knew my father well enough to know your mother would end up like mine and the women in between them."

"And yet you did nothing? You let him kill my mother, then dump me in the woods?"

"I was just a boy, Gemma. He was my father. There was no disobeying him, the consequences of doing so..." He dropped his head, running his hand through his thick locks. "I kept him from you by keeping my distance. If I'd paid you any attention, he would have hurt you to hurt me. He was an abusive prick who left a path of dead women, including my mother and yours, in his wake. He deserved the death he received."

"You killed him." I saw it now, the things I'd been blind to in my youth and in the hurt I wallowed in when he would barely look at me.

"I did. I returned to the town a year after I escaped the witch and I gutted him. I watched him bleed out as he begged for mercy. He was my first kill, the slowest one, the most inhumane. And he deserved every second of pain inflicted upon him." He wiped a hand down his face as if shoving the memories aside. "Now tell me why you're working for the witch's son."

"Sorcerer."

"Sorcerer? We've got fancy terms for him now? And which son are you working for?"

"The kind one," I answered. "He found me that day and...and he took me in."

"Took you in? What does that mean? Are you telling me you stayed in the forest with him?"

"Yes. I was poor, homeless, living on the streets, and barely surviving. He offered me something I hadn't had since the day I lost everything."

He crossed his arms, his gaze penetrating, making me uncomfortable under the weight of his stare. "What did he offer?"

"Are you asking if I slept with him?"

"Yes," he sneered.

"I did." I stood taller, not caring what he thought. What I'd done had been necessary to survive, and it had worked in my favor. "I stayed with him for a year. He taught me to hunt, to fight, to steal—"

"To fuck?"

"That, too. I was still young. I didn't know better."

"You didn't know anything. How old were you when you wandered back into those woods?"

"Sixteen."

"Dammit." He wiped his face again, his frustration showing. "Too young. You gave yourself to the witch's son, who was clearly old enough to know better than to take your virginity." His voice raised with every word, his face etched in anger.

"My mother was married and pregnant by the time she was seventeen. What's so wrong with me doing the same thing?"

"Because it's you and him."

"Should it have been you?"

"Yes, dammit!"

My mouth went wide, my heart thudding so fast it was likely to burst from my chest. He turned and walked across the room, raking his hands through his hair.

"Have you been with him all these years?" There was pain in his voice, and I wasn't certain why.

"No, I left after a year. I was a different person, and I hated being caged in one place. I wanted to see more of the world, and he didn't want to leave the shelter of his home or the life he had among the others of his kind. We parted ways. I hadn't seen him since. Not until he sent a message that he needed my services. Hunter—"

"Did you sleep with him again?"

"Does it matter?"

"Maybe."

"No, I didn't. I told you it was over. Our interaction was strictly transactional." However, there had been a lot of flirting. My sorcerer had always been hard to resist.

"And what do you get in return?"

I hesitated, not sure of what he would think of my answer. "You."

He swiveled toward me. "Me?"

"He never told me what happened to you. Refused. I inferred you were dead and that he didn't want to tell me the details, too afraid to hurt me. When he contacted me, he offered to tell me everything once I brought him payment."

"That was all? You risked your life, slept with the governor and who the hell knows who else, to find out if I was dead or alive? No other reward?"

"No."

"And what happens if you don't give him the stone? Because you have your answer. I'm right here. Why bother going after the stone now?"

I swallowed, knowing he wouldn't like my answer or how confident I'd been in taking the job. My hands trembled because I'd made the ultimate deal, too proud to turn it down.

"Gemma. What does he get if you don't bring it to him?"

"Me," I murmured, hating the look of horror on his face.

"You?"

"Yes. He wants me back. He won't take me unwillingly unless I fail to bring him the stone. Then I'm his for the rest of my life."

He sat on the bed, and I could see the quiver of the muscles in his arms. "Why would you agree to something like that?"

"Because I needed to know what happened to you. No matter how pissed I was that you turned your back on me that night, you still returned to find me. Still fought to ensure I didn't get taken by them."

"I had to protect you. I'd let you down before, and I couldn't leave you out there alone."

I gave him a half smile. "Now, do you see why I need the stone?"

"Yes." Hunter rose and rummaged through the pack he'd had last night. Walking back to me, he took my hand and laid something in it.

"The stone," I said, the astonishment clear in my voice. "You had it all this time?"

He shrugged. "It's worth a lot of money to me. My buyer offered plenty for it. Enough to take the next season off. But you're worth more than any amount of money he could offer."

I fingered the stone, watching how the magic within it swirled around with the movement.

"Now, let's go pay this guy a visit and erase your debt." I cringed and looked back at him. His scowl returned. "What did you not tell me?"

"That this is only the first thing he needs."

"Are you shitting me?" He threw his arms up in the air before storming away.

"No, there are five items I need to retrieve. Each one in a different kingdom. Each one priceless."

"Fuck, Gemma. Never take a risk like this for me again."

"Don't tell me what to do. Because, trust me, I won't listen."

"Stubborn, that's what you are. It's what you've always been. All right, where's the next item?"

"Moreling."

"Moreling? That's all the way across the realms. Isn't there something we can get on the way there?"

"We?" I must have misheard him while he was pulling his shirt over his head.

"We. I'm not letting you go by yourself. Especially with stakes this high. There's no way I'm losing you to that sorcerer or whatever he's calling himself."

"Breck." I was still trying to comprehend his words. That he didn't want to lose me. He didn't have me, although the intent was there. The words he'd whispered to me echoed in my mind, my legs clenching in response.

"Breck? What kind of name is that?"

"It's short for Breckanius, some traditional witch name. Anyway, what do you mean there's no way you're losing me?"

His eyes met mine, a vulnerability in them I'd yet to see. "Now that I've found you, I'm not letting you go again, Gemma."

My inhale was loud, the pounding in my heart painful.

"We go together. Now, why do we have to hit Moreling first?"

I searched for words, my brain not connecting to my mouth. How did I respond when he'd just said that to me? How had he moved on as if he hadn't said it?

"Gemma?"

"I...I..."

His lips turned into a playful grin. "That's a first. You speechless."

I snapped my mouth shut. He walked over to me, and my back pressed further into the door. I didn't know how my body would react to him. Didn't know if I could hold myself back from falling apart for him just from the mischievous look that had come over his face, his eyes now hooded and dark. I couldn't control my breathing, which was rapid and uncomfortable. He dragged his thumb down my neck, letting it linger where my breasts sat swollen above the dress. I gasped at his touch, feeling completely out of control.

"Make no mistake. I may not be ready to touch you the way I want to, to watch you crumble at that touch." He lowered his mouth to my neck, the scruff on his face rubbing against my skin. His breath was warm, sending heat flaring through my body. "But no other man will touch what's mine."

My moan fell unexpectedly, and his length twitched as it pressed into me. He ran his hands down my body, gripping my waist so firmly that I arched into him.

"Save it for when I'm ready to break you, Gem. I'm not ready yet, and you're not soaked enough." Not soaked enough? He had me drenched. He removed his hands and walked away. Rolling his neck, he adjusted himself. "I want you begging for me to make you come. Until then, you're my stepsister and you're off limits."

Fuck. "Then that doesn't make me yours." My voice sounded so distant, shaky, and weak. He weakened me in ways no one ever had, not even Breck who thought he had. Hunter destroyed me with just his words. I couldn't fathom what it would be like when he finally took me.

He glanced over at me. "You're mine because I say you are. You're mine because your body tells me you are. You're mine because I make you so wet that I can smell your arousal."

I'd never had a man obliterate me the way this one did. Who shredded my confidence and owned me before I'd even given myself to him. And Hunter owned me. He'd owned me the minute our bodies collided in that room the night before.

He picked up his bag and pushed me aside. "Coming?" he asked with a sparkle in his eyes. "On second hand, you're not allowed to come until I say you can."

A weird squeak sound made its way from my throat. He left the room, shoving the cloak in my hands.

"Put that on. They won't be searching for me, but they will be looking for the sexy ginger who was fucking the governor."

Damn his teasing and his insults. "I never pegged you for the dominant type," I said, making my body move as I pulled the cloak over me and tucked my braid back.

"I'm usually not, but you seem to bring it out in me. I won't need to command you when I'm fucking you, though. You'll be too ready to give me everything I want."

I gritted my teeth, knowing he was right but hating that he was.

CHAPTER FOUR

HUNTER

T he steady pace of the horse lent a calm to my thoughts, which were hard to control. Gemma sat in the saddle in front of me. I only had my horse, she had none of her own, and even if she had, I wouldn't have risked returning to the governor's home to steal it. With every step the horse took, her body rubbed against mine, reminding me of how out of sorts she made me. I'd told her the truth before we left the inn. I wasn't certain what it was between us, but it was worth exploring. It was too strong to ignore. And there was no way I was letting another man touch her before I could have her, or even after. She brought out a side of me that wanted to command her and that wasn't the kind of man I was. I was aggressive in bed, demanding but commanding a woman wasn't something that had ever turned me on. Something about Gemma and that damned annoying side of her brought it out of me. Or maybe it was how out of control I felt around her, like my body was at her beck and call.

The ride had been a quiet one. We both had contemplating to

do. There was a past between us that defined us, that had defined our lives, and now had brought us together again. Forests, witches, and desertion. A strange combination. I still couldn't get over the idea of her sleeping with the witch's son, the same one who had freed me. I owed him my life, but I didn't want to owe him Gemma. And I certainly didn't want him or anyone touching her ever again.

I swiped my hand down my face, trying to figure out what was wrong with me. I went from woman to woman. Never had I kept a woman, never had one tempted me to settle down. If I had a woman more than once, it was for convenience, never anything more. There were a few I took when I visited towns where I'd stayed before, women I knew would satisfy me. But they were quick fucks. Nothing serious or anything I had to commit myself to. I took my pleasure and left.

Never had I wanted a woman as desperately as I wanted Gemma, and never had I wanted to own one, to keep her for myself.

"You're doing a lot of huffing back there," she said, tipping her head to look at me. Her brown eyes sparkled in the sunlight, looking more amber than brown.

"You annoy me that much. Even in the silence."

"That so? As hard as your dick is right now, I'm not sure I'd call that emotion annoyance."

Damn, she'd noticed. It was hard not to. The damned thing wouldn't go down. Every time I thought it would, another image of her naked body would form, or her body would sway so her ass rubbed against me.

She scooted back a little, tilting her body forward as she leaned over the horse's mane. Fuck, I wanted to grab her hips and take her like that, with her firm ass cheeks pounding against my pelvis as I impaled her.

"Stop that," I barked, my voice entirely too hoarse. Grabbing her hips, I yanked her back, an *oof* coming from her as her back hit my chest. "We will never make it through this trip if you continue to do that."

"Do what?" That voice held such a seductive tease that I almost laughed.

"Wiggle your ass into my dick."

"But it feels good. Imagine how good it would feel sinking into my ass."

My breath stuck in my lungs, the air no longer moving like it should. I clenched her waist so hard she moaned. Her head dropped to my shoulder, the honeysuckle scent I was coming to associate with her wafting from it. But I couldn't move. Thoughts of taking her like that berated my mind. I'd done a lot of things with women, but that was one I hadn't dared attempt.

I tried to speak, but the words wouldn't form. Turning my head into her hair, I prayed I could stay on the horse because as it stood, she'd stolen all the strength I had to remain in the saddle. My hard-on was straining against my pants so badly that it was agony.

"Have you tried it?" she mumbled.

I cleared my throat, finally able to grasp my ability to speak again. "Can't say that I have."

"Shame. I hear it's tight enough to break a man. I had two men one time, and I was so full I almost passed out when I came."

Fuck, fuck, fuck. She was trying to send me spiraling to the ground. "Two men?"

"I'm sure you've had two women before. You almost had two last night."

"Don't remind me," I grumbled, glad I'd gained function enough to loosen my grip on her waist. "And yes, I have occasionally had two women. But you had two men?"

"It's no different."

"No? It's..." I wasn't sure what the word was. The thought of seeing her in that much ecstasy was erotic, but sharing her with another man left me burning with envy.

"It's what? It's okay for a man to have two women, but if a woman has two men, then it's somehow shameful or degrading?"

"That's not what I said."

"No, but it's what you were thinking." Her tone was sharp, and I didn't like how it seemed to cut into me.

"That's not what I was thinking." I couldn't tell her what I was thinking. But damn if she didn't press me.

"Then what were you thinking?"

"I was thinking it's about time we take a break and let the horse rest. We've been riding all day and only stopped for brief breaks. The sun will be down soon, and we need to find shelter."

"That's not what you were thinking!"

"Dammit, Gemma, don't push me."

She lifted her head from my shoulder, and I watched as she maneuvered her body enticingly until she was facing me. She had her legs wrapped around my waist and her pussy pressed against my hard-on. I could detect the definition of it through my pants with the way her skirt had raised.

"What are you doing?" My voice squeaked like I was a teenager again.

"What were you thinking?"

I didn't know what I was thinking because all I could think about now was that dampness between her legs and the tits that were too ample to fit in her dress.

"Hunter." I heard the warning tone in her voice.

"Gemma," I returned, pulling the horse to a stop since I could no longer see beyond her body.

"Do you want to fuck me like this?" Shit, did I ever. Was it possible for her to ride me while I stayed seated on the horse? The image made me throb, and her grin turned dangerous.

"You're a brat, Gemma."

"Do you want to pull my braid and spank me as punishment?"

I wasn't sure how far my jaw dropped, the pain from the

lunge in my pants was too distracting. Good gods, she was going to destroy me when I finally gave in and fucked her. I knew no other woman would ever compare. Irritated that she'd somehow gained the upper hand, I took her by the waist and lifted her, determined to drop her from the horse. But her legs gripped my waist, and my move only shifted her further over my unhinged dick, which rebelled against the restraint of my pants. She wrapped her arms around my neck and pushed herself down enough that I lined up perfectly with her. If those damned pants had been off, I would have been thrusting into her, and this game would have ended.

With her legs doing the work, I reached up and pulled her braid, sending her chest bowing into me, her head jerking back. More of her arousal spread over my pants as her legs clenched tighter. I leaned into her neck, taking in the honeysuckle scent that still lingered even after the long day of riding.

"You're a tease, Gemma," I murmured against her neck. Her sigh was enough to throw me over the edge of what little control remained. I ran my other hand up her leg and over her bare ass, aching to throw my resolve to the wind and take her. My commitment to that resolve was questionable. I wasn't sure why I hadn't fucked her by now, other than the titillation of the game we were playing. "You'll know when I'm ready to fuck you, and when I do..." I dropped my face into her obscene cleavage and drew my tongue along her delectable skin, "when I do, you're going to scream my name until you have no voice left. Even then you'll continue to scream it until I've filled you so much, my cum is leaking out of you for days."

The shiver through her body was the most rewarding thing I'd ever experienced. It ran from one end of her in a slow wave through to the other. Releasing her braid, I shoved her face close to mine. "Now, get off the horse before I throw you off." I squeezed her ass, sliding my hand around and dipping a finger precariously close to her dampness, wanting more than anything to plunge my fingers into her. Her lips parted, her amber eyes so shadowed with lust that they sparkled with it.

"Why are you being so obstinate?" she breathed, her chest lifting seductively.

"Because you're being such a tease. You're too easy, Gemma."

"But you want me—"

I brought my hand to her mouth to stop her words. "I want you, but you're not desperate enough yet. When I'm ready to take you, you'll know it."

Her eyes narrowed, only a glimmer of that lust remaining. "You might lose your chance, Hunter. The hunt will end, and the fox will lose interest." She pressed her body down, her hips tipping so that even through my pants I could discern every detail of her.

The dance we were playing was a dangerous one, but I wasn't about to have her twist it on me. I moved my hand past her thigh and up to her waist, the lush skin firm under my grasp. Fire flickered in her eyes as her breaths came faster. "The fox won't lose interest, and I'll take her down when she's least expecting it, reminding her who owns her now." I moved as if to kiss her. Her lips parted, ready for me to devour her, but I took her bottom lip between my teeth, biting just hard enough for her to squirm before I released it. The move had been a mistake, the taste of her there to torment me, but her reaction had been worth it. "I will claim you, Gemma. But I won't be as easy to tame as those other men you've had."

She was so flustered that her legs loosened, and I took the opportunity to lift her and drop her off the horse. She fell to her ass with an unladylike thud. The fiery scowl she gave me was the perfect payback for the torment she'd given me. I patted my horse, thankful that he'd had the patience to stand still through our playtime.

Hopping down next to where she was pulling herself from the ground, I glanced around. The space where we'd stopped was open, something I didn't like. We'd made it as far as Carenth, and the predators in this region, although slow and cumbersome, were lethal. Trolls roamed the mountainsides, venomous fairies lingered in the forests, and those were the more innocent of the beasts.

"I hate Carenth," Gemma complained, stomping her booted foot down on an oddly shaped green spider.

"It's not my favorite realm, but it's the smallest of the realms, so we'll be through it soon enough." I was surveying a spot on the edge of a stand of trees, far enough away from the risk of fairies and hidden enough to remain unseen as long as we didn't light a fire.

"We have to come back here."

I swiveled my attention to her, the tension in my jaw twofold. "What could we possibly need from Carenth?"

Her sigh was one I would have invited any other time with the way it made my balls tighten, but this wasn't that time. "The last item Breck needs is deep in Laviak."

I laughed so hard I almost fell over.

"It's not funny!"

"No, that's hilarious. Did you hear his conditions before you agreed to this? The Laviak Pits? Home to the most notorious of witches? The one that makes your sorcerer's mother look like an angel? Not to mention the lava golems that roam those pits?"

She crossed her arms, pouting her lips. Between the swell of her tits under her arms and that delicious bottom lip, I nearly took her right there.

"I did. I told you I needed to know what happened to you." Her voice had dropped to a hush, and I stopped laughing, my mood softening.

"Why can't we get what's here first?" I grumbled. The idea of going into Laviak was one I didn't want hanging over my head the entire trip.

"There's an order for retrieving the items, and I must retrieve them in that order. Let's find shelter and I'll tell you all I know."

She trudged away, toward the same grove of trees I'd spotted. I remained there, watching her and realizing how quickly the mood had turned. I couldn't believe she'd gotten herself into such a mess just for information about me.

"Are you going to stand there all day watching my ass?" she yelled, not bothering to turn back.

"It's a marvelous sight. Too bad it's covered in all that material." I led my horse and caught up with her, wishing I could see her bare ass. I'd only seen her nude from the front, and I could tell she was just as sexy, no matter which direction she turned.

"Get your mind off my ass."

"You're the one who teased me with it."

She shook her head and continued to trudge forward, the mood from earlier lost. It was probably a blessing, but I missed the banter we'd had and desperately wanted it back.

AFTER DETERMINING the best spot to camp, I turned my attention to the horse. He needed rest and water, so I led him to the small stream that was only a few feet away. The stream fed from Iceliar, a realm of frozen waterways and glaciers. Carenth was a realm of two temperatures. The cold from where it bordered Iceliar warmed comfortably through the plains and forests until it hit Laviak, a brutal, desolate wasteland of fire and volcanic ash. Legend said the first of the beasts emerged from Laviak when the gods grew angry at the mortals. They formed the beasts to terrorize us—trolls, deadly faeries, witches, shapeshifters. The list went on.

They were all just stories to me. Blaming the terrain of Laviak for creatures we found threatening and the gods for creating them.

I urged the horse to drink while I removed his saddle and brushed him down. When he was comfortable, I turned back to where I'd left Gemma, thinking she had set up camp. She hadn't, and she was nowhere to be found.

"Dammit," I grumbled, scanning the woods before trudging in. I'd told her to stay put, but just like when we were young, she had a mind of her own. I prayed there were no faeries in this grove. The nasty things were the last thing I wanted to deal with. A rustling to my left caught my attention, and I pulled my knife, cautiously walking toward the noise. As I was about to push the leaves back, the cold steel of a blade touched my throat.

"You know," Gemma started, "as big and bad as your reputation makes you out to be, Hunter, you're easy prey."

She pushed the blade further, pressing her body into my back.

"Should I be worried that you have a knife, Gemma? Are you capable of handling something that sharp?"

Before she could reply, I snatched her hand away and flipped her around, pinning her to the tree behind her. "You were saying, Gemma?"

She snarled at me, a sight that made me want to bring that part of her out to play. "You like this position, don't you?" she teased. "Is this the only way you can get it up with a woman?"

My jaw ticked, and I pushed my body against hers, squeezing her wrist so the knife fell from her hand. "I think you know the answer to that question, since you've had me hard for you in many positions." I brought my hand to her neck, watching the heave of her chest as desire flashed in her eyes. My fingers caressed the skin below them before tightening.

I yanked her to me and in one quick move spun her around, my hand encasing her neck still, my other hand on her waist. "And I promise you, I'm extremely hard right now, thinking of slamming into your tight ass." The breath she took was ragged and sexy, my hand inadvertently tightening on her neck. "I'm still deciding the best way to take you. Whether it's sinking into that ass or keeping you bent over and pounding into you as you come around me. Or if I want to watch you ride me as I hold those firm tits. Or maybe I'll take you on your back and pound that pussy while I watch your tits sway below me, your legs spread so wide I hit you where no man has hit."

Her body was trembling now, her legs moving like she was trying not to come for me. I lowered my hand, daring to slide it between her legs. Her skirts blocked my access, but heat emanated from her.

"You forgot one," she said with a moan. Her hand reached back between us, encasing my uncomfortable erection, and I almost came with her touch. "You forgot my mouth, and how you'll tear the gags from me as you fuck it unapologetically."

Good gods, my dick jumped about two feet, her hand stroking it in reaction. I could barely move, the image had me too hard.

"Or maybe you want me to take the lead and just milk you for all your worth with my tongue and my mouth until you're coming down my throat."

Shit, pre-cum had to be soaking my pants by now. I dug my hand further into her, scooping through the material of her dress and loving how her hand released me as her back arched against me.

"Which way do you want to give it to me, little slut?" I was going full-on with her now. The game had moved to the next level, and I didn't know where it was heading. I brushed my fingers along her, wishing the material wasn't stopping me from feeling how wet she was.

She moaned, dropping her head against my shoulder. My hand remained snug around her throat. "I thought you weren't the dominating type," she breathed.

"I told you. I'm not, but you bring it out in me and the idea of fucking that pretty face of yours while you're gagging all over me is about to drive me mad."

"What kind of lover are you then, Hunter? You don't strike me as a soft lover. Do you like it hard?"

The jump in my pants made her buck forward. Her legs clenched down on my hand, her muscles shaking. She was so close to coming undone that it was tempting to just give her relief.

"You never answered my question, Gemma. Which way do you like it? You don't strike me as the submissive type."

"I'll be whatever you want me to be."

"Oh no, don't give me that." I removed my hand. Her complaint was loud and almost feral. "How do you like to be fucked?"

"It depends on the man."

"That doesn't answer my question. I want to know how you like it. What breaks you? What makes you fall apart so that you can't even breathe as your climax shatters you?"

"You."

Her answer clawed through me like a rabid beast and tore at my desire, screaming for me to take her and give us both relief. I stood there, unable to pair my words into a comprehendible sentence. Our breaths were loud, our bodies rocking back and forth with the force of them. I needed her, but I resisted. Some part of me, some foolish part of me, believed this was dangerous. That the two of us should remain as stepsiblings, not crossing that forbidden line that our parents had formed when they'd married.

"Take me, Hunter, please. I want you to shatter me. I want you to be the one who wrecks me so badly, who destroys me so that no one will ever be good enough for me again. I want to be yours."

She was begging, and it was killing me. Against all rational reasoning, I pushed her away, watching as she stumbled, and then turned her wounded eyes to me.

"We can't."

"Are you shitting me? You just felt me up—"

"I didn't feel you up. Now, why did you leave my sight when I told you to stay nearby?"

She opened and closed her mouth, her ire clear in the dark shade of brown her eyes had turned. "You're a fool, Hunter. Clinging to some stupid idea that you can't touch me because you were my stepbrother years ago. Flirting and saying those things, breaking me with your words, then rejecting me over and over."

I wiped my hand down my face and turned my back on her, walking over to where I wanted to set up camp. She was right. I had no explanation. No reason not to take her. Or maybe I did. Our former relationship was an excuse, one I'd invalidated knowing it held no merit. The attraction I had for her was like nothing I'd ever experienced, and I wanted her like I'd never wanted a woman. I knew that when I finally took her and elicited the cries I wanted to hear from her, she would be the one to ruin me. That I would never want another woman. I already felt that way, and I had barely touched her. If I let myself have her, I would risk everything. My career, my life as I knew it, my heart. I had never put a woman ahead of those things before and thinking I might for Gemma terrified me.

I started a small fire, ignoring her comments. She flung the fruit of her disappearance to my feet. "I got us dinner," she groused, stomping away.

"You call a rabbit and a scrawny fairy dinner?"

"I like fairy."

"You would. There's nothing to them. It's like picking the last meat from a bone."

"Fine, then you take the rabbit. I'll enjoy the fairy. Stupid little shit tried to bite me, so I broke its neck."

I glanced at her, surmising that her mood had calmed. As I prepared the catches for cooking, I watched her grab the bedroll from my stuff. She held it up with a question in her eyes. I shrugged. "I wasn't expecting guests."

"You can sleep on the ground. I get the bedroll."

"I don't think so. You'll have to deal with my erection poking you all night while we share the damned thing."

She eyed me, pursing her lips. I could see her thinking something through, and from the look on her face, it would not be to my advantage. "Sharing it is then," she replied before turning her back on me and proceeding to spread it out.

Whatever she had in mind didn't bode well for a full night's sleep. And I wasn't so sure if that acknowledgment pissed me off or excited me.

CHAPTER FIVE

GEMMA

The fairy meat ripped from the bone with some effort. I'd always found them to be chewy, but the taste was worth the effort. Hunter sat across from me, picking his rabbit clean. He stared into the small fire, avoiding my eyes until the last of his meal was gone. Tossing the bones into the fire, he finally glanced up. The flames danced in his green eyes and threw shadows on his face, emphasizing his muscular jaw.

"Finish up. We'll need to douse the fire soon before we attract a vinecti."

The chill that ran up my spine set my nerves on alert. Vinecti were beasts that roamed the prairies of Carenth at night. They were half troll, half basilisk, and they were terrifying. They slept until the height of the moon, then hunted. Although they were dumb and slow, once they caught their prey, there was no chance of surviving. They squeezed their victims to death, breaking every bone in their body before eating them. I shivered again, thinking of it.

"We have enough time for you to tell me what it is the witch's son has you collecting and why we need to do so in order. I want the truth, Gemma. If you want my help, tell me everything."

"I never asked for your help," I said, trying to cover the fact that I enjoyed his company, even if he was broody and hard to resist. His stubborn need to not fuck me was driving me insane. I'd told him the truth. I wanted him to break me so badly that I would never want another man again. I knew when he finally took me, he would take me to oblivion and there would be no going back. Just the thought had me clenching my legs.

He raised a brow, a crooked grin forming. "Well, you're stuck with me. I need to make sure nothing happens to that body of yours before I get to taste it. And with your history, I'm not risking another man getting the pleasure of enjoying that climax I've been building in you the past two days."

I glared at him, not wanting to admit that I wanted him to be the one who set that climax free. It was so ready for release that every nerve in my body was on edge.

"Now talk," he said, holding my gaze.

He wouldn't like what I had to say, but I'd been hasty when I'd made the deal with Breck. He had answers he'd always held from me, saying it was better if I didn't know. Now that I knew Hunter was alive, it made me question why he'd never told me. If maybe he'd been afraid of me finding out the truth and leaving him. It couldn't have been from jealousy. I'd had a crush on Hunter when we were young, but it was nothing like what had a hold of me now.

"Gemma," Hunter said. "We're growing short on time."

We were. The moon was almost at its peak. "Fine. I'll tell you what Breck told me, but it's all I know." Taking a deep breath, I began. "In the early days, after the gods spawned the creatures of the night in the pits of Laviak, the witches were many. They bred with the creatures to enhance their powers, and over time, they became something other than witches. All but those in Spindara, our homeland. Those witches remained pure to their origins, knowing they needed to do so to retain their power. They only bred with other witches, keeping their powers untainted by the blood of the beasts that roamed the rest of the world."

"That's nothing I didn't already know, Gem," he huffed. "Tell me what I want to know."

"I'm getting there. Stop being impatient," I replied with the roll of my eyes. "When the last of the witches faded from existence in the other realms, the gods ripped their magic from the beasts they had become and stored it in a stone." I pulled the seeing stone from the bag closest to me and brought it out. The magic within swirled in a smoky consistency. "The gods locked the magic of the witches in Simeril in the seeing stone. That of the witches in Moreling in the earth stone, Iceliar in the water stone, Tronekrin in the wind stone, and Laviak in the fire stone. All five make up the balance of the elements of our world—earth, water, wind, fire, and spiritual sight. Breck needs the stones before his brother, Ernan, gets them."

Hunter sat back, his eyes scrunched, arms crossed. "And what happens if his brother gets them?"

"He'll have the power to rule the world, destroy it, recreate it, whatever he wants to do. But Ernan is nothing like his brother. He's pure evil. He murdered their mother—"

"Not a bad thing," he argued before scrunching his forehead in thought. "But your witch's son told me another witch murdered their mother. Why would he tell me something different from what he told you?"

I could see the distrust that had already taken hold grow deeper, his eyes narrowing with each second he waited for my answer. An answer I didn't have. It did seem odd that Breck would have told him something different. "Fear maybe? When did he tell you that?"

"The night he freed me. The same night he let you go."

"He freed you?" I couldn't hide the reaction, my brows lifting in surprise. All the times I'd asked him what had happened to

Hunter, and he'd refused to tell me even though he'd always had the answer.

"Seems he was keeping more secrets from you than you suspected. I wonder what else he didn't tell you when he made this deal with you."

I didn't want to think what else there could be. I'd trusted Breck, I still did. "If he misled me, he had a reason. I trust him, Hunter."

He screwed up his eyes, his jaw going rigid before saying, "I don't. Now tell me why I shouldn't be thanking his brother for murdering their mother."

I remained silent for a second, wondering if his mistrust would hinder my quest. "In the circle of witches, it's the worst of crimes. He now makes his home in the center of Laviak, far from the other witches, and he wreaks havoc where he can. He is everything we fear in the witches, Hunter, and if he gets his hands on those stones, he will enslave the people and take the world for his own."

Hunter ran his hands through his hair, leaving the curls scattered, the look softening his features. "Shit, he's the terrifying witch of Laviak? That adds another layer of complexity. Why do you need to get the stones in order?"

"To find the wind stone, you need the earth stone. For the fire stone, you need the water stone. To take the seeing stone, you cannot have the other stones present."

"And what happens when Breck gets all five stones? He'll have the same power. Who's to say he won't use it?"

It was a valid question, but I knew Breck. I'd spent a year of my life with him, loving him, giving myself to him, letting him school me in the ways of the world and the ways of my body. I was the person I was now because of him. "He'll destroy them."

Hunter leaned forward. "Destroy something the gods made? If that story you told me is true, those stones are indestructible. They need to be left where they are."

"Ernan already hunts the stones."

"Then why isn't Breck getting them himself? If his brother can, then he can."

"Neither of them can. A witch can't hunt the stones. The power of the gods shields them from a witch's touch. Only once retrieved from their places of rest and brought together can a witch even begin to manipulate their power. Even if I took the seeing stone to Breck now, he could do no more than move it with his magic. He cannot touch it or access its power."

Hunter stood, his fists bunched, and I could see the tension rolling from him. "That's even more reason to leave them. This isn't right, Gemma. If the gods hid those stones from the witches, there's a reason. The gods never meant for anyone to find them or bring them together."

"Breck won't do anything bad with them."

"And you know this why? Because you fucked him? Because you lived with him?"

"Because I loved him once."

He stopped his walking and stared at me. A glimmer of pain sat in his eyes before he hardened them.

"I was young, Hunter. He was everything to me until I realized he wasn't. What I felt for him was..." How did I say it wasn't what I felt for Hunter? Even after only two days, the emotion burned in my chest, building to something it shouldn't be already. That puppy love I'd had when we were kids was still there, and it was blooming with every minute I spent with him. "It was adolescent love. I know that now, but at the time I didn't. He was my world. I had no one else. My mother was dead. I thought you were dead. Your father abandoned me. I had nothing, and I'd been on my own for so many years that it was nice to be with someone who cared for me and loved me."

His jaw tightened before he turned his back on me. He drew some water from the water bag and doused the fire, plunging us into darkness save for the beams of moonlight that were streaming from between the clouds.

"Get some sleep," he muttered before sitting down, his back against a log.

Anger seethed through me. He had no right to be upset with me for something that had happened over a decade ago. Something that had been a part of the foundation of who I'd become. For loving someone else when I hadn't had him in my life.

Rising, I stormed over to him, hiked my skirts, and straddled him.

"What the fuck, Gemma?" he complained, trying to push me away.

I squeezed my knees around his waist and tipped my body into his, loving how his length grew.

"You have no right to be mad at me for something I did in my past. You've slept with plenty of women, Hunter. Shit, you had that tavern wench the night before you found me, and you were planning to take her again that night."

"And you had the governor—"

"Don't turn this on me. You've fucked your way around this world, and you judge me?"

He grabbed my knees to push me back, but I lowered them, wrapping my legs around his waist. My clit rubbed enticingly against the bulge in his pants. I needed to stop tormenting myself like this. I wanted release so badly that I was about to hump him like a dog. His hands pushed my dress further up my legs until they sat just below my hips, his fingers dipping dangerously down.

"I never fell in love," he said, squeezing my flesh. My moan was one I couldn't keep from slipping free.

"I was a teenager. I didn't know what love was."

Sliding my hand up his chest, I longed for his shirt to be off so I could touch the definition below.

"But you loved him."

"I did. Hunter, why does it matter? You thought I was dead."

His hands left my skin, and a soft cry escaped me at the loss of his touch. My body was screaming for him, and he was going to turn me away again. I wanted to cry. I wanted to hit him, to scream at him. But he encircled my waist, his hands sliding upward until they were gliding over my chest. They stopped where my breasts swelled precariously above the neckline.

"I searched for you, Gemma." His voice was a mumble, deep and sexy. "Searched for you in every girl I saw and, as I grew older, in every woman I saw. I searched every realm looking for you. At first, it was guilt, but in time, I saw it was more than that. It always had been."

His fingers slid below the material, meeting my nipples, and I trembled at his touch.

"I pushed you away because I didn't want to admit that even though you annoyed me, I loved you. That any time another boy would look at you, I wanted to punch him. That I struggled with those thoughts because you were my stepsister, and it was wrong. You weren't old enough for me to think that way about you, and I was too many years older. So I kept you away, I teased you, and called you names, and kept you at a distance because none of it was right."

He removed his fingers, and I bit back my need to scream for more of his touch. He loved me, he always had, and that admission was worth more than any amount of gold. It sent butterflies colliding in my belly, and I didn't know what to say or how to act. Because I'd always loved him. He had been my first crush and that had never gone away, no matter how I felt about Breck. Nothing I'd had with him compared to how Hunter made me feel.

"So, you see," he said, his voice deepening as his fingers trailed my neck. "I couldn't let myself love anyone else until I knew with certainty that I had really lost you."

His thumb brushed my cheek, lingering on the corner of my lip. I turned toward it, sweeping my tongue across it, and watching his features change, the softness overtaken by lust. I thought he would give in when his hardness twitched against me, the sensation sending desire surging through me. He dragged his thumb along my bottom lip as his other hand tightened on my neck. A gush of arousal fled me, and I knew he'd noticed. His wicked smirk was all the evidence I needed.

"But then you tell me you gave your heart to someone else, Gemma. What am I supposed to do with that?"

"You deal with it."

His moves were so fast I didn't have time to react before I found myself below him, his body on mine. He slid my skirts up again, this time embedding his fingers into me. I arched into him, crying out at the sensation, my body alight with fire. He thrust them further, and I grabbed at the ground for something to hold on to as I pushed my pelvis forward.

"You're mine, Gemma. I won't tolerate sharing you with anyone. I want to kill him for holding your heart before I could. To watch him suffer for touching you before I could. I want to burn anyone who has ever touched you." He pulled his fingers from me, and I cried out again, but he stopped my cry as his fingers hit my sensitive clit, and I bucked against him.

"I want you to come for me, Gemma. And when you do, I want you to know I will be the last person you ever come for. The last person who brings you to ecstasy."

"Please, Hunter," I begged, needing him to bring me release. Every part of my body was tingling so badly I could barely stay still.

"I don't think you're begging enough. I need you to beg more. I need the memory of those other men, of that witch's son out of your mind and replaced with nothing but me and the way I make you fall apart."

"Please, I need you, Hunter. I've always needed you. I searched for you, I traded my life for you. I've always loved you, even when you pushed me away, even when you left me that

OF CANDY AND BETRAYAL

night. Even when you were screaming for me to run, and I did, hearing them drag you into that cottage while my feet continued to obey you. I loved you then, and I still love you."

His fingers stopped, my climax so close that it was agony. He removed them and sat up. My mind was a mess, trying to determine why the pleasure had stopped and why he hadn't taken me.

He brought his fingers to his nose and sniffed. My stomach clenched at the rapture on his face. Bringing them to his mouth, he slowly licked each one, his eyes closing as he moaned. When he was done, he leaned back over me, mumbling, "You taste exactly how I imagined you would." He rubbed his cheek against mine, the feel of his stubble sending sparks through my body. "Get some sleep, and no playing with yourself. You will wait until I'm ready to make you come."

He rose while I gawked at him. I tried to form the words to yell at him, but they wouldn't cooperate. I was too flabbergasted that he was walking away. He was such an ass. His pants were so tented it had to hurt, yet he'd denied me and himself again. The sensation of his fingers inside of me was still between my legs, and I crossed them, trying to keep it there.

"Uh, uh. None of that. You come when I tell you to come, not before."

I pulled myself to my elbows, scowling at him. "You're an asshole."

"But I'm an asshole you can't resist, pretty thing. Shit, you really do bring the aggressive, dominating side of me out." He rolled his neck and sat across from me. The moon was bright again, and I heard rustling far in the distance. "Go to sleep, Gem. This is not the place for your cries of pleasure. I don't need to fight a vinecti when I'm in the middle of fucking you."

I dropped my head to the ground with a groan, cursing the damned creatures of this world and wishing I could kill them all and have Hunter fuck me with their blood still dripping from my hands.

THREE DAYS PASSED. Three quiet days with Hunter barely saying a word to me. The sexy teasing we'd been doing stopped, and I wondered if he'd reached his limit. There was only so far we could go before he broke down and took me. He hadn't said another word about love or the emotions we'd confessed to each other. It was almost as if it hadn't happened.

When we reached the border of Moreling, we came upon a small town. I couldn't explain how happy this made me. The possibility of sleeping in a bed, of bathing and eating proper food, was almost unbelievable.

But Hunter passed through, not bothering to stop. The irritation that had been building since that night boiled over, and I squeezed my legs to stop the horse.

"What are you doing, Gemma?" Hunter's annoyance layered his tone.

"We are stopping in that town. I need some actual food, I need a bath, and I need something besides this horrible dress to wear."

His hand tightened where it sat on my stomach. "We keep riding until we reach the mountains where the witch's son told you the stone should be." He refused to call Breck by his name, his jealousy entirely too elevated for someone who was barely talking to me.

"What is your problem, Hunter?" I tried to turn around, but he kept me in place with his hand.

"Nothing but the annoying predicament you've gotten yourself into."

"I never said you had to go with me. I'm capable of doing this on my own."

"No, I'm not risking you spreading your legs for another man to gain another stone."

I hissed, tired of his unwarranted jealousy and possessiveness. "You don't own me, Hunter. You walked away the last time you had your chance, and you've made it clear since then that you don't want me." His fingers dug into my waist, and I bit back the moan that was on the cusp of escaping. "You've barely said a word to me since you shoved your fingers into me and tasted them."

I could feel his reaction, his length growing immediately and pressing into my back.

"Now, either take me back to that town and find us an inn where you can thoroughly fuck me or stop acting like I'm yours."

The shortened breaths that were coming from him were calling to me in a strange, undeniable way. He was still for far too long, and I worried about what was going through his mind. His hand moved below my skirts, the touch of his skin against mine sending currents charging through me like stallions on the run. He moved along my thigh and over my ass before dropping between my legs to tease along the dampness that had gathered. I let my head fall to his shoulder, knowing he was only teasing me again but not caring because I craved his touch now.

"I do own you, Gemma. And I want you so painfully that it's a constant ache burning through my body. But you gave your heart to another man, and you need to be punished."

"Fuck," I said through gritted teeth. "Get over it, Hunter. You've fucked your way through the realms, and I don't care."

"But you don't own me, Gem. I'm the one in control here, not you." He wasn't wrong. I'd lost control the moment his body touched mine in the governor's home. I'd never had control. My body was his to command. "And if I say you need to be punished for giving away what's mine, then I'll punish you the way I want to."

Giving away what was his. I should have balked at the words, but they clawed their way into me and grounded themselves. I wanted to be his. I wanted him to own me, to claim me, to make it so there was no other. "You've punished me enough. You've barely talked to me and haven't touched me." He pulled me further against him, tilting my pelvis, his fingers reaching through my folds and plunging into me. I arched my back, but he held me in place. He had pushed my body up so that I was resting on his lap more than on the saddle, giving him access to bury his fingers deep in me.

The horse shifted his stance, sending Hunter's fingers even further. "Please, Hunter. I need you."

"What do you need from me, Gem?" He swirled his thumb around my clit as his other hand climbed to my chest, encasing my breast.

"I need you to fuck me."

"None of that yet. I told you, I need you drenched when I finally take you. I'm just warming up. Now, what do you need from me, Gem?"

He thrust his fingers into me again, the fire in my body an inferno seeking release.

"I need you to make me come."

"Beg for it, pretty thing."

I groaned, his hand moving to my neck and gripping it. The move stimulated every part of me because, as fierce as I was, I loved the way he aggressively owned me.

"Please, Hunter. Make me come."

There was a low rumble from his chest before he guided his fingers back into me. His hold on my neck never released, and being so vulnerable to his power further stimulated my growing climax. His fingers were magic, filling me the way I wanted him to fill me, then sliding out to rub my clit. I was panting, gyrating against his hand as my release came crashing through me, shattering me into an oblivion I'd never reached. I trembled against him, pushing down on his fingers as the impact of my orgasm took hold of my entire body.

"That's it, Gem. Gods, you're so beautiful coming against my hand like this. I can't imagine what you'll look like coming when I'm buried to the hilt in you."

I could no longer hold back the cry that had been building, his words unleashing it. I continued to writhe on his hand until my body gave out, and I slumped against him. He released me, freeing his fingers, and I could hear him cleaning them, his groan feral as it rumbled through his chest.

"Fuck, you taste so good." The hoarseness of his voice sent my arousal climbing again, but he urged the horse forward. I still couldn't get over how well-trained this horse was.

"Do you get women off like this as a habit?" I said, hearing the breathiness of my words.

"Nope, that was a first. In fact, I've never let anyone ride him. They only get to ride me."

I glanced over at him, seeing his sexy smirk. It irritated me how possessive and jealous he was over my past, yet he flaunted his own.

"I think if you want to own me—"

"Oh, I do own you, pretty thing. I think what I just did to you proves that."

I growled, but he only laughed.

"That proves nothing except you're good with your fingers."

"Ha, I'm good with everything."

"We'll see. But if you want to prove it, I want no more talk of the women you've had. If I can't mention my past without you going off the rails, then you can't mention yours."

"Jealous, are we?"

"No, just irritated at how possessive you are."

He jerked me against him. "I'll be as possessive as I want. I'm not losing you again, Gemma. I will kill every man I must to ensure you remain mine."

His eyes were deadly, but they didn't stray from the road ahead. I wasn't certain how to take his threat. Part of me loved it, loving how he coveted me. The other part feared it. I didn't have time to dwell on it. He steered the horse off the road and through a small field until we passed a rock formation. On the other side, lay a pool of crystal blue water with steam rising from it.

Hunter hopped down from the horse and stretched. I could see how prominent his hard-on still was, and that stirring of need whispered through me again. Whispered...it was more like a bear roaring in my face. He eyed me with a devious grin.

"I do like the way your cheeks flush after you come, Gem."

The way he called me the nickname he'd used when we were kids had a completely different effect on me now than it did then. My knees almost buckled when he said it.

"This doesn't look like an inn with a soft bed to me, but I suppose it will do." It was clear he wouldn't do any more than he had to ease my need for him, so I moved closer to the water, marveling at the ice-blue color of it. The water from Iceliar was freezing, but when it moved through the ground and into the warmer climate of Moreling, it made for a wonderful hot bath. These springs were a luxury to travelers like us who needed a reprieve from our long journeys.

"Are you joining me?" I said, turning to him and reaching for the ties of my dress.

He moved quickly, reminding me of just why he was renowned in the circles in which we ran. There were many paid for hires in the kingdoms, but Hunter was as sought after as I was, and no one crossed him. He was lethal and efficient. And he took bids even I didn't touch. Murder for hire wasn't anything I delved into, but Hunter did, and the world knew it. Those hands that had brought me to ecstasy earlier had taken the life of many a man and beast, and the thought of it sent the embers of my desire burning through me.

Picking me up, he tossed me into the water, where I landed with a loud splash. I kept my scream locked inside of me and frowned at him.

"Get clean. I'll be back in a few hours. We need supplies, and the air is already growing colder. We'll need heavier clothes."

"Pants!" I yelled, hating this aggravating dress I'd been stuck wearing. "Something decent with pants now that you've ruined this monstrosity."

He mounted the horse and gave a chuckle as he urged the horse away. "I like the dress. It's easier to finger fuck you in, and when I'm ready to bend you over, it'll be easier to lift."

He rode away before I could respond, leaving me fuming and unable to determine if the surrounding steam was coming from me or the water.

CHAPTER SIX

HUNTER

I rode off, hearing Gemma's complaints as they followed me down the road. I hadn't intended to leave her there, but I needed to get away from her. Having her body clamp down around my fingers, seeing her chest rising with those enamoring heaves, and hearing her moans as she'd fallen apart had been almost too much to bear. As it was, my hard-on was screaming at me for not relieving it. She'd been glorious, and I wanted more. I still couldn't figure out why she brought out this commanding side of me. There had never been a time when I was weak regarding sex. I was more aggressive than my counterparts. But with Gemma, I needed to control her, to break her and have her crumble for me. I needed to have her beg, to hear her plead for me to give her more, and to watch her crack with my words. Smoothing my hand over my face, I ignored the musk that still lingered, the memory of her taste returning.

I wasn't sure if she hadn't broken me already. Hearing her say she'd given her body to the witch's son had driven ire through my blood. But hearing that she'd loved him, that he had held her heart before me, had sent a white-hot fire blazing through me. It shouldn't have. I knew it was irrational when we'd led separate lives for fifteen years. When I'd taken every woman I could through every kingdom during that time. It didn't bother me that she'd been promiscuous, although it was unusual for a woman to do so without being deemed a whore—a double standard of our norms that had always seemed foolish to me. Women who had more lovers were always more exciting in bed. And I knew, without a doubt, that Gemma would be worth every second I delayed fucking her. She was experienced, maybe more than I wanted to admit, but she was also confident and sure of her body. And that was something that turned me on to no end. While I enjoyed a submissive, bashful woman from time to time, it was the fiery ones who turned me on the most. Gemma was a woman with a reputation built on her strength and her fearlessness. She was a woman men feared to name because to do so risked death, from her or from those loyal to her.

She hadn't meekly run from that forest and settled down with a nice farmer's boy. She'd faced death head-on, fought beasts, killed creatures of nightmares, and stolen some of the most precious jewels. And she'd returned to that forest three years after I'd lost her. Returned for me and found the witch's son.

The reins dug into my skin as my hand tightened around them. I wanted to kill him, to watch him suffer for touching her before me, for having her love before I did. That irrational envy slithered along my skin and encased my chest, restricting my breath. The horse jerked his head, sensing my change in emotion, and I loosened my grip. My reaction was uncalled for. It meant nothing that she'd once loved him...but to me, it meant everything. I should have been her first—her first kiss, her first lover, her first love, her first everything—and I hadn't been.

I shook my head and continued on, promising that I would be her last. There was no way I would let him have her, no matter what deal she'd made with him. I would find the stones with her, hand them to him, and take her away from him forever. She was mine now, and I wouldn't let him lay a single finger on her again.

FEAR STRUCK me like a knife in the gut when I returned to find Gemma nowhere near the spring. I'd been gone a few hours, buying supplies, finding her pants in a town where women didn't wear pants, and procuring a room at the inn. I'd taken the time to bathe, a luxury that was well needed, before I'd headed back, leaving everything but her clothes and some food behind in the room.

Searching along the spring, I spied her footprints, knowing she was too smart to let them lead me to her. She was playing with me, testing me. Having a mercenary for a lover would be a challenge, but it was a challenge I welcomed.

I stopped my search, thinking of where she was leading me and where she would have hidden to gain an advantage. Rocks surrounded the spring, hiding it so few knew of its existence. I'd used it on occasion when traveling out of Carenth, knowing I had no time to stop in the town where the inn was. The mountains of Moreling stood in the distance, the barren ice plains of Iceliar far to the north.

Since I hadn't seen Gemma when I'd been on the road, nor as I'd neared the spring, that meant she was hiding to the right of me, likely tucked behind the rocks. She was good. A sloppy man would have followed her trail and fallen into her trap, but I wasn't a sloppy man. I thought through my options on how best to steal the advantage back. Feigning concern, I ran back to the horse, cursing under my breath so she'd think I was still looking for her. As soon as I rounded the rocks, I slipped out of sight.

I carried a spare set of reins with me now after a vinecti snapped one while attempting to eat my horse. From then on, I'd had my reins specialty made with buckles so I could easily remove or replace them. And I always carried a spare. I snagged them from my saddle bag before moving behind the rocks. Twisting them around my hands, I left some slack, then silently crept around to find Gemma crouched and watching for my return. Her hair was still damp, lying in wet strands over her back. She'd ditched the dress, opting for just the underskirt, which she'd somehow tied to cover her chest and the rest of her body. It clung to her wet skin, revealing her curves below. I almost faltered, I was so taken by the vision.

I crept closer, ready to wrap the leather around her neck when she turned, a naughty gleam in her eye.

"Are you going to tie me up, Hunt? You didn't ask if I was that kind of girl." All my years of training melted. She snagged the leather from my hands and wrapped it around her wrists, my hard-on thudding against my pants as if she were pulling it on a leash. She'd taken the control I had earlier and sent it descending off the cliff where I could no longer reach it. "Are you that kind of boy?" She snapped the leather between her wrists, my heart leaping with the sound.

"I don't need to tie you up to make you come for me, Gem." I was struggling to steal my control back, my eyes taking in the body under her soaked outfit. My hand grabbed the reins, and I pulled her to me, her body blocked only by her tied hands. "You'll scream for me easily, pretty thing." What was wrong with me and why was I giving her this nickname? I'd lost it somewhere during our trip, or maybe even on that first night.

Her lips parted, and all my resolve to keep us playing like this went crashing to the ground. I ripped her hands free and grabbed her by the neck, crashing my mouth into hers. My body was an electrical storm, lightning surging, thunder pounding as I came alive. She tasted like honey and smelled like the clean, crisp water she'd bathed in. She pawed at me, her hands dragging me closer as they pulled at my shirt. There was desperation in her moves that set me on fire, but I didn't want to take her quickly. I wanted it to be slow. I had waited this long, building to this moment, and there was no way I wouldn't savor every second. I wanted her begging for release, to hear her cry my name as she pleaded for me to destroy her.

Taking her arms, I pinned them behind her, drawing back to look at her. Her cheeks were a gorgeous pink, her lips swollen from the force of our kiss. Her nipples were dark below the white material, hard and taut, and ready for my mouth to suck on them. She was panting, her eyes wild with lust. She was alluring, and she was mine.

"You're not doing this to me again, Hunter," she said, the amber of her eyes flickering with anger.

"Not doing what, Gem?" I dropped my mouth to her neck and tasted her skin, my tongue sliding toward her chest.

"This."

"This?" I went lower, pulling her nipple into my mouth, the thin material blocking my contact but allowing me enough access to feel her skin pebbling below it.

"Gods yes, this." She moaned, pushing her breast further against my mouth. She wanted it and gods how I wanted to see her come again. "Hunter, don't stop."

That was all I needed. I dragged my teeth along her nipple, reveling in the mewl that fled her mouth. I shoved her against the rock where she'd been hiding and tore the scraps of fabric from her. Every dirty thought I'd had since that first night came flooding back at the sight of her. I wanted to take my time, but I'd been craving her for too long, and I knew this was going to be a struggle. My hands ran the length of her body, touching every bit of skin I'd longed for as she worked my shirt off me. Threading my fingers through her hair, I brought my chest against hers, sparks flaring through me at the contact. I kissed her again, her lips parting to let my greedy tongue through. Her kisses were demanding but still soft, her mouth delicious, and I thought kissing her for eternity wouldn't be a bad thing.

As she reached for my pants, I stopped her. She let out a sad mewl, and I laughed against her mouth.

"Patience, pretty thing. You're going to come for me again before I fill you." Shit, there was that dominating side of me I'd never known existed, but it was turning us both on, so I wasn't about to stop doing it.

I spread her legs with my thigh, pushing my fingers into her waiting warmth. She was soaked again, and my growl reverberated through my chest at the thought of being deep inside of her.

"Beg for it, Gem. I want to hear you beg for me to make you come."

Her legs squeezed, but I stopped them with my thigh, plunging my fingers further into her. My body reacted the same as it had the first time I'd done it, and I struggled not to just take her like I wanted to. Dropping my face to her breasts, I licked and sucked her firm skin, loving how she squirmed under my touch. I rubbed my thumb over her clit, and she pushed her pelvis against my hand. She was a needy thing, and I was about to satisfy that need the way I'd been imagining for days.

Lowering myself, I dropped to my knees and spread her legs, her moans vibrating through my body. I reached up and squeezed her breast, pinching her nipple before I dropped my hands to her ass and tilted her to my face. Plunging my tongue into her, I growled as her sweetness filled my mouth.

"Hunter," she cried, answering my command from earlier that she scream my name. The sound reverberated through my body, sending my need for release surging. Her hands threaded through my hair, pulling at it with every moan that fell from her lips. I tongued her clit, my fingers squeezing her ass cheeks as her arousal dripped to my mouth. Her legs were trembling, the muscles quivering in her thighs. She was bucking against my mouth, her climax climbing, and I'd never been so turned on. I brought my fingers to her, thrusting them in as I sucked her clit and threw her over the edge. She screamed my name again, her climax tearing through her so fiercely that her entire body shook around me. Her fingers gripped my hair as she lurched against me, my tongue never stopping until she pushed me back.

Giving her one long lick, I stood, grabbing her waist as her knees gave out.

The flush of her cheeks was glorious. "That's what I wanted, pretty thing."

Her fatigued eyes sparkled, and she yanked me to her, her tongue swiping along my chin as she cleaned up the evidence of her climax. The move made me so hard I was throbbing. Never had I been with a woman who didn't make me clean my face before she kissed me. Gemma was cleaning it for me. She sucked on my chin, then slid her mouth up and bit my lip.

"You're right," she said, her voice holding a sexy rasp. "You own me."

I smiled as my lip fell from her teeth. "Was there ever any doubt?"

"No, I suppose not. Now fuck me like I know you want to."

And oh, how I wanted to. There would be no walking away from her this time. She had me too primed for a climax, too ready to have her body gripping me as she came again. She reached down and unbuttoned my pants, and this time, I didn't stop her. I kicked my boots off, continuing to hold her gaze. My pants fell, and she encased me, her hands stroking me, her fingers rubbing the pre-cum that had leaked while I'd pleasured her. I pushed her hands away, grabbing her ass and picking her up, settling her over my tip. She was so wet that it took all my control not to continue driving into her. She felt like home, like security, like comfort. Her legs wrapped around me, and I held her there, lost in the amber flickering in her eyes.

"Hunter?" she breathed.

"There's no going back," I said in a moment of vulnerability, the aggressor in me hiding in the background.

"Back to what? What were we before this? Nothing more than two kids brought together by circumstance then torn apart. We're not family, Hunter. We're lovers."

Her words were enough to ease my hesitation, and my body pulsed with anticipation when she said, "Take me, Hunter."

Those words were all I needed to hear. I tipped her ass, pushing her harder against the rock and smothered her mouth with my lips just as I penetrated her. Her cry was mine to take, and I took it as I continued to thrust into her, lost in the exhilaration of being inside of her. I could never have imagined how good she would feel. I'd greatly underestimated it, and the harder I took her, the better it was. I pushed aside the vulnerability and took back my control. Her ass was firm in my hands, her body soft against mine, her breasts squishing into my chest and urging my release forward.

My orgasm pounded in me, vying for release, and as her legs quivered around me, her breathing short and rapid, I knew she was ready to come again. I didn't know if I could maintain enough control to get her over the edge, but I wanted to have her come undone around me. I wanted her to call my climax forward and to answer her call. My pace slowed, my hand moving between us, taking her nipple in my fingers and twisting it gently as I let her dictate our rhythm. I continued to kiss her, not wanting to break the contact, to leave the warmth of her mouth. The shake of her legs increased, her muscles clenching around me, leaving me no choice but to obey my body's need for release.

I dropped my hand, leaving the safety of her mouth, and looked into her eyes while I held onto her. My thrusts increased, my climax cresting to waves that I knew would drown me. As she fell apart, her body clamping down around me, I broke with her. The waves pounded through me as her muscles spasmed, urging me to fill her until I was shaking so hard I could barely stand. I leaned into her, my head falling to her shoulder as I tried to regain some semblance of feeling in my legs. I'd never come so hard. I was lightheaded, my body acting as if it were no longer my own.

She wrapped her hands around my neck and forced my head up, her eyes searching mine.

"Worth the wait?" I asked, giving her a coy smile.

She threw her head back and laughed before answering, "Well worth it."

Dropping her legs, I brought her away from the rock and against my chest. "Care for a swim?"

"Do you have any stamina left in you?"

I lifted a brow at the insult. "I have plenty of stamina, and I think you should be worried because I plan to use you the rest of the day and well into the night."

Which was exactly what I did.

I LEFT Gemma sleeping and headed down to find us some breakfast. We'd left the spring where I'd first given into my need for her just before it grew dark, taking shelter in the inn. The bed had proven less comfortable than the ground, but we hadn't spent our time sleeping. I'd taken her repeatedly until we'd both succumbed to exhaustion. I felt like a new man, but an unsure one. Unsure of how to act around her or where we went from here now that we'd become something more than I'd been with any other woman. We were both mercenaries, both leading our own lives. Lives that had now merged. And then there was this endless quest we were on to find the stones and get rid of the witch's son once and for all. I didn't like the bargain he'd made with her. He'd seemed like a good guy, helping her escape and freeing me. Gemma had even lived with him for some time, and he'd never harmed her. Yet, if she failed to gather the stones, he would force her to stay with him. Making her a prisoner. Something about it didn't sit right with me.

"...too close to the border, if you ask me."

I caught the last words of the two men sitting at the bar while I waited for our food to be done. It seemed strange for them to be drinking this early in the morning, but to each his own. I'd seen worse.

"Morning hash and fresh eggs for you and your bride, sir," the innkeeper's wife said, drawing my attention away. She set a large plate in front of me, the food not as appealing as what was waiting for me back in the room.

My bride. It sounded odd, but I'd needed to make an excuse that was respectable to get the lodging. Neralp was a town that looked down on anything that offended them, and sex in any form other than through marriage was something that greatly offended them.

"Thank you, ma'am." I paid her enough coin to cover the cost and a little extra for her effort, then took the plate and utensils toward where the rooms were. I couldn't help but stop at the bar first.

"Morning, gentlemen. I overheard your worry about the borders. My bride and I have traveled from Simeril and were hoping to start a farm and a family close by. Should we be looking elsewhere?"

Lying was something that came naturally to me in my line of business, but pretending the woman sleeping in my bed was my wife was something foreign to me.

"Ah, newly married. And from Simeril. What brings you so far from home?"

Damn nosy townspeople. "My wife prefers the countryside, and Simeril is so overrun by towns now that she wanted to leave the realm. Spindara had been her first choice, but the witches that plague those lands are not something I want her near. I can keep her safe in Moreling."

"Aye, you can, but stay away from the mountains in the far west, on the borders of Tronekrin. There's strange beasts roam those mountains, and men who venture there never return." Exactly where we needed to go. I'd been to the mountains where the shapeshifters ruled, taking the form of massive beasts that looked like bears but were the size of trolls. Each of their claws stood the height of a tall man, their teeth strong enough to tear through a stone house with ease. It was a place I didn't care to venture again, but Gemma's quest made it unavoidable.

I feigned a shiver. "Thank you for the warning. But what of the border of Carenth to Moreling?"

The two men looked at each other, and then leaned closer to me. "We don't speak too loudly of it, but it's best to stay far from the land that sits close to where Laviak lies in Carenth. There is a witch who rules the pits of Laviak. Some say he is the most fearsome of them, taking his power from the pits themselves. As his power has grown, Laviak's infection has spread. A black mist covers the land and spreads into Carenth. You should stay far from the borders of the south. Here, we are too far north, the air from Iceliar protecting us. But to the south of us, the infection looms."

I didn't know what to think of the story or if it held any merit. But I knew the witch they spoke of. The brother had made his home in Laviak. The witch's terrifying son. I remembered how he'd loomed over Gemma that night in the woods, talking about how he wanted to keep her, the hunger clear in his eyes.

"Thank you, kind sirs. Your help is much appreciated, and I will be sure to avoid that part of Moreling."

"Do that. Good luck to you and your wife," the one said before turning back to his ale.

On my return trip to our room, I contemplated their words, which were likely stories spread to keep anyone from venturing too close to Laviak. It was a place to avoid, a land of fire and lava. It had taken a great deal of money to convince me to trek into that wasteland in the past. Now, I had no choice but to return. If the words held truth, then the son of the witch, brother to the one who had stolen Gemma's innocence, was more powerful than I had suspected. There could be no other explanation, no other witch to blame.

The witches had dwindled in numbers. Their counterparts, the wizards, had turned on them. Leaving them and making their way to other kingdoms to work as advisors to the kings and leaders of the lands. There were so few that it didn't make an impact. Their numbers were low, and Spindara was the only realm where they remained. None would have made Laviak a home, daring to venture into a land where the gods had cursed others of their kind. None but the witch's second son who had defied the gods by living in the cursed wasteland. I had a suspicion there would be no avoiding him if we wanted to find the fire stone.

Gemma had said we needed to go to Laviak last to retrieve the fire stone. The danger I'd thought she was in at first was nothing compared to what I realized she'd now gotten herself into. Fighting shapeshifters and trolls was one thing. Fighting a witch was an entirely different level of threat. One I didn't know if the two of us could escape this time.

CHAPTER SEVEN

GEMMA

The smell of food touched my senses, waking me from the arms of sleep. I blinked my eyes to adjust to the morning sun shining through the window. Something heavy pinned me down before I could lift myself. Hunter. At the thought of him, my body grew warm. He'd given me more pleasure than I'd ever experienced last night, and my need for him had only increased.

"I thought I wanted food to break my fast," he muttered against my ear, "but I changed my mind. I'm hungry for more of you, pretty thing."

My legs convulsed at his words. How he could still be hungry was a feat considering how many times he'd taken me. Although, I was ravenous for him now that he was touching me. His hand followed my curves, taking time to slip under me to my breasts and play with my nipple before continuing down between my legs.

"I don't know. That hash seems pretty tempting," I teased as he nibbled my neck. Who was I kidding? I wanted him to take me to oblivion again, like he had over and over the night before.

"More tempting than this?" His finger slid between my folds, dragging along my clit, then easing into me.

"Mmm, maybe." I was trying to sound tough, but my voice trembled.

"Did I give you too much pleasure last night?" he asked, removing his finger. I held back the cry at the loss of his touch. He lifted himself from me, pulling my hips up so that I was on my knees. I groaned, remembering how he'd taken me from behind at the springs, tormenting me until I was so wet that he used it as leverage to claim my ass. The thought sent a shiver through me.

"No, I don't think I gave you enough, Gem."

I'd imagined a lot of things with Hunter. From what it would be like to find him, to discovering that he'd been dead all this time, to finding him and having him tell me how he'd loved me all these years. But never in my wildest fantasies had I imagined him to be the way he was with me, demanding, aggressive, possessive. All things I normally would have turned my back on, but with Hunter it made me even wetter for him.

He pressed against my back, his hand encasing my neck as he pulled me toward him. "I want you to tell me how much you want me to fuck you, pretty thing."

I trembled, my legs quaking as he squished my breast in his other hand, playing with the nipple until I thought I might crumple.

"Haven't I told you I don't beg?" Who was I kidding? I'd been begging him for days.

He pinched my nipple, squeezing my neck with his other hand. A rush of arousal flushed through me, and my knees buckled. He held me up, saying against my ear, "Beg me for it, Gem."

"Fuck me, Hunter, please." I hated the degradation, but it titillated me as well. I would never have begged. In fact, I hated being submissive to any man. I'd made a reputation of being a bad-ass, and I was proud that men treated me as their equal. It had taken years of proving myself to get to that point. And Hunter had slashed me down to my knees within days.

He sat back, releasing his hold on me, and I wondered if I'd said the wrong thing. Dammit, he drove me mad and now he had me questioning myself. "Take my cock out, Gem, and show me how much you want it."

I glanced back at him, meaning to question him, but the sexy half-grin he was giving me had me melting over his commands. He moved from the bed and stood, lifting his shirt over his head to reveal his muscular chest. I'd touched and licked every indent on that man's chest the prior night and I was still hungry for it. I sat back up on my legs as he stood there, waiting for me to obey him.

"You know, for someone who doesn't do the whole dominating thing, you've got it down."

"I'm just enjoying myself, Gem. And fuck if you aren't sexy when you're submissive."

I pursed my lips, not moving. "And what if I'm tired of being submissive?"

He raised a brow, trying to look stern, but the twitch in his pants gave him away. Hunter may have liked to make me do his bidding, but I suspected he liked his women with some backbone. And I had plenty of backbone. I crawled over to him, running my hands up the legs of his pants, then over the bulge that sat between them.

"I don't particularly like my women submissive," he replied, confirming my suspicion as I slowly unhooked his buttons.

I stopped and sat back, trying to hold back my laugh, because that's exactly how he liked me. "And how do you like your women, Hunter? Because you have me confused."

He threaded his hand through my hair, pulling it and jerking my head back. "Is this confusing you, Gem?"

"Well, to be honest, yes."

He pulled harder, forcing my chest forward where it met his other hand. He kneaded my breast, making my thighs quake with his firm moves. "I don't like submissive, but I do enjoy controlling you, Gem. You've always been bratty, and you seem to have grown a little too confident."

"I *am* confident."

"Oh, I know you are, and I love every bit of that part of you." There was that word again, the one we'd said in our desperate hours, the one that laced our need for one another like a light fog. Acknowledged but barely seen because neither of us was completely comfortable saying it. "But you beg so beautifully that I need to hear you beg me. And you look so gorgeous on your knees that I need to keep you there. Now take my fucking pants off so I can use that fantastic mouth of yours like I've wanted to since the day I found you."

I whimpered. Damn, I whimpered like a wounded animal. His words clamped down on a part of me that loved the way he talked dirty to me, the way he owned me. And I was certain that with his aggression, he would own my mouth and use it like the slut he wanted me to be. Anticipation crept into me, and my hands shook slightly as I finished freeing him. I'd always enjoyed going down on men. There was something controlling about it, but that was because I'd always controlled the process. Pleasing them with my tongue and my mouth at my leisure. It was the only way I would allow it. I commanded the power in the bedroom, but Hunter wouldn't be one to let me lead. He was going to drive this like he'd driven every moment last night and the days before. And he was the only one I would ever trust enough to submit to that.

I took his length in my hand, enjoying its thickness as I stroked it, and sliding my thumb over the leak of pre-cum that had oozed from his tip. Peeking up at him, I met his eyes, seeing the darkness that lay in their sage hue, the lust that shadowed it. My tongue dragged along his head, and I watched him fight his reaction before his fingers threaded into my hair, pulling it again. This was going to be a game of control, and I was prepared to lose. I slipped my tongue along his shaft, noticing every veiny indent and loving how it pulsed with need.

He slid a hand down to rub my breast, but as I lowered my mouth, taking his tip into it, he froze, a deep rumble coming from his chest. I took him further, closing my eyes to the thrill of it and the sensations that were buzzing through my body. A yank to my hair forced my eyes open, and I looked back at him.

"Eyes on me, Gem. I want to watch as you choke on my cock."

Shit. My knees clenched because I knew what was coming, something I'd never let any man do. Even Breck had understood that I needed control when pleasing him this way, and he had been my first. He could easily have been rough on an innocent girl who didn't know the ways of men, but he hadn't. And in letting me lead the way, he'd helped me see that I held power in the bedroom. That was before Hunter had come along and stripped it from me. Before I'd willingly handed it over to him.

In one final move of strength, I pushed against his hand, dragging my tongue along him. Sitting back, I said, "I let you own me now, but I get to ride you next time until I break you." He hissed, his teeth clenching, his dick pulsing in my hand. Yes, Hunter liked a strong woman, and I would show him how strong I was. I had let him role-play as the aggressive alpha for too long, and I wanted some of that power.

He brushed his thumb along my cheek, then over my bottom lip. "Let's see how well you take it first. If you're a good girl, I'll let you have your way."

"And if I'm not?"

"I remain in charge, and that ass is looking mighty tempting this morning."

I parted my lips, running my tongue along them.

"Fuck," he muttered, fisting my hair and shoving me forward.

He was aggressive and rough, but never enough to hurt me, just enough to make me completely soaked. Holding me still, he used me like the slut I wanted to be for him, my body an inferno that only grew with each thrust of his pelvis. My gags were the only sound that accompanied the spit that was drooling from my mouth and dripping down my breasts. Somehow, that only helped to bring me closer to release. I couldn't get over how turned on I was, and as his grunts increased, he thrust so far back that tears flooded my eyes. With a groan, he exploded, splashing down my throat while I was still mid-gag. He shoved me further down, and I took what I could, savoring every drop of him until he finally stilled. Jerking me from him, he peered down at me. His breathing was sporadic, his eyes alive with color, and every part of me thrilled that I'd brought him that pleasure.

He released my hair and wiped his thumb across his tip where a dribble of his release remained. I opened my mouth, and that sly smile overtook his face as I licked the remnants from his thumb.

"You look so sexy soaked in my cum and your spit, Gem. Now lay down. You've been a good girl, and it's my turn to taste." He shoved me back, yanking my legs forward and spreading them as he dropped to his knees. His tongue hit me before I could even react, causing my back to bow with the sensation. My climax was right on the precipice, so close it was reverberating through every part of me.

"Shit, you're so wet," he muttered against my clit, taking it between his teeth and pulling gently on it.

It took only minutes for him to shatter me. My climax tore through me so hard that I grabbed his hair, twisting it and shoving his face further into me. He never let up, his tongue bringing me ecstasy, my body convulsing uncontrollably. And he didn't stop when I tried to push him back, my body so sensitive with the aftereffects of my climax that I needed a few moments of air. He continued, pushing his fingers into me while his tongue ravaged my clit, catching the downward spiral of my orgasm and sending it hurling again. I cried out as it built quickly, my body a raging storm looking for a way to escape.

Moving from me, he unexpectedly dropped next to me on his back, his breathing labored. My legs were clenching with my unfulfilled orgasm. I looked over at him, scrunching my eyes as I tried to determine why he'd stopped bringing me the pleasure his tongue had been giving me.

"I believe your exact words were you wanted to ride me until you broke me, Gem. Now ride me and let me see those cum-covered tits bounce while you fuck me."

His dirty talk urged my impending orgasm closer, and I didn't hesitate to climb on him. Settling myself over him, I enveloped him, his thickness filling me so that my muscles clenched down on him, my climax bucking for release. He gripped my hips as I began my movement, running my hands the length of my body as I tilted back to take him further.

"Good gods, Gemma, you're gorgeous." The commanding tone was gone, replaced by a softer one full of wonder and love. And it melted me.

Sliding his hand over my stomach, he dropped it and fingered my clit, his other hand reaching to my breast and caressing it. The sparks that were assailing my body were profuse, every nerve on edge as he brought me to the brink of ecstasy and shoved me over. I fell, my cry tearing from me as I lost all control of my body. He took over as I succumbed to my descent, grabbing my hips and thrusting into me with such a fervor that my orgasm wouldn't stop. It dipped, then soared and continued to soar until another climax hit me. He groaned, joining me, our bodies one as we tumbled with our release. It raked through me with an intensity that stole my breath until I fell against him, unable to hold myself up any longer. His muscular arm wrapped around me, and he pushed into me one last time, holding me tight.

We remained that way, tangled with each other, catching our breaths, and reveling in the bliss of our climaxes. It felt perfect. He felt perfect, like the home I'd lost and never found until now. He was home, my grounding, my sanity, and I could have stayed in his arms forever.

His kiss on my hair brought me from my thoughts, and I picked my head up to look at him. I didn't know how I loved this man as deeply as I did. Perhaps I always had, the crush developing with every year I'd searched for him. A fantasy that was now my reality.

"What are you thinking, pretty?"

"Just wondering if I've always loved you."

His eyes sparkled with mischief. "Were you fingering yourself at night, thinking about me all these years?"

I let out a laugh. "I had plenty of men to do the job for me while we were apart."

His smile faltered, a grimace replacing it. He was possessive, and I liked the way it made me feel. "No more talk of your past escapades. I'm the only one you think about, the only one you finger yourself to, and the only one who gets to fuck you."

I traced his chiseled jaw, my eyes following the path of my fingers. "Am I the only one you'll be thinking of when you're stroking yourself?"

"I won't need to stroke myself. I've got you for that."

I narrowed my eyes at him. "Is that all I'm good for?"

He smacked my ass and threw me from him. Climbing over me, he said, "No. You're good for fucking, sucking, and tasting. I'm sure I'll discover a few other things you're good for, but I'll have to wait. We've been here too long. We've got another two days' journey until we reach the home of the shapeshifters. Clean up and get dressed."

Raising myself on my elbows, I watched as he pulled his pants on, buttoning away what I was craving to have inside of me again.

"Damn, Gemma. You've got quite an appetite, don't you?"

I rose and walked over to him, loving how his eyes followed the curves of my body. "You make me hungry, Hunter. I was ravenous before, and I'm still not satiated." And I wasn't. I could have fucked him all day if we didn't have the blasted stones to retrieve.

"You'll have to satiate yourself with cold hash until we camp tonight. Then I'll satisfy that appetite."

With a sigh, I dressed, his eyes following the material as I slowly hid my body from him. He'd found pants for me and having them on was a relief. I hated bulky dresses.

"Those damned pants are going to make it hard for me to fuck you while we travel," he complained as we left the room.

"Think of it as a challenge." I ran my hand through my long strands of hair, leaving it down instead of braiding it.

"You were challenging enough. I need no more challenges from you."

"I was challenging? I was ready to let you take me that first night."

He stopped and faced me, wrapping his arm around my waist and smashing me into him. "That was the challenge. Making myself wait until you were really needy. I didn't want to take you the first night like any other woman. I needed this to be worth waiting for. And trust me, Gem, you were well worth the wait."

He released me and continued forward. Standing there, I watched him walk away, wondering if this was all a dream. I was here with Hunter. We'd given ourselves to each other repeatedly after days of holding our need at bay. Now we were heading back out to our deadly journey, a journey that would decide my fate. It was one we could fail and with that failure, our happy ending would come crumbling down like a candy house. The thought sent the hairs on my neck standing at attention as if it weren't just a thought but an impending possibility.

THE JOURNEY to the Shilank mountains took three more days. Home to the shapeshifters, the mountains sat in the far west of Moreling. The roads became clearer, eventually dwindling to paths that finally disappeared. No one wandered to the mountains. To do so spelled death. Hunter and I were the only ones mad enough to take on this journey.

Hunter had purchased a horse for me in the last town, and I missed his closeness. Thankfully, we stopped every few hours to rest the horses, and he took advantage of every moment when the horse wasn't blocking his access between my legs. He teased and played, working me to the crest of pleasure and leaving me that way until we stopped again. By the time we made camp, I was so desperate for release it was nearly killing me. He liked me that way, pleading for his touch, begging for him to bring me to climax.

Each night, we shared the bedroll like we had at the start of our journey, but now we left our clothes off, keeping our moans contained so as not to attract any creatures. I couldn't wait until we were off the road and back at an inn again. Staring at the towering mountains before us, I knew we wouldn't be sleeping comfortably for quite a while...if we even made it out of Shilank.

"Have you ever seen a shapeshifter?" Hunter asked, bringing his horse next to mine.

"No. This is the one part of the world I try to avoid. Have you?"

"Once. I had a job that required collecting the hide of one. A revenge pay. The beast had snuck into a town south of here and stolen the man's wife. I don't really know all the details, but the pay was good."

"Why would one steal his wife? Did he kill her?"

Hunter shrugged. "No clue. I try not to ask questions with kill hires. As long as they aren't children or women, I don't ask."

"So you have scruples as a killer?" I asked with a raise of my brow.

"Mercenary," he corrected.

"Funny how that title covers so many of us, yet we don't all stoop to the same level." I urged my horse forward.

"You're really going to judge me? You weren't judging me while I was pounding you last night."

"True, nor was I judging you when your tongue was devouring me this morning. But right now, I'm judging you."

"Fuck you, Gemma." There was playfulness in his voice. "I do what I need to survive. At least I don't whore myself like you do."

He left me there, my mouth agape as I tried to think of a comeback. I hated how quick he was at slinging his comments and how slow I was to sting back. Damn him.

I caught up with him, shooting him a dirty look.

"We both do what we need to survive, Gem. There's no changing who we are. But you will never whore yourself for a job again. I don't give a shit how much coin you lose or what it does to your reputation to turn the job down. If it involves anyone touching that body that belongs to me, it's off the table."

"And if anyone does touch me?"

He snapped his head toward me, his eyes dark with a lethal edge to them. "I will kill him, painfully. And if I find out you've let that someone touch you, I'll fuck you in his blood and let it stain your skin until I'm satisfied you're ready to beg for my forgiveness."

I swallowed back the fear his words had caused, the hackles rising on my neck. "And what will you make me do to earn that forgiveness?"

His eyes narrowed, the pupils tiny against their sage. "I'll bring you to the cusp of orgasm day after day until you're screaming for me to make you come. I'll fuck you so hard you'll wish you'd never dared touch another man, but I still won't give you that release. I'll keep your legs spread and your hands tied so you can't satisfy yourself. And I'll fuck you like that repeatedly, so you remember who owns your pussy and whose cum fills it.

Don't even think about fucking around on me, Gemma. I promise you won't like the price."

He rode off, leaving me there to contemplate the possessive reaction he'd had. There was a side to Hunter that was dark and twisted, a side that hadn't been there when we were young. One that years of living on his own, fending for himself, and shielding himself from the wounds of his father's rejection had created. I didn't blame him. I rarely let anyone in. To do so risked pain, and I'd had enough pain. I'd seen my stepfather murder my mother, too stunned to run when he and Hunter took me to the woods that night. Too frightened to say anything, to let Hunter know I'd witnessed the bloody act. Running back to my bed and hiding under the sheets until his father had dragged me out that night, saying we needed to find herbs to make her better.

In my mind, I'd known she would never be better. He'd stabbed her so many times, her lifeless eyes looking back at me. But the irrational side had hope, believing that maybe I hadn't seen what I had, that maybe all she needed was something to take the wounds away. And then Hunter and his father had left me, severing any hope, any faith I'd had in men. Hunter's return had partially rebuilt that, but when the witch had taken him, that faith had shattered again. When Beck had refused to tell me what had happened to Hunter, it had crumbled further. I'd held out, giving him my heart or what I had left of it, hoping he would be the one to heal it. But he hadn't been, and I'd finally left, knowing there was nothing there for me but lost hope and wishes. That the love I'd had was something twisted. Something I'd manifested into love in the hopes that everything he represented, everything that house represented, wasn't what I remembered it being.

So I understood why Hunter had said those things. Why he would threaten me, covet me so that he would hurt me and anyone who dared touch me. Because if I turned from him, if I gave myself to someone else, it would shatter what little we were building, what little he was giving of himself, trusting me with.

I urged the horse forward and caught up with him. "Should we camp at the base or just move forward?"

"Move forward. How do we find the stone? Did he give you anything besides finding the shapeshifters?"

"He said the seeing stone would show us."

"Damn witches. Did you ever stop to think he was setting you up to fail? Why not just tell you I was alive when you were fucking him?"

I pursed my lips, not liking the vitriol in his voice. "I don't think he wanted me to know."

"Exactly. He was a greedy bastard and wanted you for himself."

I chewed my lip, knowing it was the truth. "He didn't want to tell me because he knew I still loved you," I admitted, looking at the mountains and not Hunter. "That's why I left him. I told him it was because we'd outgrown each other, that I was tired of being stuck in one place for so long. I hadn't been lying, but I hadn't been completely truthful. He wouldn't tell me about you, and I didn't like the secret that stood between us."

"It stood because he didn't want to lose you to another man."

"But he did anyway. I left him years ago, Hunter. There was plenty of time for me to find another man."

"No, he knew you never would because you would continue to look for me. And he didn't think you'd ever find me. You were naïve to take this job, Gemma. He knew you'd fail, and you'd end up back with him. If you succeeded, he could have easily lied and told you I was dead. End of story, you'd be his again. I don't know why the bastard didn't just lie to you in the first place."

"I don't think he was worried when I first found him. I told him I wanted to beat the shit out of you for abandoning me that night. Maybe you should thank him for keeping me from you."

I glanced over to see his reaction. He kept his eyes guarded, but I saw the tick in his jaw, the veins that were thick in his neck. I'd gotten to him.

"Don't worry. I would have gone easy on you. Consider yourself lucky my anger turned to lust over the years, or our meeting would have gone differently."

His laugh cascaded around me. "I still would have had my fingers sunk deep inside of your wet pussy, Gem."

"Prick," I mumbled.

"Keep that up and I'll show you how much of a prick I can be. Now where do we find the earth stone?"

I gripped the reins, trying not to let him see how his words affected me. "I told you, with the seeing stone."

He studied me and I could see that he was trying to figure out how the other stone could help us.

"Just trust me." I held my hand out, waiting as he reached into his saddlebag and handed me the stone.

I rolled it around in my hands. In the sunlight, the mist-like consistency in it looked different. Colors glittered within it, making it look like the sparkling rock candy I'd once had at the traveling fair.

"How do you use it?" Hunter asked.

"Like this." I raised it to my eye, peering through the glittery haze and watching as the colors cascaded within it until they combined, turning an array of browns that centered in the stone. Bands of tan emanated from the brown in pulsing waves and around them an image of the land formed. Not the mountains, but green space dense with vegetation. I held the stone out further, seeing that I'd shifted my position unknowingly, aiming my sight to the valley between two mountains. An oasis of trees and tall grass stood there, climbing their way up the indent that sat within the connection of the two.

"It's there," I said, pointing to the green patch.

His eyes squinted as they turned from the space of land back to me. "There?"

"Yes."

"Fantastic. The shapeshifters roam the mountains, but their

den sits between them, right in that patch of land where you're pointing."

"Shit."

"Shit, indeed. Are you sure we can't just turn from this and live a happy life settled down in Spindara, raising a few brats while I fuck you every night?"

This time, it was my turn to laugh. "First, you don't strike me as the settling down type. Neither of us would be happy with that. Second, how did we get to having kids?"

He shrugged. "I'm sure it would happen at some point. Little trained mercenaries."

"Oh, wouldn't that be fun? No kids. You're not tying me down with kids while you go off and hunt monsters."

"I'll tie you down any time I want, Gemma." The tremble that skittered through me was too great to hide, and his mischievous grin grew. "Damn, that's an image that will be hard to get out of my head."

"Have you ever tied a woman up, Hunter?" I could hear the quiver in my voice because the thought sent mixed emotions through me.

"Nope, but you seem to be checking off all my firsts."

"Wait, what other firsts have I checked off for you?" There weren't any I could think of because nothing he'd done to me seemed like he was new at it.

"Let's go." He trotted away, leaving me to wonder what he'd done only with me. I knew this dominating side of him was all mine, but I didn't think that was what he meant. He didn't give me time to question him further. Nor to return to the idea of us settling down and raising a family. The thought should have sent me running, but something about it warmed my heart.

Pulling his horse to a stop, he hopped off and tethered it to a tree, gesturing for me to do the same.

"We can't take the horses any further. It's too dangerous. Grab what you need, we walk from here."

The weather had warmed some since we'd begun moving south, but it was still the cool season. Hunter had gotten us gear when we'd stopped in the town, and I hated taking off the coat that was keeping me cozy. It was too bulky, though, and I needed freedom to move my limbs. Hunter tossed me a knife once I was ready.

"What's this for? I have my knife."

"You need two. There's no reason for you to be running around with only one."

"But I keep a spare blade in my boot."

"That tiny thing is not a knife. It's a nail file. When they shift, these beasts have hides that are thick to cut through. Take the extra knife."

He turned and started toward the valley. I tucked the second knife away and followed him. Watching him work was enlightening. His eyes were focused and hard, his brows pinched in concentration. Every muscle in his arms was strained with tension, and I could even see the ones in his back pressed taut against the material of his shirt. This was the side of him that drove the aggressive side in the bedroom, the one that enjoyed owning me as his pretty thing. That name made my breath catch each time he said it. I crashed into him, my mind on nicknames and sex.

"Gemma." The warning tone in his voice did nothing to calm the flutters that had chosen this inopportune time to invade my lower belly. He glanced back at me, his eyes dancing with amusement. He pushed me back into the stone behind me and grabbed my chin. "This is not the place for dirty thoughts, pretty thing."

His kiss stifled my moan, my body coming alive as he slid his hand up my shirt, plucking my nipple until it was hard and sensitive.

"I can't take you here, Gem. Your cries would bring them running, and their males might fight me for a piece of your wet cunt."

The shake of my knees threatened to topple me. His dirty talk reached into a part of me that fed on it. It was a side of me that I'd never known I had until Hunter had awakened it.

"Have I tormented you too long today? Waited too long to bring you release?"

"Yes," I breathed as his other hand reached between my legs, having slipped into my pants when his words were destroying me.

"We're about to walk into what likely will be our deaths."

"We're not there yet." What was I doing? He was right. This was dangerous, and I wanted a quick fuck. The mere risk of it had me soaked.

His eyes lit with excitement. "You want to play at death's door, Gem?"

I gripped his shirt and pulled his lips to mine. "Fuck me, Hunter." It wasn't a plea this time; it was a command, and he shivered against me as he answered, "Gladly." His fingers plunged into me, and I kissed him harder, burying my moans in his mouth as he brought me close to climax. My need for release scaled quickly with all the build-up he'd given me through the day.

I tore at his pants, freeing him, my fingers stroking along his length that pulsed in my hands.

"Dammit, Gemma, this would have been so much easier in a dress." He shoved my pants down, tearing them from one leg, and picked me up, penetrating me so hard I had to bite my lip to silence my scream. He pounded me, our grunts muffled between our kisses. I registered the rip of material as his hand dug for my breast, but the touch of his skin against my flesh made the sound irrelevant. My body was a chaotic mess of stimulated nerves one touch away from coming undone. As I sensed his climax closing in on him, mine hit me like an avalanche of rocks, battering me so that my body was no longer in my control. I convulsed in his arms, his orgasm exploding through him as mine coaxed it forth. He buried his head in my shoulder, his grunt silenced against my skin as I clutched to him, too worn from my release to do more than that.

"Gods, Gemma," he muttered, not moving from my shoulder. He was holding me so tight that he was almost crushing me. He pushed into me one last time before dropping my legs, which shook like jelly once they were free of his hold. "Don't pull this shit again. That was dangerous."

"But it was so good," I said, my breathing still strained.

He crashed his mouth against mine, his hand moving between my legs. "Make sure you don't let a drop of my cum leak out of you. If any of these animals try to take you from me, I want them to smell that I've marked what's mine."

The pinch he gave my clit sparked currents in my belly, and I tried not to squeeze my legs in reaction. He backed from me, tucking himself away while I struggled to pull my pants back on. When I'd managed to do so without falling over, I looked up to see him watching me, his arms crossed, a devious look in his eyes.

"You're a liability. No more games when we work." He pulled me against him, dropping his face and licking my breast, which I'd only now noticed was hanging free. The shirt had been the source of the ripping. His tongue circled my nipple before he pulled it into his mouth and sucked.

"Gods, Hunter, stop," I moaned softly. He was waking my body again, and there was no way I could think if he had me worked up again. He didn't stop nipping and sucking until I was pushing against him. His leg wedged between mine, his thigh pressing against me. "What are you doing, Hunter? You said we needed to work."

"I know what I said, but that was before your tit sidetracked me. Come for me once more, Gem."

"Are you mad?" The words barely formed, coming out as a choppy mosh of syllables.

"You drive me mad, Gem. You and this body." He pulled more of my breast into his mouth and my body reacted. The pressure of his thigh stimulated me so that I was soon clawing at him to bring me the release his mouth and leg were promising. "That's it, pretty thing. Fall apart for me."

I bit my lip again as his words sent my climax pummeling, my body spasming against his until nothing remained for me to give him. I collapsed into him, hating the chuckle that he gave me. "Put those tits away before I give up on this hopeless quest and steal you away where I can fuck you for the rest of my life. And I won't give a shit what some asshole of a witch's son says about it."

He pushed my arms from him and walked away, adjusting himself and mumbling about how hard he now was. It served him right for torturing me like that.

I fixed my shirt as best I could and pulled myself together. I supposed if we were going to die here, we'd both die satisfied. Well, at least I would since his hard-on looked extremely uncomfortable.

"You're going to take care of that when we get out of this," he said, noticing my eyes had fallen to it.

"We'll see. Your cum is dribbling from me right now, so I don't really think you need anything taken care of."

"I thought I told you to keep that inside of you."

Shooting him a look, I replied, "I doubt that's possible, but if it were, you fucked that chance up when you had me dry humping your leg."

"That was a memorable sight. I like it when you're out of control and desperate, Gemma."

"I'm never out of control." It was a complete lie. I was out of control every second I was in Hunter's presence.

He stopped suddenly, bringing a finger to my mouth to silence me before stooping down. We had rounded the corner of the base of the mountain and were at the cusp of the valley. I looked to where his eyes had focused and dropped next to him. A man was resting against an entrance to a cave that led into the mountain. Man wasn't the exact word for him because I'd never seen a man as large as this one. He was so tall his shadow seemed to stretch forever. He was broad with muscles that looked the size of my torso. And naked save for a scrap of leather that barely covered his private parts.

"That man is huge," I whispered.

"Wait until you see him in bear form."

"Shit, I don't think I want to."

"Then find the stone. I'll keep him occupied."

I turned sharply to Hunter, knowing he could read the horror etched on my face. "Occupied? How do you occupy that?"

"I'll think of something. Find the stone, and we may just have leverage to get out of here. If they can't touch it, you'll hold the power."

He ran off before I could reply, approaching the shapeshifter as if he were seeing a buddy at a tavern. I stared in wonder as the man tilted his head in curiosity before they exchanged words. With each word, the anger morphed the man's face until, with one ear-shattering roar, he transformed into a bear twice the size that he'd been. I stumbled back before remembering Hunter's life now depended on my ability to find the stone. I hadn't planned to have that hanging over my head, especially not minutes after he'd had me quaking against him.

Trying to ignore the fight that was proceeding between the two, I raised the stone and scanned the area. The swirls of color appeared only when I landed on the cave entrance.

"Great," I muttered, clutching the seeing stone and sneaking on the outskirts of the space until I came to the cave.

I glanced back to see Hunter hurling through the air. The cry that the sight elicited, I silenced behind my hand. The impact he'd taken was hard, and I cringed, but he jumped to his feet, looking only slightly dizzy. My time was short if I wanted to keep him alive, so I turned my attention to the cave, stepping in. The light faded with each step until I came to a large opening. Torches lit the room before me and on the floor lay dozens of sleeping bears —shapeshifters. I covered my mouth, stopping the scream that was clamoring to escape. The cold season was just ending, but it wouldn't turn over to the warm season for a few more weeks. The shifter outside the cave had been a guardian, his only purpose being to protect his clan while they slept.

My heart was thudding so loudly I feared I would wake them. Bringing the seeing stone up, I glanced around, trying to determine where the earth stone was. I'd almost given up until a shimmer of color coming from the far end of the cavern caught my eye.

"Fuck," I muttered. I'd need to go through almost all the shifters to reach it. Knowing my time was short, I tucked the stone away and quietly removed my boots. I wanted no chance that I would wake them. I checked around my body for anything that could fall or disturb them, then took my first steps.

Each bear I passed brought more anxiety to me. They were enormous, and we were lucky there was only one to fight. I wondered if Breck had known they were still hibernating. He'd been insistent I start the journey without delay. He'd schooled me on the shapeshifters and the other witch descendants, explaining how they had lost their power, and the gods had transformed them into the creatures they were today. All but the few who had turned their backs to the enticing flesh of the beasts who roamed the realms where they had lived. The witches of Moreling had forsaken the gods, satisfying their carnal urges with the bears who roamed the mountains. Their offspring eventually became the shapeshifters, their power over the land sealed in the earth stone after the gods punished them.

The seers had watered down their abilities and their heritage by mating with my people and so their power of sight had faded, the gods storing it in the seeing stone. It had sat in the capital of Simeril since the day the gods had formed it.

The water wielding witches, who grew too familiar with the sea creatures in Iceliar, the gods had cursed to live as half siren, half fish. Their power formed the water stone. Those with the power over air in Tronekrin, the gods had cursed not for the relations they'd chosen but for forsaking their gifts. Those witches had seen their magic as a curse, their zealots claiming they were an abomination and trying to cast the powers out. The gods, in their anger, stole their form and their power, sealing their magic in the wind stone. The disembodied spirits of the witches now haunted the deserts of Tronekrin as wind wraiths. They stirred the sand and blinded their victims, ensuring they lost their way and died from the elements. The bones of their victims lined the deserts as a warning to never venture there.

The final of the stones, the fire stone, contained the power of the fire witches. Those who controlled the element of fire, the deadliest of the witches. The gods punished them for trying to overtake the other races of witches, stripping their power and locking it in the fire stone. The gods had then trapped their bodies in molten lava, transforming them to become the golems. Their punishment was especially harsh—their souls locked within the flames taken from the Laviak pits and encased within their shells. Living a tormented existence, they wandered Laviak, trapping those who dared to stop on the paths throughout the pits, turning them to ash and feeding on their souls.

The only remaining witches lived in Spindara, my homeland. They were witches who had refused to follow the foolish ways of their families and fled to Spindara. There, they mated with witch families of the other kingdoms, betraying their original roots. By mixing the purity of their lines, the power that passed to their offspring was twisted and foul. It became something unspeakable in most, like Breck's mother who feasted on the meat of children. In some, like Breck, it settled as something good. In others, like his brother, it remained twisted. Because these witches were not specifically from one family, they remained protected from the wrath of the gods. Our realm was the only one with witches who still held magic.

The shapeshifters, although deadly, were the least frightening of the cursed witch families. At least that's what I had thought until I found myself surrounded by their sleeping forms.

At the end of the cavern lay a pond, sleeping bears on each side. I lifted the stone, looking everywhere but the water, hoping the earth stone was in sight, only to find it when I gave up and turned toward the water.

I threw a silent temper tantrum. There was only one way to reach the stone, and it was one I didn't find appealing. I peered into the water, which was sparkling and clear. Thankfully, the shifters hadn't been using it for their toilet. At the very bottom of the reservoir, peeking from below the sediment, lay a brown stone with waves of tan and white running through it. It reminded me of a piece of caramel with chocolate on the outside, a delicacy I'd only had once from a fellow mercenary who had traveled the seas.

There was no choice but to plunge into the water and retrieve the stone. If Hunter was still alive, the stone would be my only way to save him. I stepped into the water, took a deep breath, and plunged into the frigid unknown.

CHAPTER EIGHT

HUNTER

Having underestimated the shifter's strength and overestimated my own, I found myself on the ground yet again. Silently cursing Gemma's foolishness for getting herself into this mess, I vowed to punish her appropriately if I made it out alive. And if I ever laid eyes on that wretched witch's son, I'd slit his throat before he had a chance to use his magic on me.

The beast brought his paws around me, daring me to use my knife and cut him. I'd tried multiple times and only made contact a handful of those times. The last shifter I'd faced had been smaller and easier to conquer. It had been a vicious battle, one I'd sworn I'd never brave again. Yet, here I was. He roared in my face, saliva slopping from his sharp incisors. I prayed for a quick death, wishing I'd taken Gemma one more time before stepping into death's path.

"Let him go or I torch them all!" Gemma stood in front of the cavern, soaked from head to toe and holding two torches.

The shifter roared, rising to his back paws and turning to her. I took my opportunity and rolled from him, jumping to my feet and plunging my knives into his sides.

"No!" Gemma screamed as the beast roared, flailing from side to side, trying to free the knives which were still gripped in my hand.

He succeeded, the movement sending me flying into the mountainside. The impact rattled my teeth, reverberating through my body like my bones were being tossed around in a sack.

"Gemma, don't," I tried to warn her, but the blow had knocked the wind from me, my words coming out in a hoarse wheeze.

"Don't hurt him, Hunter. He's just trying to protect his clan."

Was she serious? These were shapeshifters who could squeeze their victims to death in the grip of their paws.

The shifter transformed, the man returning. "You stand before the resting place of my people and hold fire. You are as much a threat as he is."

"No, I'm not. I needed to get your attention."

"You have it. And now I'll kill you for daring to set foot in our lands."

I brought myself to my knees, my vision still blurry, my entire body aching. So much for punishing Gemma tonight. I'd be lucky if I could even move to touch her.

In four long strides, the shifter covered the distance between him and Gemma. He was too close to her for my comfort. I forced myself to stand, then to move my legs, praying he didn't make it to her before I could kill him.

"Don't come any closer." She held a brown stone with waves of lighter brown hues in front of her. The earth stone. She'd found it. Pride welled in me before fear shoved it aside and clawed at my chest. What was she doing? Antagonizing a shapeshifter was bound to bring certain death.

But he stopped moving, backing two steps away.

"The earth stone. How do you have it?"

"I'm here for it."

The muscles rippled in his chest. "You will not take what is ours."

"I will because it's needed. Now let us leave this place."

"That stone will not leave this valley. It is the source of our power and our strength."

"A source you cannot touch or harvest. Losing it will not bring any harm to your clan. But keeping it here limits your potential. With it, I can collect the other stones and destroy them, ending the hold the gods have on your people and those of the other lands."

I balked at her. Ending the hold was a strange phrase to use. It could end their existence, severing the hold the gods had. Or it could end the hold on the magic, returning it to the witches. Witches were vile, repulsive things we dealt with regularly in Spindara. If what Gemma said was true, it would unleash them in every realm. Their numbers were low, but they were still an annoyance we were better off without.

He took a step closer to her, and I fisted my hands so tight the tendons were straining below my skin.

"And why would you want to help us?"

Gemma didn't miss a beat, nor did she turn from his penetrating gaze. There was no fear in her eyes that I could find. "Because I once experienced the kindness of a witch, and I don't believe you're all as bad as my people make you out to be."

He laughed, a sound that nearly shook the surrounding mountains. "Trust me, we are. And you would be wise to fear the kindness of any witch, especially one who still holds the power and the title. I am no longer a witch. The gods stole that title from my clan ages ago."

My thoughts exactly. I didn't trust *her* witch's son, just as I hadn't the night he'd freed me. But Gemma did, and I had to trust her instinct, no matter that her words left me concerned.

"Let us go and you'll discover the truth in my words." She put the stone in her pocket. Maneuvering the two torches, she worked her shirt off without dropping them. Fire blazed through me at the sight of her breasts bouncing free, a red-hot heat that seared me from the inside out. She squeezed the water from her shirt, dousing the torches before throwing them on the ground before him. "I won't hurt your family."

It took him two swift steps, and he was upon her. I lunged, but my movements were stiff. He had her in his grasp before I could get anywhere near him.

"You betray me, and I will hunt you down and rip your body apart." He grabbed her and turned her toward me, one hand cupping her breast while the other held her neck. Rage seethed within me at his audacity to touch what was mine. "If she does not do as she has said, I will hunt your woman down. I will make you watch as I fuck her until her screams run with blood. Even then I will fuck her dead body as I force you to watch my cum coat her blood."

He shoved her toward me, and I snatched her hand, dragging her to me.

"Leave now before I change my mind." He stalked away, leaning against the cave wall and assuming his station as guard again, his arms crossed, his eyes beady and deadly.

I pulled Gemma along, ignoring the pain that was pulsating through my body. When we were far enough away, I released her hand. "Put your fucking shirt on."

She snapped her head to me, anger twisting her face. "What the fuck is your problem? I just saved us, and you're throwing a tantrum?"

I jerked her to me. "You didn't save us. You promised some-thing you can't ensure and showed your tits to that shifter.

Nobody touches you, Gemma. Nobody even looks at this body. It's mine."

"Are you shitting me? You're angry because I took my shirt off?" Her laugh was wicked and unexpected.

I grabbed a handful of her hair and yanked her head back. "No one touches you. No one even sees what belongs to me. And you let him do both."

"I was saving us," she snarled.

"With your tits?"

"You're an asshole, Hunter."

"You haven't scraped the surface, pretty thing. Now put your fucking shirt back on."

I shoved her away and stormed off. My anger was uncalled for. I knew it, but I couldn't calm it. Between the danger she'd put herself in, the beating I'd taken from the shifter, and seeing him with his hands on her, I was so far over the edge I was a snake coiled and waiting to strike.

Throwing the reins of her horse to her, I climbed on mine and set out, hoping to distance us from the mountains quickly. I wanted no chance the shifter would change his mind and come after us. I had an inkling he'd only been toying with me, playing with his prey before he was bored and ready to kill.

After a few hours of quiet riding, I found a small hill of stones tucked away enough to provide shelter. No predator would bother us here. None were brave enough to stay within a few miles of the shapeshifters. Even the deadliest of beasts avoided their kind.

I rolled from the horse with a pained grunt, Gemma turning her eyes to evaluate me. She raised a brow, but I didn't bother to talk to her. My anger had subsided, but she didn't need to know that. I snatched the reins from her and led both horses to a grazing spot, making them comfortable before returning to our makeshift camp. Gemma had started a fire and rolled out the bedroll. I'd been looking forward to playing with her in it before my body had become a sack of flour for an enormous beast to pummel.

Sliding down against the rock formation, I rested my head, watching as she dug some bread and water from the pack.

"Why are your clothes wet?" I asked. I'd been too stubborn to ask earlier when they'd still been water logged.

"Oh, now you're ready to talk to me? Your nasty possessiveness calmer now, is it?"

"Don't make me punish you, Gem. You won't like it."

"I doubt that. You can barely move." She threw a crust of bread to me.

"I can move enough to make you come."

The laugh she gave annoyed me, and I hardened my eyes, grimacing at her.

"I could be buck naked on top of you, and you wouldn't have the energy to make me come."

"Is that a challenge?"

Her eyes lit, and she walked closer to me. My dick woke with a painful lurch.

"So you want to know why I'm soaked?"

"Are you?" I asked, understanding her double-meaning, or at least hoping I had.

Her lips turned to a seductive smile that lessened the discomfort of my aching body. She drew her shirt over her head, freeing her breasts. I watched her walk closer to the fire, laying the shirt out to dry. Her pants came off next, and she did the same thing with them. I wasn't watching anything now but how her body was moving.

She came back over to me, my eyes taking in every glorious inch of her. "While you were playing with the shifter," she said, straddling me in an unexpected move. "I was making my way through a den of hibernating bears." She wiggled herself down further on me, taunting me with the warmth that was emanating from her. Caressing her breast, I drew her to me, nipping at her bottom lip. "The stone was at the bottom of their water source, wedged deep in the sediment."

My hand froze. I hoped she hadn't gone into that water and risked drowning even though I knew she had because she'd come out as soaked as she was between her legs.

"You went into the water?"

She nodded. "I took a swim. The damned thing was lodged in pretty far, but after a few tries, I freed it."

I squeezed her breast, loving the flare of desire that sparked in her eyes. "So, not only did you share the body I own with that shifter, but you risked your life in that cavern?"

"While you had the shit beaten out of you." She gently touched a cut on my forehead. "I came out in better shape than you did, so get over my tits being out and stop being jealous about it."

"These are my tits," I said, cupping them both and fondling them.

"I didn't give them away," she said, giving me a pouty look. "I needed my shirt to douse the torches."

"I don't think that's what he was paying attention to. And dammit, Gemma. You made a promise to that shifter, and if you can't keep it—"

"You'll protect me."

I loved the surety of her voice, the power she handed me in those words. But I wasn't so sure I could protect her. "If you don't succeed and that asshole takes you from me—"

"You'll take me back."

"Gemma, I'm strong and I'm good at what I do, but against a witch? Even one without magic would be hard for me to handle. I don't think I'd win that battle and if I lose, the shifter will hunt you down."

"And if you lose, I'm Breck's, and he'll protect me."

Envy slithered through me, coiling around my insides so tight that I squeezed her breasts painfully hard. She cringed, backing away, but I grasped her neck and put her flush against me, whispering in her ear, "That witch will never touch you again. I will rip every ounce of magic from his body and tear him to pieces with my bare hands if he even so much as looks at you with that expectation."

Her chest was rising in uneven bursts against me, her legs tightening around my thighs. I dragged my lips across her cheek and kissed her with all the emotion that had plagued me over the past hours. She pushed at my shirt, working it from me. Her fingers touched every bruise as she stopped to look, keeping her body and her lips from me.

"Leave them be, Gem," I told her. She glanced up at me, concern in her eyes. "I've had worse."

"Maybe, but you aren't doing anything tonight but resting."

"The fuck I'm not."

She sat back, putting her hands on her hips. "Hunter, you're a mess."

"I'll heal. I'm just bruised and sore. Nothing's broken. And I can guarantee that part of me still works just fine."

I could see her fighting the smile, but she shook her head. "Nope. I won't be a party to causing more damage."

She rose, but I grabbed her wrist, moving my other hand to her ass and shoving her body into my face. Her cry was delectable as I nibbled on her skin.

"You're not denying me my pleasure, Gemma." I pushed her closer, spreading her legs and sliding myself down to sink my tongue into her. "You're dripping," I muttered, nipping her clit.

"Hunter—"

I stopped her words, pushing my tongue deep into her and savoring the sweetness of her. I was relentless, my tongue and fingers working in tandem until her body was quivering. She moaned, and it sent my erection pounding against my pants. Her fingers were pulling at my hair, her pelvis bucking against my face, and I could sense she was close. I wanted her to come, to fall apart on me as I owned the most sensitive place on her body, claiming it again and reminding her who she belonged to. With a cry that clawed through my body as it ripped from her throat, she came, her climax drenching her. I continued to suck and lick until she was trembling.

Pushing from me, she stumbled back. "That wasn't nice," she complained in a husky voice.

"That was retribution for sharing your tits. Now get back over here and ride me. I need you coming while I'm deep inside of you, pretty thing."

The shiver that ran through her was stimulating, and I couldn't wait to be deep inside of her. But I knew she was right. I wasn't up to par and pushing myself would leave me hurting even more in the morning. I unbuttoned my pants and freed myself, stroking my length as she watched with hungry eyes.

"You're letting me lead?" she asked, her tits swaying with the movement of her hips as she moved over me.

"Relinquish my control to you?" The thought had my dick twitching in my hand. She lowered herself over me, and I lined myself up, groaning as she slowly enveloped me. She really was soaked, and she was so tight that I wasn't certain I could last long.

Leaning against me, she brushed her lips over mine. She was confident and seductive, and I loved this side of her as much as I loved it when she submitted to me. I didn't like submissive women, but I'd only been with a handful who were aggressive. I wasn't the type to submit, so the result was always a struggle for dominance that left a nasty taste in my mouth.

Gemma tested everything I'd enjoyed with women. The controlling side of me thrilled with commanding her and watching her break. The aggressive side loved how she let me own every part of her and dictate how we progressed in every part of our new relationship. And the calmer side of me, the one who got hard just at the thought of her feistiness, embraced that part of her. That was the Gemma who was now riding me like I was the one thing she'd been craving since the last time I took her.

Her hands slid up my chest, gripping onto my shoulders as she threw her head back. Mine were tight around her waist, giving me leverage to meet the dropping of her body with my thrusts. She pushed her breasts out as her back bowed, and I pulled one in my mouth, relishing the moan that filled the silence of the surrounding night. I sucked and bit her nipple, swiping my tongue around it before dragging my teeth along it. The skin around it had pebbled, and as I licked it, I could feel the small ridges of her excitement.

She stopped her movement, and I tried forcing her rhythm again. "I'm in control," she said against my mouth before lifting herself, my hardness flopping against my stomach. I gave her an annoyed look, but she shoved my hands away and turned. With a groan, I realized what she was doing. Resting on her knees, she leaned her ass toward me, and I watched her envelop me before she rode me, that firm ass mesmerizing me with its motion.

Grasping her hips, I tried to calm the impending climax her move had caused. I pulled her against my chest, ignoring her complaint and taking a breast in my hand while my other reached for her clit. Her cry as I played with it lit my soul on fire, making me throb at the sound.

"I don't know if I want to relinquish all the control to you. I need to break you, Gem. Come for me, pretty thing."

She lurched forward, but I held her steady. I remained embedded deep inside of her as her muscles clenched, her legs squeezing tighter with every second she grew closer to her orgasm. Until finally, she came undone with a cry that called to the most feral part of me. Her body shook, her channel spasming so tight that it nearly forced me over the edge. Pushing her forward, her hands fell to my knees, and I yanked her down on me, driving her hips to meet my pelvis. I continued slamming her body back. The sound of her ass cheeks hitting me drove me to where I could do no more than heed my body's call. My climax washed over me like the pounding surf, drowning me with every wave of release.

"Gods, Hunter, fill me," she cried, and I stilled her against me, pushing with a last thrust into her, my fingers so tight on her hips that they were leaving marks in the flesh.

She fell against me, and I released her, bringing my hands up to cup her breasts as we both caught our breath. She shivered, and I pinched her nipples before picking her up from me and pulling her into my arms.

"You are something, Gem," I mumbled into her hair before finding her lips and devouring them. She pushed me over, the hard ground scratching against my back, and laid on my chest.

"You're not too bad yourself, Hunt. I'd say we make a good team."

"That we do, Gem." It was the truth. We had made a good team getting the stone, and we paired perfectly together in every way.

I held her to my chest, stroking my fingers through her hair, wondering at how that one moment in the Governor's home had changed the course of my life so immensely.

THE NEXT FEW days were long and tedious. My injuries healed thanks to the nursing Gemma gave me with her body. Any thought of aching muscles and bruises disappeared as soon as she tempted me, and that was often. We didn't talk about the events with the shapeshifter again. My anger about her exposed chest had simmered, but her words regarding the stones still bothered me. She'd laughed it off when I'd questioned her about them, saying she'd used them as a lure, not realizing the shifter would fall for it. But I wasn't entirely sure I believed that. I stayed quiet, preferring to remain ignorant than admit to myself that she might be lying to me. The thought left a strange, gutted sensation in my chest, and I didn't like it.

"So, the wind stone," she said, bringing her horse to a stop as the terrain before us dipped. The grass slowly gave way to the desolate sand that defined the realm of Tronekrin.

"Guarded by nasty wind sirens," I answered, stopping beside her. "You ready for this?"

"Not sure. I try to avoid this part of Tronekrin. The coastal sides are more enjoyable. The desert, not my thing."

"I don't know that it's anyone's thing since it's a haunted cemetery of wind witches. Most of us avoid jobs in this area. I can't even think of anyone who was idiotic enough to step foot in this desert."

"Stint did."

"Stint? That bastard braved the wind wraiths of the Cursed Desert?"

"Uh-huh."

I scrunched my brows, thinking of Stint, who was a massive beast of a man, taking a job out here. "How do you know?"

"Because he told me after we finished fucking." Her voice had a teasing tone, but it didn't help the fury the words caused in me.

"Stint fucked you? That moron touched you?"

She looked over at me, amusement in her eyes. "He's not a moron. And no, I fucked him. Rode him so hard I nearly broke him, but it was worth it. He's got a cock the size—"

"Gemma." Her name came out as a snarl through my clenched teeth.

She arched her brow. "That jealousy of yours is sexy, Hunter. Should I tell you about my other conquests just to see how hard you take me?"

"Don't tempt me to bend you over and show you how hard I'll take you right here, pretty thing. And when I see Stint, he'll be lucky if he can walk when I'm done with him."

She dropped from her horse, giving him a pat. "He could barely walk when I was done with him."

A blaze of heat whipped through me, and I gritted my teeth so hard my jaw pulsed with pain.

"Really, Hunt. With all the women you've fucked over the past fifteen years, I don't know why you'd expect that I was sitting around all prim and proper, saving my virginity for you. What fun would that be, anyway?" She led the horse over to a small stand of bushes, tethering him before looking back at me. "I wouldn't be able to handle half your size if I hadn't choked on a few others before letting you own my mouth."

Even with the anger fuming within me, the rise in my pants was noticeable. I frowned, trying to ignore the sensation. Leading my horse to hers, I dismounted and, after getting him settled, stomped over to her. With a quick move, I had her hair twisted around my fingers. Her neck went back, her lips parting perfectly.

"Need I remind you that this mouth is mine? That this body is mine? That you are mine?" The shiver of excitement that trembled through her had me throbbing. Her amber eyes were lit with it. "I don't want to know what you did before I made you mine. I am the only one who gets to use you like the slut you are." Shit, I hadn't meant to sound like such an ass, but she stirred the ire in me. She did it purposely. I had a feeling it turned her on to watch my anger seethe until it drove me to this point. And I knew this version of me left her soaking. "Now drop to your knees and show me that mouth is mine."

"Here?" The frantic quality to her eyes had my stomach knotting in anticipation.

"Here. If I'm going to sacrifice myself to a wind wraith for you, you can prove to me it's my cock you worship."

A whimper fell from those luscious lips, and it was a sound that stroked my dick as if her hand were holding it. I pulled her against me, making sure she could feel how hard she had me. Reaching up her shirt, I took her breast in my hand, her nipple

119

pebbling with my touch. This probably wasn't the place, but I didn't care. I wanted her, and there was no way I could concentrate on surviving with a hard-on this bad. Pushing her shirt up, I took one of her breasts into my mouth, loving how her nipple hardened even more while I sucked on it. I flicked my tongue against it as I plunged my fingers down her pants, finding the dripping arousal I'd known was there. My dominating ways left her drenched, which was why I couldn't help but continue them. If this was going to be our dynamic, then so be it, because it made my girl come undone in ways that drove me mad.

Her hands twisted the material of my shirt as I kissed her, my tongue entangling with hers. The moan that came from her reverberated against my chest, causing my heart to beat uncontrollably. I shoved two fingers into her, and she lurched forward, her kiss growing more desperate.

"That's it, pretty thing. I want you to come on my fingers." I really wanted her coming around me as I pounded her, but this definitely wasn't the place for that. Her breaths grew sporadic, her fingers so tightly wrapped in my shirt that I thought the material would rip. She was cresting, her climax so close her muscles clenched around my fingers. I pulled them free, pushing her away from me.

Her cry was one that gripped me with its wounded sound, but I ignored it. I brought my fingers to my mouth, running my tongue over the essence that remained, savoring every lick. She looked at me with eyes that were fiery and dangerous, her legs twisting tightly. I'd left her pissed and wanting, but I wasn't getting her off that easily. "Take your shirt off and drop to your knees, Gemma, like a good girl."

The surprise on her face as her mouth gaped was glorious. "But I—"

I grabbed her by the neck, loving the groan my move set free, and pulled her to me. "I said drop to your knees. I'm going to fuck that mouth so hard that your orgasm will tear you apart with its intensity. Now on your knees, pretty thing, before I change my mind and leave you without release."

There was a tick in her jaw, and I wondered if I'd gone too far. I was waiting for her to tell me when I crossed the line, when I pushed too far with my control of her. But each time, she surprised me.

She fell to her knees and pulled her shirt off before yanking me forward by the pants. With each button she unhooked, my dick danced in expectation. Her moves were aggressive, stirring the desire in me. Threading my fingers through her hair, I met her eyes as she stroked me, her tongue reaching out to lick the dribble of pre-cum that spurted in anticipation. Her eyes still held that fire, and I loosened my grip on her hair, letting her have control for a moment. She descended on my shaft like I was her sustenance. Each drop of her mouth left me breathless, my ability to take that control back lost as she devoured my cock.

"Fuck, Gem," I moaned, my grip in her hair tightening. I hit the back of her throat, and she gagged, the sound like a siren's call. She moaned at my reaction, the vibrations bringing me closer to my release. I pulled her from me, loving how saliva dribbled down her chin, tempting me to drop and lick it from her. "Play with yourself, Gem. I want to watch you come before I fill that pretty mouth of yours."

Her body trembled, lurching toward me as if I'd pulled a leash on her. That image sent all sorts of strange feelings through me. I really didn't know what it was about Gemma that left me unhinged like this, and I wasn't sure I was too comfortable with the man she drove me to be.

She slipped her hand in her pants, my length quivering at the sight. I rubbed her breast, pinching her nipple before stepping back to watch her take over. I'd left her on the brink of climax, so I knew it wouldn't be long before she was coming all over her fingers. Stroking myself, I watched her squeeze her tit, her other hand fluttering in her pants. I wished I'd ripped them from her so

I could see her fingers plunging in and out. As it stood, just watching her like this had me so hard that it was likely I'd break with her.

Her lips parted, her head falling back as a cry came from her. Her body was trembling, the flesh of her tits moving in ripples.

"Eyes on me, Gem."

She jerked her head forward, her amber eyes hooded with pleasure, and my climax edged closer. Just as she came, her body a beautiful rhythm of shakes and quivers, I laced my fingers through her hair and shoved her down on me. Her hands flew to my knees as she braced herself, the muscles in her arms still shaking while I fucked her mouth. She met every thrust with a gag that ripped my climax from me in pieces. And in one overwhelming plunge, I exploded, holding her head so tight while I filled her that she choked.

I released her, staggering back, my orgasm still pummeling through me. I grabbed my dick and pushed out the remains with one last grunt, watching as it splashed over her breasts. Gemma was still on her knees, catching her breath, and I wondered if I'd taken it too far. I hadn't meant to hurt her, but seeing her like that had worked me up so badly that I'd lost all control. I expected to see daggers in her eyes, to see her lips tight with anger, but instead, I found a sparkle in her eyes. She looked so sexy it threatened to make me hard again. Spit and cum were dripping from her nipples. Her stomach muscles were trembling, and there was a pink hue to her cheeks.

"Fuck, you're beautiful," I mumbled, my voice hoarse.

She motioned me back to her and looked up at me with those big eyes. I rubbed my thumb over the cum that was collected on my tip and brought it to her mouth. The sight of her running her tongue over it clawed through me. I helped her stand and brought the hand she'd pleasured herself with to my mouth, swirling my tongue around her finger. Her taste sent an erotic sensation rushing through my body.

The mix of spit and cum over her breasts left me feeling like I'd marked her, making her mine in yet another way.

"Now I'm ready to face the damned wraiths," I said, fixing my pants. I rolled my neck, trying to stay on my feet. My knees were weak, and I didn't know how I was going to fight wind wraiths in this state. I supposed it was better than doing it with a raging hard-on. "How do we find the stone?"

She'd made her way to the horses and was using the dress she'd worn the first part of our trip to clean her chest up. My eyes followed the way her tits jiggled as she cleaned them. I needed to look away before she got me worked up again, but the movement had me too entranced. She gave me a knowing smile before covering them with her shirt. I watched as she weaved her hair into a long braid, her fingers moving nimbly with the task before she turned back to the saddle.

Digging around in the saddlebag, she said, "With this." Her hand opened to reveal the earth stone.

"And how is that supposed to help?" I scratched my head, not understanding how these stones worked. And I didn't want to think about how she knew. The thought stripped away the remaining pleasure that had been settling in my core. That damned witch's son. I swore I'd kill him when I saw him.

She gave me a side-glance. "Are you ripping through the leather of your belt for any particular reason?"

"No," I answered tersely, shoving my hands down. "Just figure out where the stone is so we can get this over with."

Shaking her head, Gemma walked past me, toward where the oasis-like green grass turned over to endless sand. I could see she was having trouble walking steadily, and I couldn't help smirking at the thought that I'd caused that crooked walk.

"I can feel you smirking behind me," she called without turning.

"Can't help myself. You need a hand walking?" She shot me a dirty look, but I could see the corners of her mouth fighting her smile. As she neared the sand, I ran to her, yanking her back. "Don't go in."

"Why not? We need to find it."

"And you'll find it through the stone."

Huffing, she put her hand on her hip and frowned at me. "That won't put the wind stone in our hands. We need to go into the desert."

"I'll go in. You just figure out where it is."

The change in her demeanor was swift, anger lining her eyes as the amber in them faded to dark brown. "You will not pull that masculine shit on me, Hunter."

"I'm not pulling masculine anything on you. I know what you're capable of, Gemma, and defeating a wind wraith is not one of those things."

"How dare—"

"You will die."

"Then I die. I'm not letting you sideline me because you think I'm too weak, that I'm just some girl who can't handle this."

"I don't think anything of the sort." She was irritating me with her constant need to prove she was invulnerable. My emotions vacillated when I was with her, from craving to annoyance. "The wraiths like to blind their victims, to leave them wandering the desert until they die of thirst and hunger or heat stroke. But that's just what happens to the men when the female wraiths attack. It isn't the females you need to worry about, Gemma. They simply play with their victims and feed from their confusion. The males sleep while the females play unless a female walks into the sand. Then they wake, and the female wraiths slink away."

I'd seen it once, traveling with a team of mercenaries, ready to brave the wind wraiths and bring back a bit of their essence for a buyer. Stint wasn't the only one who had been foolish enough to venture into the innocent-looking trap. We'd lost three out of the five of us. I hadn't wanted to tell Gemma, knowing how confident she was. It was the only time I'd ever worked with a team and the only time I'd ever come back empty-handed. I knew when to admit a feat was too much, which was never until that moment.

"They are particularly cruel to females. I've seen what they do, Gem. I won't let you set foot in that desert."

"You said you'd never been in. You lied to me?"

"I didn't lie. I've never stepped into that sand. I watched two men on my team get swallowed up by that desert, and one woman get eaten alive." The horror of watching Krina's death remained imprinted on my memory. She hadn't been the most likable mercenary, but she hadn't deserved what they'd done to her. "They circled her so she couldn't run, the sand flinging in their current, tearing through her clothes first. It coated her from head to toe as their shapeless forms raped her in the only way they could. The sand shredded her from the inside out, her skin then tearing from her limbs with their greedy attempts for touch in a form that gives them none. By the time they were done, there was nothing left of her but the echo of her screams and the white bones of her body." Those screams had taken me years to forget, and I'd never once second-guessed my choice to flee the desert. They'd destroyed her within minutes before I could even reach the edge of the sand.

Gemma's eyes had grown large with terror, her skin pale. There was a slight tremble in her lips, a tremble I hadn't brought to her this time.

"Did the witch's bastard give you any clue how to beat these things?" I swallowed back my fear, knowing I needed to be the one to go in. I wasn't about to let that asshole have her, even if it meant I spent days wandering the desert as the wraiths taunted me. And I sure as fuck wouldn't let her walk into that desert.

"Cover your eyes." Her voice came out in a hush. "Cover them with a cloth thin enough to see through but thick enough to block the sand."

"Great, that should be easy," I replied, sarcasm tainting my words.

Peering back at our gear, I contemplated what I could use. I pulled Gemma against me, saying, "Don't move past this spot. I don't want you even tempting those things to drag you in there." She didn't argue, instead she leaned against me as I wrapped my arm around her neck. "I don't care how fearless you are, Gemma. I will always protect you."

"And I won't always let you," she returned, grasping my arm and pushing it tighter around her. "But this time, I will."

I kissed the top of her head and let her go. "Stay. You move an inch, and there will be punishment involved."

"Oh?" she replied with too much excitement.

I laughed as I walked away. "You might not like my punishments, pretty thing. I'll ensure you don't come until we've found every one of these damned stones."

I heard the hiss that came through her clenched teeth. My laughter continued until I returned with a strip of the underskirt of her dress. The same dress she'd used to clean herself up earlier. I tried to ignore the way my balls tightened at the thought. Gemma had a hold on me I couldn't explain, one I didn't want to remove, no matter how it affected me.

"Did you find it?" I asked.

"Yeah, look." She passed me the stone, and I held it before me, watching as the streams of tan within it writhed like snakes. They twisted and curved into each other before separating and pointing to our right. The tails coiled in so there was no confusion about the direction they were pointing.

"Gods, that's bizarre," I muttered, rubbing my eyes to check if I'd really seen it.

"That's magic. But I can't tell where it's pointing. You'll need to take the stone with you and keep referring to it."

"That should be fun while the wraiths batter at me. If they discover what I have, they may try to break it from my hold."

"True. Hold tight to it."

I glanced at her, hoping she could read the irritation on my face. "That's helpful."

Her lips pursed as she stared off into the distance. "I try," she mumbled absently before gazing back to where our things were. "Stay here."

Before I could reply, she ran off. There was bustling as she dug in the bag, then fooled with the gear for the horses. She came running back to me with that damned dress and the reins.

"What are you doing?" She had me completely confused by this point.

"Hush and wait."

She stretched out the reins, unbuckling then knotting them together. The dress she tore into long strips, one after the other, which she then tied together before attaching them to the connected reins. She grabbed an end and looped it in my belt, binding it.

"I had no idea you were into bondage, but I can play along with that."

She snapped the other end at me, the leather from the reins stinging my skin.

"Do that again, pretty thing, and I'll be slapping your ass with that leather." The thought had my pulse racing. I'd never been into rough play, but I could see Gemma bringing that out in me, just like she did the control.

Her eyes twinkled with desire. "They're not for my ass or for tying me up." There was a slight rise in her pitch on the last words. "They're to keep you anchored." She gave a tug and pulled me over to her. "Now get in there so you can come back and show me how you want to use these on me." By her last word, she'd wrapped the reins around her wrists. Tugging them, she gave me a wicked grin, sending my bulge straining against my pants.

"It's not nice to tease, Gem."

"Who said I was teasing?" She released her hands and snagged the strip of cloth from me, bringing it up to cover her eyes. This time, my cock jumped so hard it almost pulled me over. Shit, I didn't know what she was doing to me or to my body, and I wasn't certain how I felt about it. Never had a woman had this much control over me.

"Give me that before I come in my pants," I said, ripping it from her. Her only response was a playful giggle, which I found both annoying and cute.

Unexpectedly, she grabbed my face and kissed me. It was a sensual kiss, one that claimed every part of me and sent me reeling with emotion. "Come back to me," she mumbled.

"I will and when I do, I'm going to tie you up for the rest of the night and do naughty things to you."

"Is that a promise?"

"Damn right, that's a promise." I kissed her once more and gently pushed her back. Gazing into her eyes, I realized what a hold she had on me. Below my aggressive, dominating façade lay the heart she'd claimed, one that had only ever been hers and always would be. She was it for me, and that acknowledgment was a terrifying one for someone who had never settled down. I'd never let myself get close enough to anyone to risk losing myself, but Gemma had changed that.

"Stop staring at me and go before I change my mind and head in there myself," she said, crossing her arms.

It had been the right thing to say to focus me. I'd die before I let her walk into that desert. I turned from her, flexing my muscles and stopping at the edge of the sand.

"Here goes nothing." Bringing the material to my eyes, I tied it tight. It was thin enough to offer some sight, but having it on was disconcerting. Taking the stone from my pocket, I lifted my foot to take my first step.

"Hunter," Gemma called. "I love you."

Smiling, but not looking back, I replied, "Save that for later,

Gem. I want to hear you screaming it when I'm fucking you so hard that you're coming around my cock."

I heard her sharply inhale, and my smile grew. She may have broken me, but I was breaking her with every dirty word I said to her. I dropped my foot into the sand. Each step further I took from her, the sand churned, and the heat grew. I glanced at the stone, watching the waves coil and shift. The air grew thin, the sand rising to form the first wraith. As the grains stung my face, I wondered why the witch's son would have sent Gemma on this journey. No man who truly loved her would have ever wanted her anywhere near the twisted evil that made up the remains of the world's witches. The thought of him lit the fire in my chest, the one that wanted to strangle him and watch him take his last breath at my hands. I looked at the wraith, whose shape I could discern in the cloud of sand.

"Bring your best, bitch, you're going to need it." The wraith roared, but I ignored it, walking straight through it. The sand pelted me with a vengeance, but the wraith didn't attack.

I continued toward the stone, ignoring the wraiths and discovering that they held no power if I didn't fight back or show fear. It was the emotion they fed on, the fear that instigated them. Perhaps that was why the witch boy had sent Gemma. Maybe he had more faith in her fearlessness than I did. The thought hurt, and for a second, I wavered. A wraith sensed my change in emotion and attacked.

Dammit. I shoved the thought away and walked through the storm of sand, pushing against the force that was trying to lift my blindfold and turn me around. Restraining myself from fighting back or showing any reaction, I glanced down at the stone. The surrounding storm calmed again as the waves in the stone shifted. I was getting closer, but the lead Gemma had fastened on me to help me find my way back was slowly running short. Praying the stone was close, I continued, ignoring the pull that was growing on my waist and the nudging fear of what Gemma would do if she ran out of that lead.

CHAPTER NINE

GEMMA

The sand swallowed Hunter up within moments of him walking into the desert. I could see his form through the wraiths that surrounded him, and I clenched my hands so tightly on the leather reins that they cut into my skin. Every second he was out there, I resisted the urge to pull him back with the anchor. The wind storm around him settled, moving from him, and I breathed a sigh of relief. He'd found a way to avoid the terror of the wraiths, something that further solidified my appreciation of his skills. My mind began sifting through my knowledge of the wind wraiths and their desert of death. The things Breck had told me, the things Stint had said, the stories that were whispered in passing or after too many drinks.

The line grew taut, the slack lessening with each step further Hunter took from me. Those steps were confident, never letting up, even when one wraith moved to attack him. He walked right through the thing, its form scattering. It was as if Hunter feared nothing. The last of the reins straightened in front of me, and there was a tug as Hunter took another step.

Fearless. That's what he was. He wasn't fighting, and he wasn't frightened. Breck had told me not to let the wraiths get to me. That was the secret. As Hunter took another step, the last of the lead almost slipped from my hands. I caught it and took a step into the sand. Closing my eyes to the blinding storm I knew would rise around me, I took a few more steps and dug my heels into the ground. Hunter stopped moving, and I prayed that meant he had found the stone.

The wraiths circled me. I could feel their presence, their form pressing against me. I didn't move, scrunching my eyes tight so they wouldn't force them open. "I am not afraid of you. You are nothing but air and sand. I am form. I am strength. You will not break me. Only one man has that privilege."

They shrieked, the storm battering me, but I didn't flinch. I knew if I showed any fear, they would devour me as they had the mercenary Hunter had told me about. I wondered if he'd slept with her, then shooed the thought away, not wanting any emotion to slip through. Minutes ticked by and the storm continued to rage. They were trying to get me to falter, their sandy forms sliding over my skin, up my shirt. At one point, it even seemed as if rough hands were on my breasts, pawing at them. I gritted my teeth and stayed calm, the sensation dissipating as if my lack of reaction had destroyed the wraith. With each passing minute, my worry for Hunter grew. Just as I let it slip through my show of fearlessness, the line slackened. He was there, returning to me.

I took a step back, wrapping the loosened lead around my wrist and tugging so he'd know which direction to go. I took another step back, the wraiths screaming all around me. And another step and another until I stepped outside of the desert. The difference in the terrain under my boots was noticeable, the heaviness of the air fading. I continued to tighten the lead, backing further away as a precaution since I still had my eyes squeezed tightly shut. The reins grew slack, and my heart thudded so hard it knocked a tortured cry from me. My mind immediately attributed the lack of resistance to Hunter's demise, but large hands encased my cheeks, holding me steady and kissing me. My heartbeat calmed, my eyes opening to see his green eyes looking back at me.

"You're alive," I said, the words just a hush in the relief that encased them.

"I promised you I'd come back, and," he took the reins from me, snapping the leather between his hands, "I promised to use these on you while I do naughty things to you."

Goosebumps emerged on my skin, a shiver accompanying them. Hunter brushed his hand over my hair, his eyes following the sand that fell from it. He raised a brow, his eyes narrowing, so I gave him an innocent shrug.

"You haven't been a good girl, have you, Gemma?"

"I had no choice, Hunter. It was that or lose you in the desert."

"You had a choice, and you made it."

I frowned, but excited nerves were behind it. "So you wanted me to drop the lead and let you find your way back on your own?"

His jaw clenched, and I could see he was trying to appear angry, even though I'd bested him. "I told you not to set foot in the sand."

"And I chose to disobey you."

His eyes shimmered, and he gripped my hip, bringing me hard against him.

"You're not winning this argument, Hunter."

"Oh, I'm winning it. And I will teach you to disobey me."

I couldn't help but laugh, which only seemed to annoy him more. Bringing my face close to his, I bit his bottom lip, dragging my teeth along it. There were small grains of sand on it, and they ground against my teeth. "I don't obey you, Hunter. I choose to let you lead, but there will be times when I choose to make my own decisions."

The green in his eyes danced with amusement.

"Where's the stone?" I asked, pushing at him. He didn't release me, but he brought out a plain white stone and held it before me. I took it from him, turning it back and forth in my hands. Only then did the magic appear, the white loosening from the shape of the stone and turning to swirling funnels within what was now a clear vessel. The movement mesmerized me. "It's beautiful."

"Yes, it is," he replied, a faraway tone in his voice. I peered up at him, seeing that his eyes were still on me, filled with adoration. The blush that covered my cheeks was warm, and I dropped my eyes, the weight of that look holding so much within it.

He tipped my chin, forcing my eyes back to his. "I love you, Gemma. Every fearless, frustrating, annoying, rebellious, and submissive part of you."

His kiss was warm and tender, the intensity of it interrupted only when grains of sand played on our tongues.

"I think it's best if we find someplace to rinse before you show me how sexy you are with nothing but this leather holding your wrists together," he teased.

"That would be a wise idea. Let's find someplace we can share that bath." Anticipation rippled through me at the thought.

"Mmm, so I can have some fun before I get to my dessert."

I tugged the reins, leading him behind me as I walked to the horses. "Come on, I want that dick clean before you fuck me with it."

His groan was delicious, and I was looking forward to hearing more of them. When he groaned, it came from deep in his chest, rumbling through him.

We packed the horses back up and rode off, leaving the wind wraiths behind. It took us another hour of traveling before we discovered an oasis with a cool spring. There, we washed away the sand, and Hunter made good on his promise to test the leather out, taking me to places that I didn't know anyone could. Ones I never wanted to forget or leave behind.

Hunter lay spread out on the grass outside the spring. We'd stayed there for two days, doing nothing but enjoying each other's bodies. It was what I imagined being in the heavens with the gods was like. His arms held me tight every night, his kisses layering my body.

I dropped next to him, my body still wet from rinsing our sex off in the spring.

"Let's stay here, Gem."

I picked my head up, leaning my chin on his solid chest. "Here?"

"Yes, let's hide away here. We can live off the land. I can live off your pussy if need be."

I giggled, nuzzling his chin with my nose. "We can't live here forever, Hunter."

"Why not?" He turned his body into mine, pulling me against him.

"Because there's nothing here."

"Nothing but you and me, and that's all we need." He was serious, and that scared me. I drew back some.

"Hunter, we're not the settle down and stay in one place kind of people."

Hurt passed over his eyes, causing an ache in my chest.

"We could be," he whispered. There was a vulnerability to his words, one I didn't want to destroy with my response. I stayed quiet, seeing the understanding there.

"Hunter—"

"No, you're right," he muttered, lying on his back again, his arms going behind his head, no longer holding me. "We're not that type. Get some sleep, Gemma. We'll leave in the morning."

He said no more, closing his eyes and closing me off in that one move. The conversation didn't come back up, not in the morning as we packed up, nor for the days we traveled through Tronekrin. The absence of it left a distance between us. It was subtle, but it hovered over us. His emotions grew guarded, his words gained an edge to them, and I wondered if I'd been wrong in shutting him down. If I should have agreed and remained in our oasis, far from the reality that awaited me, hidden from the shadowed man he had become.

"ARE you sure we can't get the fire stone before the water stone?" Hunter asked again. I'd told him multiple times now, but he kept asking, as if I'd change my mind.

"We can't."

"We're passing through Laviak—"

"Hunter, stop asking me. Breck was very specific. The water stone must be in hand before fire; otherwise, the fire stone remains unattainable."

"Fucking witch's son. You realize we're days still from Iceliar, yet Laviak is mere hours from us."

"Yes, I realize that. Spindara is hours from us, too, but we're not going there."

He grumbled something about going there to kill the witch's son. His jealousy amused me. I hadn't slept with Breck in years, hadn't spoken to him until he approached me with this job. Yet Hunter acted like he was still my lover. It made me wonder if he had some insecurity about Breck that he wasn't sharing with me. There was no reason to be jealous. I didn't love Breck. What I'd had with him had been nothing to what I felt for Hunter.

We continued on in an uncomfortable silence that only grew the closer we came to Laviak. By the time we were deep on the paths of Laviak, it had grown to a festering wound. Laviak took up the southwestern corner of Carenth. To avoid the Laviak pits, we would have had to add an extra day of travel west through Moreling, then back into Carenth. Or go east through Spindara, then back into Carenth. Hunter took the direct route, and I'd been questioning his intention the entire time. There was no turning back now. We were too far in to do anything but head directly through.

Hunter stopped his horse. The anger I'd seen increasing in him was now coating him like a cloak that left deep shadows around his face.

"What is it you're not telling me, Gemma?" he barked.

I reeled back, hating the tone he was giving me. "I've told you everything."

"No, you haven't. What is it your witch's son wants with the stones?"

Now he was *my* witch's son. The stewing Hunter had been doing for the past few days, the same emotion I'd sensed from him as we'd grown further from the desert, that I'd noticed in his movements, in the aggression that he'd had each time he'd taken me since, was pouring from him.

"I told you. He wants to destroy them." It wasn't entirely the truth, and I didn't know why I was so keen on leaving out the entirety of it.

"You told the shifter the stones could bring back the glory of the witches. That bringing the stones together would restore their power. He doesn't want to destroy the stones. He wants them to bring the witches back."

His gaze was penetrating, as if he could see right through the mistruth I'd given him.

"You lied to me, didn't you?"

"I didn't lie."

"Dammit, Gemma! You said you were just saying that to the

shifter, that it was only to mislead him. You fucking lied to me, not to him."

I'd never seen him so angry. The veins were swelling in his neck, his jaw so tight I could see the muscles in it.

"I didn't lie."

"No, you didn't tell me the complete truth, and then you lied to cover it. What else have you been lying about?"

"Nothing."

"No? You're not planning to take those stones back and spread your legs for the witch's son like you did for me?"

Now, it was my turn to be angry. The ire boiled in my gut. "Why would you even say something like that?"

"You fucking lied to me, Gemma! You led me on this mission for these blasted stones, risking my life for what? For him?"

"You came on this quest with me! I never invited you. You could have given me the seeing stone and walked away."

"The fuck I could! That stone was mine. And you know what? Now they're all mine. I'm sure my buyer will offer a pretty penny for the three I have, and your fuck buddy can buy them from him."

"You asshole. Those are mine."

"No, nothing's yours any longer, Gemma." The layered meaning behind those words shredded me like a rusted knife. "You've been lying to me this entire time, fucking that sick bastard...dammit, you probably fucked him right before we met up. Was that after or before he whored you out to the governor?"

If I'd been off my horse, I would have slapped him. Fire seethed in my belly. Yes, I'd given him a mistruth, but the way he was acting was out of bounds. "You're a jealous, possessive prick, Hunter. Too caught up in yourself and your needs to see what you're blind to. Well, fuck you. I don't need you. I've been fine all these years without you. You want those stones, you take them. I'll find the others on my own then steal them back from your buyer."

I turned my horse, not wanting to look at him, hoping he would realize what a mistake he was making and how his words had hurt me. He muttered a few profanities before he rode off in the other direction. My heart dropped. The fragments that were left from the wounds his words had caused collapsed, leaving an ugly ache in my chest. I remained there, fighting the tears that were begging for release, before riding my horse hard in the direction we'd been heading. The opposite direction from where Hunter had ridden.

My mind couldn't comprehend how his one question had morphed into his leaving me. He'd been relentless in questioning me about the stones, about why Breck needed them. I should have known he was suspicious. And yes, what Breck wanted to do was terrifying, but there weren't enough witches to do harm, and what were a handful of flesh-eating witches in the world? Nothing but a nuisance. I had needed to find Hunter and finding the stones assured I would. Now I wished I hadn't found him, that I'd gotten the stones on my own and that Breck had lied and said he was dead. My heart would have hurt, but not nearly as much as it was hurting now.

Something startled my horse, and he bucked, throwing me from his back before running off.

"Shit! No!" I screamed after him. But he was gone, and I was stuck in the middle of Laviak alone, with no gear, no food, no Hunter.

I ran my hands over my face and calmed myself. The pits were enormous, and I had no idea how far I was into them. Maybe I'd find the horse if I continued in that direction...if the golems didn't find me first. I walked for hours, the lightless pits growing even darker as night fell. Hunter was never coming back, and with the thought, my heart broke even further before I covered the pain with my anger. How dare he accuse me of sleeping with Breck before that night. As if I'd only been using Hunter to find the stones. There was no truth to it, but somehow he'd convinced himself of it. I'd noticed the change in him slowly over the last few days as his questions increased, and I continued to deliver the same answers.

He'd brought me so much pleasure the night we'd found the wind stone and the days that followed. All until I'd made the fateful mistake of turning down his offer to stay there. I'd known it had hurt him, but I hadn't realized it had shut him down completely. That, somehow, in my fear of letting myself have that comfort, I had crushed him. And now he'd left me. I knew Hunter enough to know he wouldn't be back, that he wasn't the kind of man to come crawling back. That his pride would lead him to some new adventure where he'd take other women to cover his pain until he was over me completely. Although, I didn't know that either of us could get over each other completely. I knew I couldn't.

Sighing, I put my emotions aside, hardening myself to them as I'd done for years. Now that I'd opened my heart, it was difficult to close it off again.

The Laviak pits were sweltering and dry. Their mythology spoke of them as the birthplace of the creatures that roamed our world, spewing from the pit of the underworld where the worst of the gods ruled. I stayed on the path, knowing to venture from them risked sinking into molten lava that would scorch my skin off and lead me to an indescribable death. If the lava didn't get me, the lava witches would. Golems. They were what remained of the fire witches, stripped of their power and cursed to spend their existence in fire form. They made the wind wraiths look welcome.

On and on, I walked until night had fallen and the smoke from the pits blocked the moon. My only light was the flames that soared sporadically outside my path. I didn't dare sleep for fear of rolling into the lava. No creatures were foolish enough to wander the Laviak pits, only me. And only the golems, which I'd been lucky to avoid. Eerily lucky.

Stopping to rest my weary body, I leaned on a large stone that may have once been a pile of lava. The heat was almost unbearable. I leaned my head back, trying not to think about Hunter and how he'd left me. I knew how his mind worked. He saw my lie as betrayal, even if I hadn't meant it to be. I'd been lying to myself just as much, knowing how disturbing the thought of Breck using the stones to bring back the witch powers was. But for Hunter to twist that lie into a belief that I was using him, that what I had with Breck now was anything more than a business arrangement, was hurtful. The mere fact that he thought so little of my need to find him, that he seemed to forget completely that the only reason I was on this quest was to learn the truth about him, stung so that it was almost impossible not to be just as angry at him as he was at me.

The longer I sat there, the more that anger grew. Damn him for throwing what we had away so easily, as if it were nothing more than the contents of a chamber pot. If he didn't want my love, if what we'd had was so easily untethered, then perhaps I'd been wrong to love him.

My thoughts drifted as sleep took over against my will. I hadn't realized just how exhausted I was, both physically and emotionally. An uncomfortable heat woke me, and I forced my heavy eyes open. Morning had come, lighting the ugliness of the pits. I looked down to discover the source of the heat was a spark from the pits that had landed on my shirt. Jumping up, I patted the burning patch until there was only a scorched hole left. I ripped at it, tearing the bottom half of my shirt from my waist. The air against my open skin should have been refreshing, but this was Laviak, a place where refreshing wasn't a concept.

The sun continued to rise as I walked on, using the torn piece of material to wipe the sweat from my forehead. I'd only ventured into Laviak once for a buyer who wanted a piece of molten lava to show his friends he'd braved the pit of fire witches. It was good pay, but I'd wanted to strangle his lying rich ass the entire time. The trip had only taken me to the edge of the pits, not this far in.

To be honest, I didn't know how far I was or if the other side of the pits was steps away or days away. If it was the latter, I was dead.

I tried not to think about it as I continued my journey, but the heat made ignoring my thirst nearly impossible. There was no water source here, no vegetation. It was a vast land of nothing but fire and lava. The air on the path grew thicker, a layer of smoke hindering my vision and seeping into my lungs. The hairs on the back of my neck rose, my heart rate increasing. The fire witches were near. I'd taken a wrong path. Instead of spanning the outskirts of the pits, I'd walked directly into the middle of them, where the golems roamed within the flames.

I cursed Hunter for leaving me behind. Cursed myself for trusting him, and for lying to him. I'd gotten myself into this mess, and then he'd left me in it. I stopped walking, running my options through my head. Without the water stone, there was no way to retrieve the fire stone. And I had a distinct feeling there was no defeating the fire witches without whatever magic the water stone held. This wouldn't be like the Moreling desert. Ignoring these creatures was not how I would defeat them.

I contemplated turning back, but there was nothing behind me but the slow death of dehydration. Of course, there was nothing ahead of me but death, either. Damn, I was going to kill Hunter if I made it out of this. Cautiously, I moved ahead, the smoke clearing to reveal a patch of black tar-colored land. All I'd seen thus far had been a myriad of paths that intersected and continued in different directions. This was different. This was a place where the paths met, and within it stood a forest of charred trees. I couldn't see past the trees to make out what lay beyond them. I would need to walk through them to continue my journey. I looked around for an alternate path, knowing there was none. As I turned back to the trees, I stepped back, my heart leaping to my throat. Statues now stood before the trees. Statues of hardened stone, black and gnarled. Their expressions were horrifying, the positions of their bodies contorted. It almost looked as if people were in the stone, suffering an unimaginable death. I swallowed. What little saliva I had left stuck like a lump in my throat. Hesitantly, I took a step, remaining on the outskirts of the area. It took a lot to frighten me, but the thought of being close to those statues was terrifying.

As I continued moving, my hackles rose further, my pulse thumping so fast it was a wonder I hadn't passed out. My eyes grew large as one statue moved. A scream stuck in my throat when its fiery eyes opened and looked directly at me. A golem. Its frozen expression of agony broke and it let out a piercing wail. I couldn't move, fear holding my muscles hostage while the other statues broke free from their stasis. They lumbered toward me, each movement a strange series of clicks and segmented moves. Another one screeched so loud I thought my ears had burst.

The sound was enough to wake me. Adrenaline took over, and I ran, the creatures increasing their speed. Several of them shifted their bodies faster, blocking my way. I turned to go back, but my path was hidden in the smoke. I looked back at the things, watching in terror as they contorted their limbs, dropping to all fours and staring at me with those eyes of fire. A scream tore from my throat, shredding the dry consistency of it like sandpaper.

These were what remained of the fire witches. Cursed by the gods for daring to think themselves more powerful than the other witches. The story of how the gods had punished them to live their eternities in the flames of the pits was wrong. Their punishment had been worse, made into creatures from the depths of the underworld, their agony eternal as the gods turned them to living stone. No one knew because no one had ever survived.

I would never share the truth because this was my death. Another blood-curdling scream clawed from the deepest part of me as I looked from side to side, desperate for a way to escape. But there was none. The witches, who had dropped to their hands and feet, skittered closer, their heads twisting so their eyes were now resting where their mouths should be. I whimpered as they descended upon me, fear gripping me so intensely that my vision wavered. The exhaustion, the dehydration, the terror were too much for my body to handle. In one last act of mercy, I passed out. The horrifying fiery eyes of the witches lunging for me were the last thing I saw before blackness took over.

CHAPTER TEN

HUNTER

The expanse of Iceliar stood to every side of me. Once again, I questioned why I was here, not liking the answer that came each time. When I'd left Gemma in Laviak, I'd been beyond angry. She'd betrayed my trust, lied to me to cover the truth. I didn't know what to think anymore. Or if anything she'd told me was the truth. I'd left her, not looking back, not once stopping until I found myself in Spindara, the last place I wanted to be. I headed north, wanting to be as far from Spindara and the memories of my youth, of Gemma, of the witch's son as I could. But my horse was tired, my body weary, my guilt heavy.

I'd left her, just as I had when we were kids. But I'd gone back then, and this time, I hadn't. She was resourceful. She'd find her way out, and if she didn't, I convinced myself I didn't care. I found an inn in a small town on the border of Spindara. I'd been traveling for days and was ready for a distraction. Something to get my mind from Gemma. I took one, then two, fucking them both until the early hours of the morning when I sent them both from my bed. Neither had given me the satisfaction Gemma had, but the release had felt good. Having my mind on another woman's body had been a welcome distraction. And both women had left me drained. I slept the rest of the day, then headed out, focused on getting back to Carenth and as far from memories of Gemma as I could. But each day of travel brought thoughts of her back. Each woman I took in the different towns where I stopped only reminded me of how I missed her touch and how no other's would ever satisfy me the way hers had. And so, I'd continued forward, the days passing until I found myself in Iceliar.

The frozen river of Ikanthi lay before me, untouched. The ice upon it was so thick it spoke to the fact that Gemma had never made it. Something had stopped her path. Whether it was the cursed spirits of Laviak or the witch's son, I didn't know. Neither comforted me, but the latter at least held hope that by turning my back on her, I hadn't caused her death.

I turned my horse from the home of the water stone, not caring if it went undisturbed, and looked south, knowing where I'd go next. To face my past, to face my guilt, to face Gemma's lover and my undoing. Spurring the horse on, I fled Iceliar and made my way back to Spindara. It took many more days, days that gave me no comfort, my mind playing through every possibility of what I'd find. Gemma in his arms, riding him like she had me. She now his, with nothing to stop him from taking her. She'd failed her mission, and he owned her because I no longer did. I'd given up my claim on her no matter how it hurt. It made it easier to imagine she was pleasuring him than to imagine she was his prisoner. The prior brought anger to shield the pain in my chest. The latter only compounded the pain. If she was there unwillingly, then I'd been wrong about leaving her, wrong about not listening to her, not letting her explain why she'd lied to me and shutting her down. I didn't let myself think of the alternative to either scenario—that she had never made it back to Spindara to explain her failure. That she lay dead somewhere in the Laviak pits, the cursed witches feasting on her bones.

As days turned to nights, I only slowed my pace to stop in a few towns to ease the ache the ride was causing in my muscles and the one in my heart. I dabbled in a few women, letting their bodies replace hers, letting them take my mind from my guilt and pain.

"You've got it bad," the brunette at the bar where I'd stopped said to me. She had pretty blue eyes that reminded me of the sky on a cloudless day.

"I suppose I do."

"She must have really broken your heart." She leaned over the bar, her breasts spilling over the top of her dress. "Do you need something to take your mind off her?"

Fuck, I really did. It had been four days since the last town, and the Endless Forest was looming a day's ride ahead of me. My expectations were high that I'd find Gemma and regret the days I'd wasted riding there. That she'd be doing the things to the witch's son that she'd done to me. I wanted to take that image from my mind, the one that I'd planted there over the long, dull hours of traveling.

I picked up my ale and took a long swig, my eyes never leaving hers. When I lowered it, I said, "I do. Do you like it rough?"

"I'll like it any way you want to give it to me. Meet me round back in a few. I'm due a break."

She walked away, but I remained at the bar, glancing over at her until she finally left, heading to the back of the building. I tossed some coins on the bar and followed, looking forward to a reprieve from my incessant thoughts of Gemma. I walked out into the dingy alley to find the woman leaning against the wall, the sleeves of her dress pulled down her shoulders, her breasts spilling out.

As I grabbed her neck, her gasp was loud, bringing back memories of Gemma—Gemma's neck in my grasp, the way her heartbeat would always rise, how her chest would heave—and I couldn't leave my hand there. Shoving it down to her breasts, I caressed them, unable to get the thought of Gemma's from my head, no matter how I tried. It was like this each time, and this time I wouldn't let those thoughts disrupt my pleasure.

I hiked her skirts up while she freed my hungry length, playing with it with expert hands. Too expert, and my alarms went off. I pushed her hard against the wall, bringing my hand back to her neck and squeezing it tight.

"Are you charging me for this?" I growled.

Her eyes were wide, providing me with the answer I needed. "How did you know?" she choked out.

I dropped my hands and backed away, my body screaming at me. "Because I know a whore when I see one." Although I'd failed to recognize it this time because my mind had been on Gemma like it always seemed to be. I'd assumed the woman had worked at the bar, an assumption that had been based on her deliberate actions, deceiving me so I wouldn't suspect she was anything more than a barmaid. "I don't pay for sex. There are plenty of women willing to give it to me for free."

She grabbed at my shirt, yanking me to her. "I'm clean, I promise. I'm particular about my clients, and you're paid up. You want to fuck her, fuck me instead. Take me like you want her."

I released her neck, contemplating whether it was worth it. The thought of taking Gemma from my mind and finding any amount of pleasure was tempting. I wrapped my fingers around her waist, ready to hike her skirts up and fuck her like she'd said, ready to strip the memory of Gemma away for a few minutes even though it never worked. My fingers twisted into her skirt, and I pulled her flush against me as her lips parted, but her words repeated in my mind, 'you're paid up'. It seemed an odd thing to say.

My eyes narrowed as I backed from her and tucked my aching member away. "What the fuck do you mean 'I'm paid up?'"

She swallowed, her eyes darting to the end of the alley. My

instinct flared, and I grabbed her wrists, pinning them to her sides.

"What did you mean?" I snarled, seeing the fear in her eyes.

"It means I paid her to see if you were really over my Gemma," I heard from the end of the alley. "And once again, you proved me correct. It didn't take you long to replace her."

I let the woman's wrists go, and she scurried off. Turning my head to the end of the alley, I faced the owner of the smooth voice, looking him over with a mix of envy and anger. He'd aged, growing into his thin features, his gray hair messy still, his blue eyes a dark navy. The witch's son stood across from me, appraising me as much as I was appraising him.

"I'm surprised Gemma let you fuck her so hard, but then again, she's always had a thing for you."

My hands clenched into tight fists, and I gritted my teeth. "What did you do to her?" I said, my voice strained.

"Me? Last I saw, you had her mouth around your cock, but now you're running around the kingdoms fucking every woman who will spread her legs for you. Easily taking the prey I set in your path to test you. So I ask you, Hunter, what did you do with my stones and my Gemma?"

I wondered briefly why he'd put his stones before Gemma. It seemed an odd order. "You don't have her?" I asked, relieved that all the images flooding my brain these last few weeks weren't true. Guilt quickly replaced my relief with the knowledge that I'd so easily found pleasure elsewhere. A sense of dread followed along with an understanding of what it meant that she wasn't with him.

"You had her, and I was nice enough to put up with you touching her." He stepped closer to me, his blue eyes shifting to a darker shade, the angular slope of his cheekbones reflecting the anger I sensed in his words. "She was told to bring me the stones or bring me her body. A body you have now used and lost. So, I'll ask you once more," his magic flickered around him, tingling along my skin, "where the fuck is Gemma?"

"I thought she was with you," I answered, straightening my back so the inch I had on him would be more noticeable. I was twice his size, but he had twice my strength with the magic he held.

He flung me against the wall without lifting a finger, the action knocking the breath from me. "I don't have her, and I don't have my stones."

"Fuck," I mumbled, reality sinking in.

His expression turned lethal, his hands so tight his knuckles shone white from the bone. "What did you do?"

"I left her." Saying the words aloud brought the guilt down upon me like an avalanche. The nagging feeling came back with a vengeance—that I'd made the wrong decision, that I'd been rash, too lost in my jealousy and too quick to accuse her of betrayal to comprehend the dangers of walking away from her.

"You what?" he roared, his magical hold on me tightening.

"I left her. We had an argument, and I ended things." Abruptly, without recourse, without thinking. And now she was dead. Anguish invaded me, spreading through every part of me, and I fought against the way it was ravaging me.

"Where did you leave her, Hunter?" he asked, his teeth gritted so that his lips barely moved. "The last time I spied you together, you were on the border of Carenth, fucking with glee. The next time I looked, she was nowhere to be found, and you were having quite the time with two women, neither of whom was my Gemma."

"She's not your Gemma," I sneered.

"And it would appear she's no longer yours." He dropped his hold on me, and I stumbled slightly as my feet hit the ground. "I do hope those women and the ones you've taken since were worth it."

"They weren't," I mumbled, rubbing my wrists that were still tingling from his magic.

OF CANDY AND BETRAYAL

"Where did you leave her?" His voice still held an edge, but his expression had shifted, the concern showing behind his eyes.

"In Laviak."

The concern yielded to rage. "You left her in Laviak? With my stones?"

"No, just her. I have the stones."

He tilted his head, his steely eyes studying me. "You left her and took the stones?"

I nodded, noting the excitement in his voice. His concern about Gemma was no longer present.

"Where are they?"

"They're safe."

His jaw ticked. "So you stole the stones—"

"I took what was mine. I retrieved most of those stones and the seeing stone was for my buyer."

His eyes widened. "Your buyer? Interesting."

"You don't even care about Gemma, do you? All you wanted were the damned stones."

"Make no mistake, I want them both. I dealt with you fucking her while you were hunting the stones with her. I would not have dealt with it when she returned them to me."

"Because you didn't intend for her to return with them, did you?"

"If anyone can retrieve all five stones, it's Gemma. But you went and left her in the pits. That means she's either dead, the golems having feasted on her, or..." He stopped, his teeth clenching, that calm exterior shifting so that his eyes were blazing. "My brother has her."

"Your brother? The one who was going to share me with your mother for dinner?" That was a possibility that hadn't crossed my mind. I'd completely forgotten Gemma had told me he was somewhere in Laviak.

"Yes. And she'll wish death had claimed her if he has her."

My heart wrenched, coiling in so tight its beats resounded through my body.

"How do we save her?"

"Not we. You. You are to bring me those stones, then finish what she started."

"Fuck off. I'm going to get her. If there's a chance she's still alive, I'm going after her."

His lip curved into an eerie grin. "Like you did when you left her there? How you rode back to save her from the fire witches? To save her from the dehydration and heat death she suffered if they didn't find her? To save her from my brother, who will use her like the prize she is and never set her free?"

Ire seethed through me, but I couldn't direct it at him. I was the one who hadn't gone back for her, too proud to do so. Swallowing my pride this time, I asked, "How do I get her back if she's with your brother? I can make it to Laviak in a few days—"

"You're not going to Laviak. You're going to Iceliar."

"Iceliar? Why would I do that? If she's still alive, every day will be torment for her."

"You didn't care about that when you were about to fuck the wench I hired."

I punched him, getting it in before he could draw his power. He only laughed, rubbing his jaw and saying, "Don't take your guilt out on me. I wonder what she'll think when you rescue her smelling of another woman's cunt? Will she run to your arms, or will she run to mine?"

"I wish I'd killed you all those years ago. You and your family."

"But you didn't, and it was me who saved you. Me who freed you both." He moved so close that he was in my face, but I didn't step back. I wasn't about to let him intimidate me. "Get me the fucking stones, then make your way to Iceliar or I'll find her myself, and you'll never see her again because she'll be gagging on my cock every night."

I shoved him, bringing my fist up, only to be stopped by an unseen force.

"You're not getting another strike in, trust me. Bring the stones to the Endless Forest at dawn."

He stormed off, entering the bar from the rear where I'd followed the whore earlier. A myriad of thoughts flooded my mind and the emotions that accompanied them nearly drowned me. He'd paid the wench to have sex with me, testing me for some unexplainable reason when he already knew I'd been indulging in women since I'd left Gemma. He didn't know the reason, or maybe he knew I was trying to erase her and the heartache that had been threatening to incapacitate me. But how did he know what I'd been doing? Somehow, he'd been watching us on our journey, watching me since I'd left her.

The idea was disturbing, but not as disturbing as the thought that his brother might have Gemma. Or that she had died in those pits, never making it to her destination. I would find her. The determination I'd had when I'd ridden to Iceliar returned. The need to find out if she was indeed alive, drowning out all other needs. I tore through the alley and made my way to my horse, digging through the saddlebag for the small pouch I had hidden below. I rushed back into the bar, but the witch's son was nowhere to be found. Neither was the whore, and I wondered if he'd taken her somewhere to have his way with her after watching me with her. After all, he'd watched us like some strange voyeur and likely would have continued if I'd followed through and taken her.

I didn't care, and I didn't want to wait until dawn. I strode out of the bar, mounted my horse, and rode to the outskirts of the Endless Forest, where I camped for the night, all thoughts of an inn with a comfortable bed left behind like the whore I'd taken.

THE FIRST BEAMS of sunrise bled through the open field where the small cottage stood. I wiped my hand down my face, wiping away the memories of that night that still haunted me. Walking with deliberate slowness, I approached the cottage. Dilapidated and run-down, it looked as if no one had lived in it for ages. Only a section of the door still stood, weather having beaten down the outer edges of it so that only a piece of it remained hanging from its hinges. In the daylight, I could see that pieces of candy made up its outer surface, a large colorful lollipop embedded close to me. I touched it, my finger descending slightly into its sweet consistency. It was a strange item to make a house out of, but then again, the witch had taken me and attempted to take Gemma, who had still been a child. The gumdrops and lollipops that decorated the quaint cottage would have enticed any child wandering the forest. If only they knew what was beyond the exterior, the façade of the spider's web that hid the horrors within.

I pushed the door open, pieces of it flaking away at my touch. The scent of gingerbread wafted to my nose as I brought my fingers back. I ignored the chill that tingled along my spine and stepped into the cottage. Dust and spiderwebs covered everything within it. The weather, no longer stopped by the fractured door, had rusted the metal on the large oven that sat across from me. The small cage that had held me was still intact, the bars now with that same rust color.

"I'd say it's in good shape considering I left it that night and never returned until that fateful day when I came to burn it down and Gemma wandered into the field."

I didn't turn to his voice behind me, not wanting to give him any indication that he'd caught me off guard.

"Gemma said she stayed with you here." I was afraid to hear that had been another lie.

"She did." He snapped his fingers, and the cottage came alive. The oven transformed into an inviting fireplace, a large fur before it. A small table and chairs appeared where the cage had been, a large bed opposite them. He walked over to the fur, leaning down and running his hand over it. "This was where she gave me her virginity. It was delectable."

The growl that rumbled through my chest was loud, and he peered over at me. "Does that bother you, Hunter? That I was the one who made her a woman? That I taught her the things she does to make you climax now? And oh, what a quick learner she was."

I had my knuckles gripped so tightly they almost ripped through my skin.

"And what were you doing while I was fucking her girlish body?"

"I wasn't using young girls who were too young to know they were being manipulated."

"Manipulated? I beg to differ. I brought her to ecstasy and back, showed her how a man should treat her, and the wonders of climax. All while you were traveling the world, fucking every random woman you could find to quench your thirst."

I pulled the pouch of stones out and threw them on the floor. "There are your precious stones. Now tell me how to find the water stone and your brother."

He meant his gaze to make me uncomfortable, but I didn't back down from it. If he thought he was intimidating, he wasn't. I was not Gemma.

"Open the pouch," he sneered.

"I don't take commands from you."

"No, but Gemma likes them, doesn't she? Surprisingly, since I taught her to be dominant and own her sexuality."

My urge to punch him was growing again. "I've had enough of—"

"Have you?" He stalked over to me. "I don't think you have. You had her, she was all yours, and you walked away from her."

"As did you."

"No, I let her walk away, knowing she needed to see the world, to spread her wings, to experience life beyond Spindara and these woods."

His words sounded too benevolent to be coming from him, too unselfish. And he struck me as the selfish type.

"Tell me, Hunter. How does it feel when she's coming around you? Do her screams urge you on? Does her moaning coax the cum from you until there's nothing left? It was my favorite way to make her come. She would writhe on me as she called my name—"

I shoved him away, my rage engulfing me. "Enough! How do I get the stone?"

He laughed, walking over to the pouch. "Pick it up."

"I'm not your servant. Pick it up yourself."

"I said to pick it up!" The anger was fast, like a streak of lightning in a stormy sky. He couldn't touch the pouch. Gemma had said the witches couldn't touch the stones and this one wouldn't even get near them.

"What good are the stones if you can't even touch them?"

"Don't you worry about that. Pick them up and put them on the table."

I did as he said, more than amused at how he backed away from the pouch as I approached him.

"Take the seeing stone out and keep it with you. I expect it back when you return with the water stone."

"Who says I'm returning? I plan to go to Laviak next."

"I said you were to bring me the water stone first. Then you get the last stone and Gemma, if she's alive."

I shot him a look, hoping my annoyance burned through his skin. "Fine, what do I do with the seeing stone?"

"It's connected to each pair. Like Gemma used it to find the earth stone, then the earth stone to find wind. The seeing stone will discover the water stone and water will find the fire stone."

"Why didn't we just use it to find the water stone first?" This sequence was ridiculous.

"Because if you do not collect the stones in order, they disappear from your hold and return to the place you found them."

I couldn't grasp the impossibility of that, yet he said it with a straight face, his look stern and serious.

"Take it to the edge of the Ikanthi River in Iceliar. Use it to find the stone and return to me. Only then will I tell you how to find my brother."

If the possibility Gemma was out there struggling to survive wasn't driving me, I would never have obeyed his command. But I'd hurt her enough. I wouldn't leave her to die miserably if she was still alive.

Removing the seeing stone, I tucked it in my pocket and left the cottage, not bothering to look back at him.

CHAPTER ELEVEN

GEMMA

Awareness washed over me. I wasn't dead. It seemed like I was—my head was pounding, my mouth so parched that my tongue stuck to the inside of my cheek, and a weariness hung over me, one I couldn't seem to lift. I opened my eyes, the stone floor against my face hastening my need to rise. But it was a need I could not meet quickly. Easing my hand from below me, I slowly lifted my head, spying a torch that was casting shadows of the bars of my cell over me. And within those shadows sat a figure.

Dark and brooding, his icy glare fascinated me the closer he leaned toward my cell. Even in the dim light, I could see one was a bright blue that shimmered in the torchlight, the other a milky gray that matched his streaked hair. Thick, gray locks lined with black. His eyes were intent as I studied his handsome face, the jawline that rose high, set in a grim expression that defied its softness. Full lips that were tight in the frown they held.

"Decided to live after all?" His voice was deep but soft, a dichotomy to the imposing presence he was.

I tried to talk, but my mouth was too dry.

"I suppose I'll have to waste my food and drink on you now, just for the entertainment of seeing you struggle to reach it."

Bringing myself to my knees, I moved closer to the bars.

"My brother might like you on your knees, but don't pull that shit with me. I'm not taking his sloppy leftovers."

He rose, and I saw it then, the flash of hunger in his eyes that I remembered so vividly from that night when I was a child. I scooted away, my back landing hard against the stone wall. His laughter echoed through the room.

"You're right to be frightened, pet. I am nothing like my brother. I do not hide my imperfections. You'll find no softness here. Now drink, but take it slow. I'd hate to make you lick up your own vomit."

He left, his form blending into the darkness and leaving me with uncertainty about what had just happened. In the corner of my cell sat a tin cup and a plate of bread. I dragged my body to them and with shaky hands brought the cup to my nose, sniffing its contents. There was no scent, no obvious sign of poison. I didn't have any reason to think he'd poison me when he could have let me rot in this cell or left me to die in the pits. Yet he hadn't, and that knowledge sparked a strange curiosity in me.

I took small sips of the water. The coolness in my mouth was the most refreshing thing I'd ever experienced. I wanted to gulp it down, but I knew that would only bring it back up. And even with as thirsty and hungry as I was, the idea of eating my vomit was something I found revolting. As I delayed my gratification with the water, drinking it over a tediously long period, I took stock of my surroundings. My cell was tiny, one of about five lined along the wall. There were multiple torches hung on the wall across from me, shedding light on the narrow room.

The torches were fascinating. Their flames never ceased to flicker, the force behind them unseen. All the torches burned with the same intensity, the same breath of fire. Magical in ways. Lit by the fires of the Laviak pits, eternal flames that would always burn.

Directly across from my cell sat a wooden bench, the one on which he'd been sitting. Ernan. Breck's older brother, the firstborn of the witch. I remembered how he'd begged his mother to keep me. I'd hidden in the woods, too afraid to go too far even as Breck had run after me. Only when Breck had found me and dragged me away, his hand muffling my mouth to quiet me, had I completely left Hunter. I hadn't been mature enough to realize why Ernan had wanted to keep me, but I knew now, and I wondered if that's why he'd saved me from the golems. To make me his, to force himself on me. I shivered, rubbing my arms against the chill that should not have been in this warm, uncomfortable cell. Breck had told me horror stories about his brother, how evil he was, unrelenting in his need for blood and power.

Yet, he had been sitting there when I'd woken, watching me. Given his comments from our youth, I could have attributed that to some disturbed motive, but he'd done nothing but grumble at me. Why not take advantage of me while I slept, or even when I first woke? Granted, I was certain my smell was quite foul and with how long it had been since I'd had sustenance, I likely wasn't the most attractive option. But from my experience, that didn't derail a wicked man's intent to have a woman's body. If they wanted it, they took it. And he hadn't.

I mused over the situation while I sipped my water, eventually daring to take small bites of the bread he'd left me. Another strange kindness.

The day passed exceedingly dull as I dozed on and off. I wasn't certain if it was day or night or how time was passing with no access to the sun. Of course, the smoke from the pits blocked most of its rays when it was present, making it hard to determine if it even existed. Ernan didn't make another appearance, but as I woke through different intervals, I would find fresh water and bread. Enough that I calculated three days had gone by as I sat and nibbled on the small piece of cheese he'd added to the plate this time.

I poked at my ribcage, missing the swollen feel of a full belly and the curves that were disappearing from my lack of sustenance. "You stink." I heard his voice before I saw him. He leaned forward on the bench, his different colored eyes seeming to see straight into my soul. I hadn't seen him there and wondered how long he'd been watching me make orgasmic expressions over how good the cheese tasted.

"I'd stink less if I weren't sleeping where I piss and shit." I lifted my arm and sniffed beneath it. "And if I had a warm bath to rinse the stench from me."

His lips lifted slightly. "You're not here for pampering."

"No? What am I here for then? You saved me from the golems, you've given me shelter, albeit questionable shelter, and you're feeding me. Seems like you've got a pleasant side your brother doesn't know about." I shouldn't have said it, but I was curious to see what his reaction would be.

"There's a lot my brother doesn't know about me and plenty he refuses to admit." He stood, his towering frame casting me into the shadows as he blocked out the torchlight. "Don't mistake my actions for kindness, girl, because I promise you they aren't."

"I'm not a girl," I defended, as he turned his back on me. "I'm a woman. One who will take your actions any way I want to."

He threw a glance at me over his shoulder, and I could have sworn I saw the glimmer of a smirk before he turned away and left me again. I sat there, thinking about Ernan, wondering why I was so curious about him, why he didn't frighten me the way I thought he would, and why the sound of his voice caused a flutter in my belly, the same type Hunter had stirred before he'd made it clear he no longer wanted me.

THE SENSATION of someone watching me crawled over my skin and grabbed me from the depths of sleep. My eyes opened, and I jerked back upon discovering Ernan was standing over me. I rubbed the back of my head, my reaction to his presence having caused me to hit it on the wall.

"Do you always hover over people like that?"

He ignored me and, in one quick move, picked me up and threw me over his shoulder. I yelped and clung to his waist, noticing how solid it was. His hand was over my ass and an unexpected warmth crawled through me. The reaction had me flustered. Maybe I'd been too many days without sex and my body was rebelling. Hunter and I had been relentless, fucking multiple times a day. My body missed it. That had to be the reason this grumpy, very muscular, intoxicating man was making my pants wet.

At the thought of Hunter, I gritted my teeth. My grief at his leaving had transformed into profound anger. I planned to hunt him down and beat the shit out of him if I ever got out of this prison.

Ernan dropped me to the floor, my ass landing hard, only the soft fur below protecting me from a rather uncomfortable bruise.

"Do you treat all your women like this?" I asked playfully. There was no reason to be playful, but it seemed to bother him, and I liked the way he groused when I didn't succumb to his broody persona.

"Women don't make it this far."

"You've never had a woman?"

He turned so fast, I couldn't help but cower.

"I've had plenty of women, but none ever come to Laviak." He leaned over me, putting his hands on either side of me. "I fuck them in the towns and leave them pining for more when they're being fucked by their small-dicked men."

"Do you always do that?"

"Do what?" he asked, his eyes creasing. I found those eyes so fascinating that I inadvertently reached my fingers up and touched the corner of one.

"Mask your responses in anger and bravado."

He grabbed my hand, lowering it and squeezing it so hard that I cried out in pain. "You reek," he grunted, then rose from me and pointed to the other side of the room.

Only then did I realize we were in a cavern. The air was humid but dry at the same time. I didn't know how to explain the impossibility of that description. I followed the direction of his hand and spied a large pool of water, similar to the spring where Hunter and I had stayed. The place where I'd crushed him, turning him away so that his final push against me was inevitable. Neither of us should have given our hearts away, yet we had, and in doing so we'd subjected them to damage. I'd hurt him with my rejection of his offer, and in turn, he'd hurt me by rejecting me completely. The thought brought the pain back, but I shoved it away. There was no changing the events. He'd left, and I knew him well enough to know he was soaking his sorrow and anger in other women. Something he would do until he stripped all thoughts of me away, replacing them with unattached sex.

It was something I would have done in the past, but not now. It was exactly what I'd done when I'd left Breck, burying the hurt that he hadn't stopped me from leaving, that he'd let me walk out without a single argument. I'd used men to drive him from my mind. But not this time. Hunter was a part of me, even if I hated him. I wouldn't turn back to the way I'd been and bury that emotion or those memories. Not that I'd have the chance. I doubted I would see any of the world again, my prison now Laviak, my jailer Ernan.

"Does water always make you sad?" His voice was softer than

I would have expected, and I turned to him, cinching my brows to understand how the sound had come from the same man who'd just roughly thrown me to the ground. His face had lost its hard edges, his eyes studying me with inquisitiveness.

"Thinking of the past," I admitted, uncertain why I didn't want to lie to him. The lie that had driven Hunter from me was still a fresh wound.

"I find the past is a place I prefer to leave behind."

"Then what drives you if not your past?" I wondered about this man whom Breck had led me to believe was a monster to be avoided at all costs. I saw nothing in him that supported that notion. Only a stony exterior that had vulnerabilities.

His eyes hardened, the grimace returning. "Get in the water and clean the stench from yourself before I throw you in."

He folded his arms and stood like a statue on guard.

"Are you joining me?" I couldn't help teasing him. The urge to break his moody demeanor was too tempting not to.

His lips tightened, but I saw the flicker in his eyes, the duality of them still fascinating to me. No reply came, so I shrugged and pulled my shirt over my head. Those eyes grew large, dropping to the ground quickly.

"You told me to get into the water," I said, pulling my pants off and untying the braid that was barely still intact. His eyes perused my body, but he gave me no other reaction. He was a hard one to break, and my stomach fluttered again when those eyes met mine. I had no shyness about my body. I'd traveled with men most of my life, whether they chose to entertain me or to work with me. Either way, traveling the road for months on end meant doing away with shyness or privacy.

But the way his eyes took me in, slowly with hesitation, in a way that held no solicitous intentions, had me suddenly self-conscious. There was something in his eyes that I'd not expected from him, vulnerability shadowed by adoration. Warmth flushed my cheeks and not between my legs, as would normally be my reaction. There was a strange pitter to my heart, a pull at the pieces Hunter had broken from it, and I dropped my eyes from Ernan. Turning from that heavy gaze, I waded into the water.

It was hot, and the heat sank into my muscles. He hadn't been wrong. I wreaked. I'd lost count of the days from my last bath and the water seemed to peel layers of muck from me. I dipped my head under the water, remaining there as the heat radiated through my body, repairing my strength and my mood. When I emerged, Ernan was close to the edge of the water, peering in, a look of concern on his face.

He jumped back when I opened my eyes, as if I'd caught him doing something wrong. I wanted to ease that worry, so I said quickly, "I love sitting with the water over my head. It clears the noise of the world out, leaving only me and an internal silence."

He squinted his eyes, and I could see him trying to figure out what I meant.

"You should try it sometime."

"Use soap. I can still smell you," he grumbled, pointing to a pile of soap flakes.

My eyes grew wide, and I swam over to it, inhaling the wonderful scent of hibiscus. Soap flakes were a delicacy for the rich, especially perfumed ones. They were a luxury I'd only experienced a few times in my life. Soap was otherwise in a black bar that smelled of nothing, the bar rough enough to rub away the dirt but worthless otherwise.

I moved until the ledge was waist level and picked up a few of the flakes. Bringing them to my nose, I smelled them again before I gingerly lathered them along my body. The experience was so intoxicating that I forgot Ernan was there, my hands layering my body in the scented flakes until every inch of me smelled of flowers. I slid my hands from my stomach all the way to my face and inhaled them deeply. With an excited laugh, I plunged back into the water, thinking of how the rich ladies in the more to-do towns would balk at someone like me using such a grand extravagance.

Emerging again, I rubbed the rest into my hair, closing my eyes as the lather built. I peeked over at Ernan, remembering that I was being watched. His expression was unguarded, a smile on his face until he realized I had caught him. The smile turned downward, his eyes growing guarded again. Sighing, I rinsed my hair, running my fingers through the knots as I thought about my captor. The terrifying eldest witch's son was not what I thought he would be, and with that thought, my stomach somersaulted again. I didn't know why my body was acting so strangely. I was used to it reacting to men. I had my types and broody, aggressive men were high on the list. It was the reason Hunter had always been the one for me. At the thought, my smile faltered, my heart clamping down at the excitement in my belly.

I turned away, not wanting Ernan to see. Although I didn't know why it mattered. I was heartbroken, no matter which way I turned it, no matter how I tried to hide it.

"Who hurt you?" he asked, and I swiveled toward him, my mouth parting.

"No one," I murmured. He walked closer to me, doubt in his eyes. "Do you have anything for me to cover myself with?"

His brow raised. "You had no qualms about taking your clothes off in front of me."

I pursed my lips, knowing he was right and not understanding why I had the sudden urge to cover myself from his gaze. He pulled his shirt over his head and held it out to me. Stunned by the act, I stepped from the water and took it from him, my eyes dropping to his chest to devour every defined muscle of his toned body. I pulled the shirt over my head, catching his eyes lingering on my breasts before he brought them up to meet mine. There was lust behind them, and this time, the warmth in me sat between my legs.

He stepped to me, so close I could smell the scent of fire and brimstone. "Who hurt you?" he asked again.

The way his eyes darkened, small lines forming at the corners of them, the way the muscles in his chest went taut, took my breath away.

"Hunter," I breathed, unable to lie to him. His hold on me was one I welcomed, even though I didn't understand it.

His eyes narrowed, his jaw so tense I could see the tension in them. "What did he do?" Each word came out as a growl that sent my pulse racing.

I lowered my eyes. "He broke my heart." It hurt to say the words out loud, to admit that he had left me devastated because it was the truth, no matter how I'd hidden it below my anger.

"I'll kill him and let you watch as he writhes in agony."

My mouth fell open, and I tried to find my voice, but by the time I found it, he'd walked away. Confusion wrapped its way around my mind. His response had been entirely unexpected, the look in his eyes had been deadly. I didn't know why he would even care if Hunter had hurt me, but I knew he could kill Hunter. He was a sorcerer, the son of a witch. He was a lethal hunter and any of us were his prey. I ran after him, his shirt sticking to my wet skin, the material sticky against my nipples.

"You can't kill him," I said, grabbing his arm.

He yanked free and turned on me, glaring down at me. I felt small in that moment with this terrifying man over me, unsure of what to expect from him next. His eyes fell to my chest, which was now heaving but in an entirely non-sexual way. Terror had staked its fangs in me, and my entire body was shaking. His jaw ground, his lips becoming thinner as he stared at my breasts. Time stood still, and he seemed to wage some kind of internal battle, his eyes flaring from lust to anger in a myriad of emotional variations.

"Why wouldn't you want him dead?" he asked, his teeth gritted still so his ire emphasized his every word.

"Because..." Because I still love him, I wanted to say, but the words wouldn't come out. I loved him, but it hurt so badly that I didn't think I'd ever forgive him. And the truth was, he hadn't returned for me. He had another woman's legs wrapped around him, and I was sure she was one of many. Hunter was too proud to admit his feelings, to deal with his anger or even his grief. He'd bury it and fuck the memory of me away woman by woman until he was free of me. But he'd done that in his youth and he'd never truly been free of me. And I knew no matter how the pieces of my heart slowly crumbled away, I'd never be entirely free of him.

"Because what?"

"Because that's not what you do. We're over, he left me—"

"He left you out there?" The fire returned to his eyes, the veins in his neck protruding.

Shit. "Why does it matter to you? I'm your prisoner. Why do you care if he left me?"

He moved a step closer so that his chest was against mine. I could discern his skin below my wet shirt and I inhaled at the sensation. The touch seemed to fluster him, and he went to step away, but I pressed further into him, not knowing why but needing to continue our contact.

"Why do you care?" I asked again.

His eyes searched mine, the gray one cloudy like a stormy day. "Because he left you to die. And no man who loves you would ever leave you that way." His features softened, the transformation revealing how handsome he was when he wasn't drowning in his anger. His hand reached up and moved a wet strand of hair from my collarbone, his eyes following the motion. "No man who loved you would ever leave you."

That flutter intensified in my belly, my heart ceasing its pounding for a beat. Something drew me to Ernan, although I couldn't comprehend what that something was. I didn't think it was an attempt to leave my emotions for Hunter behind. This was different—seizing another part of my emotions, co-existing with what I still felt for Hunter.

He dropped his hand, his fingers grazing my nipple inadvertently and his demeanor changed, shadowed again as he wrenched his hand back and moved from me. He turned and walked away, but my body was aglow with that small touch; it wanted more.

"Catch up," he grumbled. "I'd hate for you to lose your way and end up outside with the golems."

Panic swept through me at the thought, and I bustled to catch up with him. My eyes were everywhere while I followed him. Although the halls were dimly lit, I could make out the coarse consistency of the walls, the blood color of the rugs that layered the floor, the ceilings that had no end. I dragged my finger along the wall, fascinated by the texture, my eyes watching them rather than him. I slammed into his back, the impact sending me stumbling backward and knocking the wind from me.

He spun, his eyes holding an irritation that was palpable. "Watch where you're going before I change my mind and feed you to the golems myself."

He returned to his forward motion before I could reply, and I made a more concerted effort to pay attention to my path.

"The walls are so unique. What are they made from?" I asked, disliking the silence as the walls seemed to close in around me.

"Cooled lava. This was once the fortress of the fire witches. They were too proud in their greed for power. This fortress was an example of it, one the gods left intact. I found it abandoned yet still standing and claimed it as my own."

"Why do you live out here alone?"

"Because I choose to."

"But don't you get lonely? Locked away here with only yourself."

His step faltered, and for a moment, I thought he would turn on me again. "I live here because I don't like people," he groused. "If I want to torment myself with them, I can go into Carenth."

"Is that where you fuck the women you leave pining for you?"

This time he did stop but only to throw a door open and point inside. "Get in. You stay here from now on."

I peeked my head into the large room, then looked back at him. "You didn't answer my question."

His jaw ticked, his cheeks thinning with his angst. I was enjoying the break in his control, the way my words seemed to push him each time I spoke.

"Do you not leave women through Carenth with thoughts of only you and your enormous dick?"

The fire blazed in his eyes, but there was something under them, shaded behind the anger, a flash of vulnerability. I wondered at it. Ernan was a man who I couldn't read, but I thought perhaps he was much more than the cold, uncaring, terrifying man he made himself out to be. His reaction had me feeling bad for making the comment, although I didn't know why I'd feel anything but hatred for a man who was holding me captive. The same man who had saved me, fed me, let me bathe, and threatened to kill Hunter for hurting me.

I moved closer to him, surprised that he didn't push me away when I leaned my body against his. It caused the reaction I'd expected. I slipped my hand down over the bulge that lay below his pants long enough to know he had enough there to satisfy any woman. He grabbed my hand, his face contorting so that I thought he would kill me right then.

"Don't touch me, Gemma," he growled. "I'm not my brother."

"No, you aren't. You're much more endowed than your brother." The hard lines on his face faded, the tension fleeing. "You know my name," I said, trying to keep him in this state. I liked him this way.

"Of course I do." He looked like he wanted to say more, but he shoved me into the room.

"Good night Ernan," I said, just as the door closed behind him. A faint "Good night, Gemma" slipped through the door, bringing a smile to me. There were layers to Ernan, and I wanted to see below the layers he let others see. I thought just maybe, they were layers worth discovering.

ERNAN LEFT me in the room for days. There was nothing much to do but sleep, which I did often. I hadn't been so stationary in my life, and I discovered that my body was embracing the rest. Food would appear whenever I woke, but I never saw Ernan. He avoided me, coming into my room only when he knew I could not talk to him.

By the fourth day, I was ready to lose my mind. My body had no more need for rest, and being locked in this fancier cage was still confining, even with its luxurious bed and the delicious food Ernan was bringing me. I laid down, intent on catching him this time. It took forever, and I fought the need to move as I lay there, listening for the sound of the door to unlock. I was about to give up when I heard the click, followed by quiet footfalls as he entered my room. I peeked my eyes open and watched him set down the tray.

Silently, I sat up and waited for him to turn my way. I crossed my legs and watched his expression. The one that met my eyes was revealing. There was a sweetness to it, a gentleness that made my heart thud heavily in my chest. But as soon as he saw that I was awake, it morphed back to the stony, reticent man he wanted me to see.

I hopped from the bed and walked over to the tray, brushing his arm. A tingle cascaded its way along my skin. Grabbing a piece of cheese, I took a bite, savoring it. My favorite part of the food he brought me was the decadent cheeses he left.

"Why won't you come to me when I'm awake?" I asked, devouring the cheese in a very unladylike way.

He ignored me, walking toward the door.

"Why save me at all if you're only going to keep me locked in here?"

He stopped but didn't turn, so I went to him, standing directly in his path.

"Did you know cheese is my favorite?" I asked, changing my tactic. I licked the remaining bits of cheese from my fingers and took a sip of the juice he'd brought me. It was sweet with a fruity flavor with which I wasn't familiar.

He watched me, staying silent, which frustrated me to no end. I moved away and dropped the cup back on the dresser where the remaining food sat. The thud it made broke the silence in the room.

"I don't understand you, Ernan." I turned back to him, but he was still standing there, staring at the door. With a sigh, I continued, "You rescue me, treat me with kindness that you hide behind that broody mask you wear, avoid me yet watch over me. If you hate me so much, why confuse me with your actions? And why not let me die out there?"

He turned and stormed over to me, but I didn't flinch, regardless of how terrifying his eyes were.

Despite his angry expression, I continued, "You wanted to kill me when we were young, to keep me—"

He grabbed my arms, and I thought for a moment he would hurt me. That look as if an internal battle raged within him shadowed his face again. His grip loosened, his fingers slipping.

"I never wanted to kill you, Gemma."

"What did you want to do that night, then?"

His eyes softened, the blue a beautiful crystal shade that complimented the gray of his other eye. He brushed his finger over my cheek, his thumb settling on my bottom lip and drifting over it. The sensation was one that drifted over my soul like the whisper of the wind. Everything faded around us and Ernan was my world, the sound of his heart beating, the straining of his breath, the sensation of his touch. I leaned into it, and he gently cupped my chin, his lips pressing against mine with the slightest of kisses. My body came to life, my heart freezing its beat, the breath stolen from me. He tasted of black licorice and cinnamon and smelled of ash and fire. I leaned further into him. The gentleness of his kiss, of his touch as his hand threaded through my hair, was so opposed to what I'd had with Hunter, to anything I'd ever had with any other man. Hunter was force and strength, while Ernan was gentle and giving.

His lips parted from mine, and I leaned further into him, wanting more but finding none. I opened my eyes, my breath catching at the look in his eyes, one of sadness and conflict. I wanted to remove that sadness, but he backed away from me.

"Ernan."

He turned and left the room, leaving me wrestling with my own conflicted emotions as more pieces of my crumbling heart repaired.

CHAPTER TWELVE

HUNTER

The icy world of Iceliar lay in the distance, beckoning me on as I settled for the night. Exhaustion had taken hold of my horse and of me. I'd traveled swiftly, avoiding towns...and avoiding women, determined for some twisted reason to not touch another until I found Gemma. It made no sense because I knew she wouldn't take me back, that she would hate me for leaving her and not returning this time as I had when we were young. But if she were in the clutches of the other son, I couldn't fathom finding pleasure when she was bound to be suffering.

Sitting, my back to a hollowed-out log, I thought through my plan for the next morning. I was about an hour's ride to Iceliar— the change in the air, the icy mountains in the distance told me this. The realm's temperature difference bled subtly over the edge of its borders, leaving a coldness that remained even during the warm months. It was not unbearable, however, like one would think. A spell surrounded Iceliar, locking in the more brutal of its weather. There was no reason to justify why this was so, it simply was. Stories varied from another curse from the gods to a spell gone wrong. One story even told of a sorcerer who was so jealous when his lover took another that he imprisoned the realm in eternal winter as punishment, sealing her behind the borders of the icy land.

Whatever the reason, the realm was miserable. Once I crossed the border, the bitter cold would bite at me until I turned back.

A hawk landed on a branch of the tree across from me. Its color was distinct—white as the snow that layered Iceliar, but with ebony tips along its wings and head. It stared at me, tilting its head.

"Stealing the warmth of my fire?" I asked it, not having spoken to anyone for far too long.

It took flight from the branch and landed close to the fire, its form stretching and shifting until a beautiful, naked woman stood before me. I scooted back against the log, trying to determine if she was real or if I had completely lost my mind.

"Breck sends a message," she said, her brown eyes a dark chocolate. Her ebony hair fell in waves that lay over her breasts seductively, leaving their plump size and dark nipples exposed.

If I hadn't been so surprised, I would have been hard as a rock. But as it was, her words sobered me even further.

"Breck? Have you been spying on me? For him?"

"I have for a very long time." She drew closer, her thick hips inviting with each flick of movement. "You are a very naughty boy, and one I find extremely intriguing."

Great. Here I'd been avoiding women and Breck sent me another temptress. She straddled me before I could react, pushing her hair back to completely expose her breasts. My body flared to life as she ground against me.

"How long have you been spying on me?" My voice was hoarse, and she smiled wickedly.

"Long enough to know you fuck like a man I want to taste."

I tried to push her back, but my hand sank into her flesh,

inadvertently wrapping around her hips. "Why don't you go back to Breck and tell him I don't want any more of his women?" I had meant it to be a command, but it was a weak one.

She ground down on me again as she guided my hands to her breasts. I couldn't help but squeeze. They were fantastic tits, and they felt too good to deny myself the satisfaction of touching them.

"Breck sent me to tell you to use the sight to find the stone."

I pulled my eyes from her tits and stopped my obsessive fondling. "What does that mean?"

Her hands worked their way down my chest, untucking my shirt and unbuttoning my pants. I grabbed her hand, but she leaned closer, her other hand reaching into my pants and guiding my starving dick out.

"He also said you need to be satisfied, extremely satisfied, before you face the sirens of Iceliar."

"Satisfied?" I knew exactly what she meant, but the question squeaked from my throat anyway.

"You've denied yourself since you left Spindara. That's something very unlike you. I've watched you take women since you lost your gem."

At the reference to Gemma, I froze, that ache I'd been shielding in my chest striving to return. "Go back to your master—"

She sank over me, enveloping me before I even realized she'd moved her body.

"You need to be pleasured. To have me satisfy you so completely that the sirens will not sway you with their bodies or their words." She rose up and down as she spoke, her words casting a spell on me. I grabbed her hips again as she leaned closer, guiding her chest to my face. "If not, they will drag you to the endless depths of their icy tomb and you will fail, losing everything."

Her words were seductive, and they made sense to me,

enough sense for me to stop resisting and suck one of her delicious nipples into my mouth. I hadn't taken a woman in too many days and this one was riding me like I was her last meal. Even the strongest of men couldn't have denied themselves. Her curves were thick, and I succumbed to her, bringing her full red lips to mine and devouring her mouth. The more I let myself go to her, the more the world became a blur and pleasure riddled my body. My release came fast, my second climax slower as I flipped her, forcing her missionary and pounding into her. She ripped my control from me easily and I knew this was going to be a battle of strength, one she quickly won as magic seeped into my pores. I wavered, her long legs wrapping around me before she maneuvered us so that she was above me.

Pinning my arms with her hands, she said, "I have the power here. I am the hunter, and you are my prey."

I wanted to be her prey, to have her use my body for her own pleasure, her seductive magic distorting my senses.

"Fuck," I muttered, struggling against it and throwing her off me. I stumbled as I pushed her to her knees. "I don't like my women in control."

"It's a good thing I'm not your woman," she said, shoving her ass toward me. "Now fuck me hard, like a good boy."

I growled as her magic sank further into me. "What are you and what are you doing to me?" I asked as I thrust into her, groaning at the overwhelming sense of rapture that hit me.

"I'm a witch, you fool. And I'm bringing you more satisfaction than you've ever had in your life."

I yanked her waist back, digging my fingers into it as I penetrated her deeper. She cried out, the sound pulling me from under the spell, but only enough for me to realize I wanted to continue fucking her.

"Stop using your magic on me," I sneered, driving into her harder. She was quivering, and I wanted her to come. I wanted to break the hold she had on me. I leaned over, sliding my finger over her clit and loving how she bucked against me. The hold from her magic slipped more as her legs trembled, her muscles bearing down around me in spasms that were coaxing my release forward. With a scream, she came, the intensity of it shaking her entire body as I started pounding her again. The magic had worn off and my anger surfaced. Anger that Breck had once again played on my desire for sex, that I'd been trying to forego my needs for some warped reason that made no sense. I'd left Gemma, made it clear in doing so that we were over. What did it matter if I took other women? It shouldn't have. It didn't.

As the last of my internal conversation concluded that this witch was what I needed, my release hit. It flooded through me like the acknowledgment that no matter what I thought, I'd lost Gemma. If it hadn't been my asshole move of leaving her, it would be the women I'd used to free myself of her hold. She was no longer mine. I'd given her up.

I yanked the witch's ass back once more while the last of my release fled me, then I collapsed to the ground. She crawled over to me, taking my softened length in her mouth and sucking it clean.

"We're not done yet," she cooed, and her magic drifted over me again. I didn't resist this time. I was too exhausted. "I need to leave you thoroughly satisfied with no inkling of desire left in this body."

I didn't think there was anything left, but as she slid her tongue down my shaft, I knew if there was, she would find it. I closed my eyes, letting her magic and her mouth take me from my thoughts, a temporary distraction that I welcomed.

A THICK FOG hung over me as I blinked my eyes open. The morning light was nearly blinding, only intensifying the sensation that I'd had one too many drinks the night before. With much effort, I sat up, rubbing my eyes and wondering if I'd had the most erotic wet dream or if it had been real. A fire still burned, one that hadn't gone out in the middle of the night. Its flames ran a strange purple hue and sent enough warmth out that the night chill hadn't bothered my naked body.

That body lay sprawled out, my dick sticky with sex. But my seductress was nowhere to be seen. I dropped my head back to the ground, completely drained. The effects of her magic hung over me like a cobweb. I'd never fucked a witch and never would have if Breck hadn't sent her to seduce me. The experience had been worth whatever hangover I had now. She'd left an impression and with as many women as I'd had in my life, that was saying something. Gemma had been the only one to ever do that.

I thought about her plump body on mine, her hips in my hands, her oversized breasts in my mouth, and my dick sprung to life. It wasn't my usual spring, however. She had used it, leaving it exhausted so that even the thought of it staying hard was tiring. Running my hands through my hair, I glanced at the tree limbs, spying the white hawk watching me.

"Bitch," I muttered, and she gave a laughing screech before taking off. I watched as she flew away, wondering why she was letting the witch's son use her like that. Not that I was complaining, but it still left an unpleasant taste in my mouth. If I made it out of this alive and Gemma sent me out of her life, I'd find the witch and discover the story behind her. Maybe take her a few more times.

"Dammit, Hunter, get up and move," I mumbled to myself. There was a purpose behind what she'd done to me. She'd wanted me drained, as had the witch's son. Breck. It irked me to give him a name, but, although I would still kill him, I needed to call him by his name at some point.

I finally dragged myself up, cleaned as best I could, and broke camp. The ride into Iceliar passed slowly, and I tried to keep my mind from the prior night's activities, if only to avoid a painful erection. If what she'd said was true, that was the last thing I wanted when facing the water witches.

Once I made it into Iceliar, I pulled my coat out, wrapping up against the bitter cold. The witches lived in the waters of Ikanthi. Ice layered it so thick it was impenetrable. As I rode, I considered how I would find the stone if I couldn't break through the ice to even see it. By the time I made it to the Ikanthi River, I still had no plan. I left my horse a safe distance and approached the frozen waters. Across from me stood an ice sculpture of the god of the waters, the god the ice witches had forsaken when they'd committed their sins. This was the only land that had any reference to the gods, and it seemed strange. We never depicted them, only worshipping them from afar—those who cared to worship them. The gods were aloof, never interacting with their people, making their presence known only when the witches had misused their gifts. Otherwise, we wouldn't have known who our creators were. And even now, there was confusion about them—what they ruled over, how many there were, what they expected of us. We went through life blindly, praying they granted us eternal life when we passed through this one.

I pulled out the strange plugs I'd found in my pocket earlier, knowing the witch had left them for me. She had attached a note to them telling me to put them in my ears. The note had turned to ash once I'd read it, startling me so that I'd almost dropped the things. I put one to each ear, my head lurching back as they sank into my ears, a strange sensation of vines leeching over my outer ears and curving behind them. I had the instinct to claw them from my skin, but I knew she'd left them for a reason. Damned witches. I'd never trusted magic, and I'd certainly never trusted witches. Not that we encountered them often. There were so few that it was rare to meet one. I'd now met four.

There was complete silence, as if my head was underwater. The witch had said the sirens would lure me to a watery grave. So the myth was true. Not only did they seduce with their bodies, but they used their voices as well, luring their victims into the icy water, then devouring their remains. Only a brave few had broken the ice throughout history. Those who had witnessed it and survived returned with stories of madness and death.

I stared at the ice, wondering how the ones before me had broken it and how I was supposed to find the water stone. Use the sight to find the stone was Breck's message to me. My sight was doing nothing to assist, no matter how hard I stared at the ice. My hand brushed the seeing stone that sat deep in my coat pocket. Sight... I brought the stone out, holding it in front of me. The stone was the key. I just didn't know how the key worked.

The mid-day sun was high in the sky before me. The spell the witch had cast on me had left me sleeping well past dawn, and I'd left later than I'd wanted. But maybe that hadn't been a misstep on her part. Maybe she'd done it purposely.

I held the stone out, catching the light. The mist inside swirled, turning a dark orange the color of a gumdrop before the color split in rays. Those rays cast downward on the ice, which fractured, shattering into large chunks.

"Gods," I mumbled, my eyes wide as I observed the action unfolding silently before me.

Several larger pieces of ice rose in the air, forming a path to the ice sculpture. Only then did I notice the sparkling blue embedded within it. The water stone. Tentatively, I took my first step on the ice path. A woman's torso emerged from the water, her blue hair enhancing her stunning blue eyes. She was mouthing something I couldn't hear while her hands rubbed across her bare breasts. Another with silver hair emerged next to her, followed by a golden-haired woman. I lost count as bodies rose, their moves seductive and beckoning. If I hadn't had the witch until the early morning hours, I would have succumbed to their temptation. Two of them gyrated against each other, kissing and rubbing. I couldn't draw my eyes from them as the one began licking the blue-haired woman's breasts. My satisfaction from the witch slowly diminished, causing my path to waver. Would it be so bad to play with them? One with red hair blocked their view, her full tits in her hands as she looked enticingly at me. I reached my hand to her, her hair reminding me of Gemma's.

Gemma. All temptation stuttered to a halt as I thought of her. I staggered back, remembering what the witch had said. I needed to be satisfied to avoid falling under the spell of the sirens, but the satisfaction she'd given me had quickly faded. Thinking of Gemma hadn't helped because my body craved her, and no matter how many times I'd taken the witch, nothing could ease that craving. Clearing my head, I thought of what I loved about Gemma, letting those images fill my heart, no matter how it hurt. With every step, I pictured her—her smile, her laugh, her beautiful eyes. I turned the sexual thoughts away, focusing on only the things I loved about her. All but how I loved the way she came for me. That one I pushed aside, knowing the sirens would seize on it.

With my mind focused, I made it to the sculpture quickly. The water stone shimmered the blue of the puffy candy I'd once gotten when the carnival was in town. That had been right before my father had taken us to the woods. I'd shared the sticky candy with Gemma, staying quiet as I'd watched her marvel over the way it melted in her mouth. Her tongue had been blue, her lips coated with a light dusting of it and for a second, I'd wanted to kiss her, before I'd reminded myself how inappropriate it was. She'd barely been thirteen, and I was much older. Besides, I'd told myself, she was an annoying brat, no matter how delicious her full lips looked.

I reached my hand into the center of the statue, which wasn't ice as I'd thought. It was water, static water held in the shape of the god by some form of magic. When I grasped the stone, the water collapsed, and a shrill screech broke through my ear plugs. I spun around, seeing the sirens in a frenzy. Gone were the beautiful women, now replaced with the torsos of haggard witches, their scaly fish tails now visible. They thrashed around in the water, disturbing the ice pathway. Knowing their anger would turn on me, I ran down the path, jumping as they reached for me and dodging their bodies. Their movements were sinking the ice blocks behind me, so I ran faster. As I neared the remaining blocks, I realized I wouldn't make it. Leaping, I landed on my side and slid the rest of the way, the waves casting me over the last ice chunk and into the snow with their force.

I scooted from the shore as far as I could before I collapsed in the snow, catching my breath. A siren crawled from the water, and I backed away further, knowing that was my sign to put some distance between me and the river. Running to my horse, I tucked the stone in my pocket and hopped on him, never once looking back at the water or the sirens I knew were screaming for my return.

When I reached the border of Iceliar, I stopped and let my horse rest. The ear plugs had disintegrated the further we were from the frozen water, just as the note had earlier. I removed my coat, the bitter cold having faded once I'd crossed over into Carenth. The seeing stone I kept tucked into my pocket, but I removed the water stone, letting my fingers run across the smooth surface.

"It's a beautiful stone."

I turned to find the witch, her naked body before me.

"You did well, Hunter. Breck wants you to bring the two stones to the Endless Forest. Then you will retrieve the fire stone and Gemma."

"Do you always heed his commands?" I asked, still curious about the raven-haired witch who had brought me so much pleasure.

"Yes."

"I don't much like taking commands from other men."

"But you like to give them," she purred, moving her body against mine.

"No," I admitted, knowing I only enjoyed commanding one

woman, and I'd never truly commanded her, only controlled her...aggressively.

She moved her hand up my side as I tried to ignore the rise in my pants at her touch. "Why does Breck command you?" I asked.

"Because I am his."

I eyed her, not liking the sound of those words. "You're his lover, and he makes you fuck other men?"

She laughed, a shrill sound that reminded me she was no normal woman. "He is my lover when he wants me. He uses me as he wants and when he wants."

Her hand grasped my erection, but I grabbed it, pulling her away. "Why does he own you?"

"Because he captured me long ago when we were children. We played together, the three of us. And he captured me in a spell, binding me to him, to his will, to do his bidding for the remains of my life."

I loosened my grip on her, searching her brown eyes for any sign of deception, but I found none. "You can't leave him?"

"No. I am his eyes and his ears any time I am in bird form."

She'd told me she'd been watching me. Seeing me as I'd traveled after I'd left Gemma, watching us together before then. My mind pieced it together, and I tightened my grip on her. "You've been his since you were children? Watching for him?"

"Yes."

"Were you there that night?"

She tried to pull away from me, but I held her tighter. There was fear in her eyes. She'd given me too much information, and she knew it.

"Were you there that night? When Gemma and I were young? Were you watching then?"

"I need to go. He'll know I've taken human form when I shouldn't have."

I jerked her closer to me, holding her arm behind her back. "Tell me."

There were tears in her eyes, and I knew I was hurting her, yet she wasn't using her magic against me. I loosened my grip, my tone changing, my desperation coming through in my words. "Please. Were you there that night?"

She nodded, and I released her. She'd been there, already his prisoner, his servant, doing his bidding. My heart stuttered to a halt as the realization hit me. All this time, Gemma had defended him, telling me he was good and all this time I'd trusted that instinct I'd had the night he'd come into our lives. Witches weren't good, no matter how they pretended to be.

"Please. He'll kill me," she pleaded as I walked away.

My step faltered. She'd done nothing but help me, even if it was at his bidding. Turning back to her, I walked over and tipped her chin. I really didn't like witches, but this one seemed to be an exception, sinking into my hardened heart. "I won't tell him anything against you."

I brought her face closer, kissing her and enjoying the innocence that was there, the side of her that hadn't been present the prior night. Her body melted into mine, and I wanted nothing more than to take her again, to fuck her like I had before. To experience her without the drug of magic clouding my perception. I brought my hand around her waist, fighting my desire but losing my battle until I thought of Gemma.

"If she's not there, if she's gone," she said against my mouth. The thought gripped me like an icy vise, stealing my breath and sending my heart pounding in fear.

"She'll be there," I said, kissing her again, wanting to erase the thought of Gemma in death. To replace it with the witch.

"But if she's not..." Her words faded, and I drew back, searching her eyes and wondering if there could be more with her. A witch, my sworn enemy, a woman who had seduced me and given me an amazing night of sex.

"You belong to Breck."

Her face dropped, that innocence returning before I saw the

transformation. Her power returned to her, the innocence replaced with the seductive witch once again. "So I do," she said with a terse bite to her words. She pulled free of me, but I jerked her against me, my mouth smothering her gasp as her breath caught in her throat. She kissed me with a hunger that made my balls ache, and I knew I couldn't let her walk away yet. There was something there, nothing to what I had with Gemma but a connection. Perhaps it was the need for someone to replace Gemma on my part, and the need for escape on hers. Whatever it was, it tied us.

I picked her up, and she wrapped her legs around me, her arms encircling my neck. I kneaded the flesh of her ass, loving how voluptuous she was. Slamming her against the closest tree, I dropped my mouth to her breasts as her head fell back with a moan. I took her there, fucking her so hard she came twice. With her last climax, her body went limp as she let me use her until my release hit me like a churning storm. Her legs squeezed me tighter, her muscles drawing the remains of my climax from me.

"If she's gone, free me," she said against my ear. "I will let you own me, and we can fuck our lives away, erasing the pain of our past with each other."

I raised my head, looking into those chocolate eyes that were pleading for me to agree. For the first time, I let myself think of what would happen if Gemma were dead, if the golems had taken her, if Breck's brother had killed her.

"Promise me," she begged, kissing me.

"I promise," I murmured against her lips, knowing I would, because burying my pain in her would take it away. Although I doubted that pain would ever cease, just as the heartache remained a constant no matter how many women I tried to erase it with.

CHAPTER THIRTEEN

GEMMA

The room that had become my prison was growing claustrophobic. I needed to get out, but Ernan avoided me completely now. He'd been absent since the day he'd kissed me. Food and drink still appeared regularly, and I'd found two dresses on the bottom of my bed one morning when I woke, but I never saw him.

I was not one to be caged. I detested being in one place for long periods. So, as I paced my room for the millionth time, I came up with a plan to escape. No matter what confused emotions I had toward Ernan, I was still his prisoner, and that was all he would let me be.

The furniture in the room was sparse, but there were a few standard pieces. I moved the armoire from the wall, hoping magic from the fire witches hadn't made it. It was wood, so I suspected they hadn't. Once I'd maneuvered it from the wall, I inspected it, feeling along the back and underneath until I found the telltale sign of a nail head. Snagging the fork that Ernan had left with my lunch, I used it to wedge the nail out. It wasn't an effortless task—

forks were cumbersome, thick pieces of metal. After some struggle, I worked the nail loose enough that I could slip it between the tongs and leverage it to pull the rest of the nail out.

The nail clattered against the stone floor, and I snatched it, running to the door. This wasn't the first time I'd found myself in a captive situation. It was, however, the first time I didn't mind being the captive. My captor intrigued me too much to complain. The thought of his lips against mine threatened to deter my focus, so I pushed it aside, thinking instead of Hunter and how I'd like to gouge his eyes out with the fork. But as always happened when I thought of him, the heartache returned because no matter how I hated him, I still loved him.

"Damn my stupid heart," I muttered as the door clicked open.

Tossing the fork on the bed, I peeked out of the room. Torches lined the hall, the eternal flames of Laviak burning brightly in them. There was no sign of a guard, no sign of Ernan, so I left the room. I wandered through hall after hall, my fingers sliding along the rough texture of the walls, until I eventually found myself in a large room. It was barren of anything but a large leather chair that sat in front of a fireplace and a bookshelf with a scattering of worn books.

So, my captor was a reader. I ran my fingers over the spines of the books, reading the titles. I was lucky I could read. My father had taught me at an early age, sitting me on his lap and sounding out the letters until I could read with the proficiency of any boy. That was my earliest memory of my father, and I could almost hear him telling my mother that I needed to read, regardless of the fact that I was a girl. She'd let him have his way, watching us fondly from the kitchen as she baked bread. That had been many years before the sickness had spread through the town, taking a third of the population with it, and my father.

I wiped the tear that had fallen, swallowing back the memories and emotions they'd stirred. I rarely thought of my parents. It hurt too much. Illness had stolen my father from me. Hunter's father had stolen my mother. Her beautiful amber eyes that were the twin to mine had looked lifelessly back at me, dark bruises staining her neck, blood staining her body.

"What are you doing here?" Ernan's shocked voice woke me from my memories, and I turned before I could completely hide the impact those memories had left on my mood.

His hardened expression turned to one of concern and he came to me, picking my face up with his fingers. "What happened? Are you hurt?"

I couldn't understand the sudden change in him, the way his eyes held nothing but the need to fix whatever had upset me.

"I'm fine," I said, pushing his hand away.

He stopped me, taking my hand so that it was suddenly in his. He seemed as surprised as I was, his brow furrowing as he looked at our hands intertwined. His eyes met mine again, but he didn't let my hand go. With a gentle move, he wiped a tear from my cheek with his other hand, his eyes seeking something in mine.

"Why are you crying?" His voice was smooth, and it slipped over my skin like the finest of silks.

"Just thinking of the past," I answered honestly.

His expression fell, his eyes narrowing until that terrifying look was shadowing them again. "Why do you continue to pine over a man who left you to die? Who cared so little about your fate that he has not returned for you?"

The venom in his words caused me to step back, but his grip on my hand tightened.

"Ernan, you're hurting me," I said, as my bones scraped painfully against each other.

"You seem to welcome pain." He stepped closer to me until he had my back pinned against the bookcase. "You love a man who threw you away. Who left you just as he did when you were a child. He left you then, yet you still loved him, still fucked him. You must enjoy being hurt."

I brought my hand up to slap him, but he caught it by the wrist, slamming it into the bookshelf as he continued. "All those years apart and you still took him back, spreading your legs for him, and giving him your heart. Just as you did for my brother, who will rip your heart out and feed it to his pets. You love only those who will hurt you, fearing those who want nothing but for you to be safe." On his last words, the malice in them faded, the wounded look returning before he quickly hid it, his jaw clenching tightly.

I was unsure how to respond, but felt the need to defend myself. "Yes, I loved your brother once, but he never hurt me. I no longer love him. That faded long ago. I will always love Hunter. No matter how he hurts me, it never fades. And he came back for me that night."

"He never returned this time, did he?"

His words stung like the strike of a viper. "And what did you do that night?" I snapped. "You stood there, begging to keep me, so you could what? Rape me? Torture me? Keep me in some prison like you are now?"

He snapped, the veins in his neck protruding as he shoved me harder into the bookcase, his body fully against mine, his eyes flaring with anger. "I would have protected you. I would never have hurt you, nor touched you as my brother did, manipulating you and using you. I would have kept you safe from them both, Gemma." The anger fled his eyes. "That's all I've ever wanted and yet at every turn, you step head first into danger, willingly loving the vultures who use you and leave you."

He released my hand, intent on turning from me, but I gripped his shirt, keeping him against me. Searching his eyes, I saw it then, remembering that night, how Hunter's fear had clouded what I'd seen. How I'd sensed a connection to the strange boy who had emerged from the dark that night, with his mismatched eyes and messy gray and black hair. How I'd talked to him because I hadn't feared him, because he was the only part of that night that had given me calm. Until his brother had found me and led me from the forest. Fear had laced that encounter. But Ernan had felt like safety.

"You were trying to keep me from her?" I asked, finding my voice.

He tried moving away again, his eyes growing hooded, that broody demeanor setting in.

"Ernan," I said, gripping his shirt so tight my knuckles were aching. "Were you trying to keep me safe?"

He nodded.

"Why?" I had to hear his answer, to know the truth that was sitting so heavily on his shoulders that it conflicted him.

The gray in his one eye shifted to a lighter hue, and he relaxed, giving up the struggle against whatever he was hiding.

"Because..." His fingers brushed my cheek, his eyes following the motion. "Because I fell in love with you that night. I'd never seen such a beautiful girl, delicate yet confident, your eyes the most alluring shade of brown, almost gold in the moonlight. I didn't want my mother hurting you or my brother touching you. I knew what they did, and you were too young to fight it, too young to know better. Even when Breck found you again, you were too young." His eyes darkened, the muscles in his jaw twitching. "He took what wasn't his to take, manipulating you, using you like he always does and you...you let him."

There was so much hurt in his expression that I didn't know how to ease it. His words had touched a part of me that had sat locked away since that night. A curiosity that had driven me back into that forest, my path crossing with Breck's when deep down, I'd wanted it to cross with Ernan's.

"Who's was it to take?" I asked him. "Who should have been the one to teach me the ways of the bedroom, of my body?"

"Not him," he growled. "Never him. He stole your innocence—"

"My innocence was gone the night my stepfather abandoned

me in those woods and Hunter let him. My innocence wasn't my virginity. It was my view of life, my trust in men, my trust in anyone. Breck didn't steal anything. I gave it willingly because I needed to."

"No, you needed to have never stepped foot in those woods again, to have stayed far away from him. But you didn't. You sought him out like the brave, foolish girl you were."

"I didn't seek him out," I said, hating this conversation and how his words were making me feel so small, so stupid for reasons I didn't understand. "I was looking for you." The words escaped my lips in the desperation that was clawing at me.

His eyes grew large, his anger faltering. "Me?"

I swallowed, my heart pounding beneath my skin. "Yes. I was trying to find out what happened to Hunter." At Hunter's name, Ernan's lips thinned. He hated him. Hated him for what he'd done to me. "I just needed answers. I've always loved him. I don't think there ever will be a time when I don't, no matter how he hurts me." My voice broke, but I fought the emotion my words had made raw. "But I wasn't looking for Breck. I was looking for you because there was something about you that stuck with me, just as Hunter always stuck with me. There was something that night, something I trusted about you that Hunter didn't see. Something I saw, and I wanted to...I wanted to find out what that something was."

"But Breck stepped in your path, knowing you were coming, and stole you away with his words and his touches." His fists clenched, the white of the knuckles showing through his skin. "I've always hated my brother, but now I hate him even more."

"It wasn't a bad thing. He treated me well. He taught me a lot." I could see my choice of words hadn't been the best.

"Taught you the things I wanted to teach you. I would have waited, keeping you safe until you were old enough, until you were ready."

I leaned into him. "My mother was pregnant with me by the time she was seventeen. I was ready."

"No," he said, his fingers picking up a lock of my hair. "But there's no going back now. No turning back to that night and changing events."

"If you could..."

His lips were so close to mine that I could almost taste him. "I would worship you from afar until I thought it was time..."

"And then?"

"I would make love to you for hours, treating you like you deserve, worshipping every inch of you and claiming it as mine."

I inhaled sharply, my body burning with his words, a warmth that radiated through every part of me. "And now?"

He dropped my hair. "Now, you are someone else's. Your heart is his, your love is his. Even when he gave you up." He looked so hurt that it wrenched my heart, the pieces that were turning toward him screaming for his touch.

"There's room," I murmured, taking his face in my hands and feeling the strength of it.

"Gemma." He linked his hands around my wrists.

"Ernan, you stole a piece of me that night, one I've never realized you had. Take it." He studied me, drawing closer until his lips hovered just above mine. "Take me like you wanted and wash your brother's touch from my skin."

"And Hunter's?"

My heart froze. As much as I hated Hunter for what he'd done, my heart would never be free of him. My body still craved him. "Is a part of me you must accept."

"No matter that he hurt you? That he left you to die?"

"No matter. He will always be my first love, one that will never fade."

His hands slid down my arms, his touch sending a flurry of sparks through my body. I knew then that I wanted to experience Ernan, to know all of him and have him know all of me. That he had indeed been a part of me since the night I'd spoken to him in the Endless Forest, the night he'd pleaded to keep me.

"Make me yours now, Ernan. Keep me like you wanted to then, like you want to now. Claim the parts of me that are yours to take, that were never your brother's but always yours."

His lips met mine, the passion of his kiss almost bringing me to my knees. It wasn't demanding or forceful; it was loving and sweet and filled with a love he'd held for me all these years. As his hands skimmed my arms, wrapping around my back, he brought me further against him. His heart pounded below his chest in a rhythm that met my own. My hands ran through his thick hair, my fingers lost in the mismatched strands. I parted my lips, his tongue meeting mine in a delicate dance that sent a multitude of shivers through me. But he stopped his kiss, drawing back to look at me, desire shading his eyes.

"Gemma," he said, brushing his lips against mine again. "I shouldn't have—"

"Yes, you should have."

"No," he said, shaking his head. "You're not mine. You were my brother's first."

"And he let me walk away. He didn't keep me."

"But you're Hunter's now."

"And he walked away from me. He, too, didn't keep me."

The blue in his one eye danced alluringly in the light from the fireplace.

"No man wants to keep me as you did...as you do. Will you keep me as they chose not to?"

His fingers traced my cheek, pushing back a strand of my hair. I wanted Ernan to say yes, a part of me needing him to take what the others had given up, what Hunter had turned from. Another part recognizing that I'd wanted him to keep me that night, to find out what lay below the beautiful two-toned eyes. He'd loved me all this time, and I found that endearing. This hardened man who should have frightened me, who I'd been told would only harm me, only wanted me safe and protected.

He scooped me up in his arms, and I wrapped mine around his neck, returning the intense gaze he was holding. As he laid me gently on the fur before the fire, I knew he would be a very different lover than Hunter had been. That this would be unlike any experience I'd had with the aggressive men in my past. Ernan hovered over me, looking at me with those beautiful, mismatched eyes, and I pulled him to me, kissing him as our bodies met. His hands ran the length of my body, bringing my leg up alongside his hip. He slipped below my skirt, his breath halting as he touched my bare skin. His kiss became greedier, but his touch remained tender.

My heart was fluttering in my chest as if this were my first time and, in a way, perhaps it was. Ernan didn't taunt or torment me. He didn't do the things that normally had me so soaked I could barely contain my orgasm. But what he was doing had me climbing so fast I didn't think I'd make it long enough to get my clothes off. His fingers never sank into me, but they grazed the inside of my thigh, causing my skin to quiver in anticipation like it was awaiting some kind of penetration that never came. Instead, he raised his hand up the rest of my body, pushing my dress up with it until the bindings ripped. The sound caused my breath to hitch. With it came the feel of his fingers on my breasts, caressing them in respectful, worshipping touches that had me grinding against the bulge that was still locked away in his pants.

He lifted his lips from mine, working my dress over my head. His kisses drifted down my neck to my breasts as his hand came around my back, lifting me so I could remove the dress the rest of the way. I moaned, a sound that tore through my body like the shrill sound of a banshee. I was completely naked and his for the taking, yet still he was slow. Precise in every move of his fingers and hands and lips as they graced my skin, slowly grazing my stomach until his lips brushed my inner thigh. I inhaled, my back arching as his tongue met my flesh. It was his turn to moan and the way it rippled through the air gripped the deepest part of me, claiming me and the part of my heart that he now owned. The piece that he may have always owned. I pushed my pelvis against him as my climax barreled through me, shredding my soul into a million pieces.

I felt like I'd left my body and was floating in some oblivion where no one could reach me. My body was numb with the ecstasy that had overtaken it. He kissed my thigh, my hip, my stomach, working his way back to my lips before he picked his head up, looking at me again. His eyes were sparkling with excitement and shadowed by love. Those eyes made me feel like the most glorious woman in the world, like there was no other who held that place in his heart. I leaned up and kissed him, my hands reaching down to work him free, needing to touch him, to have him in the deepest reaches of my body so that we could be one. He kicked his pants off as I stroked him, his length hot and sticky in my hand. He removed my hand, pinning it over my head as he settled back between my legs. Deepening our kiss, he brought my leg back up, his tip sitting just far enough to leave me aching for him.

"Please, Ernan," I cried between kisses.

"Don't beg, Gemma. Never beg. It's me who should beg to touch you, to kiss you, to have you." His words, so different from what Hunter's had ever been, burned through me, igniting the recesses of my body.

Raking my hands through his hair, I pulled his lips from mine, losing myself in his gaze and never wavering from it as he penetrated me. My cry merged with the groan that rumbled through his chest. His eyes closed as he moved in me, and he dropped his head to my shoulder, holding me so tight I thought I might sink into his flesh and truly become one with him. He dragged his lips across my collarbone and up my neck, each thrust sending the desperate desire to climax surging higher within me.

I'd never been so full, so loved as I was with Ernan, and the thought sent my release tumbling, my cry ripping from me only to be captured by him. He tensed, his own release joining mine, and together we fell, breaking with the total collapse of our bodies.

His ragged breaths burned against my lips, drawing out more trembles from the bliss of my climax. Even when our bodies calmed, I clung to him, not wanting to break the spell he'd cast on me. It wasn't magic. It wasn't something he'd done to me. It was a different spell that bound the fractured pieces of my heart, the ones Hunter had discarded, to Ernan. They were his, as was I, and the thought was one I welcomed.

He rested his forehead on mine, his eyes studying me, and I slid my fingers along his cheek, wondering at this man who had made love to me like no one ever had. Truly made love to me in the most endearing, gentle manner that so opposed the threatening presence he was. He turned his mouth to my hand, kissing my palm as he rolled over, taking me with him and settling me against his chest. It was a place I never wanted to leave, tucked in the safety of him. Only Hunter had ever made me feel that way, and he had turned out to be the biggest threat to my heart.

"Why didn't you find me all those years ago?" I asked, regretting that I'd fallen for Breck and knowing anything I'd had with him was worlds from what this was.

"Because my brother found you first."

"Were you searching for me?" I raised my head to see his face.

"No. I'd already found you, just as Breck had." He turned his eyes to me, raising his hand to brush my hair from my cheek. "I watched you from afar after that night. I worried he'd find you, but my brother likes the game. He manipulates and uses until he's ready to make his move."

I sat up further, the icy fingers of fear making their way down my spine.

"I've always watched you, Gemma, but you were never mine

to take, and I would never have done what he did. He set that trap for you, leaving breadcrumbs for you to find him, until one day you wandered back into the forest. I tried to deter you, but you're so stubborn." His lips curved into a sweet grin. "Always so determined to prove yourself."

I thought back to that day. The forest had been terrifying, the sounds of wolves around me, the creak of tree limbs. I'd brought my knives out in anticipation that something would attack, but nothing did. "You were there?"

He nodded, turning his body so that he was facing me. The contact of his skin to mine caused that ache to return between my legs and I pushed further into him. He gave me a coy grin, as if knowing my thoughts. "I was always there. Not physically, but there are ways to watch from afar, to urge the howls of the wolves to travel farther than they were."

"But why? Why not show up? Appear before me?"

"And what would you have done? Would you have greeted me as you did my brother? Or would that night have reminded you I was the frightening one? The one who wanted to keep you when my brother freed you? You say you were seeking me, but what would you have done if you'd found me? I doubt you would have been so inclined to approach me as you did my brother." I dropped my eyes, knowing it was true. Entering the forest had terrified me. I likely would have run if he had appeared, the memory of watching him drag Hunter's body into the cottage that night shadowing my senses. "I stayed from your sight, and my brother stepped into your path, having led you exactly where he wanted you."

My heart came to a halt, and I looked back up at him, cinching my brows at the power of that statement. "What does that mean, Ernan?"

"Breck does nothing that does not benefit him. And you benefited him greatly."

I bristled, but he pulled me closer. "Shhh, I didn't mean

anything against you, although it pisses me off to no end that he stole what should not have been his to take from you. What you should have given freely. What should have been mine."

"He didn't steal my virginity. Gods, what is it with my virginity that bothers you and Hunter so much?"

"Well, at least we have one thing in common. That's about all," he grumbled, and I could tell in that expression that if he met Hunter again, he'd kill him just like he'd said he would. "Breck manipulated you, Gemma. He played you and Hunter from the start. He set you free because that's where he wanted you to be. Then he murdered our mother and made it look like I had done it. It forced my hand, forced me to become what you thought I was that night, what Hunter thought I was. The cruel, terrifying sorcerer, son to the most notorious witch in our kingdom. If I hadn't stepped into that role, they would have killed me. Breck fled, leaving me to fend for myself, and he freed Hunter. I think he meant to use him as well, but he found you more intriguing."

"But I ran from there and never looked back—"

"Until something called you to return, to find answers. The same something that manipulated every move and shaped you to be who you are today. I tried to stop the inevitable, knowing what he was using you for, that he would only betray your trust. I tried to keep you from the seeing stone that night."

My world came collapsing around me. Everything I'd known was now stripped away. Everything I'd thought had been me taking my destiny in my hands, me controlling the world that had been so traumatizing as a child, shattered. None of it had been my doing, none of it free will. Even Hunter.

"You...you were his buyer." I stared at Ernan, unable to close my mouth for the shock that grasped me. "Gods, you sent him there..." I sat up, trying to make sense of it all. His hand rubbed my back as he sat with me. I knew he was observing me while I sifted through the confusion that addled my brain. "You knew I was there and sent him in my path." My words broke, emotion gripping me. "Knowing—"

"Knowing you loved him and that he'd searched for you as many years as you had for him."

I turned to him, my eyes burning with the tears that were pressing behind them. "But if you loved me, why would you give me to another man?"

"Because I loved you. Hunter was strong and smart, like you. I knew he'd keep you safe, knew he'd help you with the other stones and ensure nothing happened to you. Well, until the asshole left you here."

"He left me because I broke his heart." The words fell from my lips as I realized they were the truth. "He wanted to stop searching for the stones, to stay in the oasis we found in Tronekrin. To stay with him and never leave. But the idea frightened me. I turned him down and hurt him, even though he didn't tell me. It stewed in him until he finally broke in Laviak, and we fought...and he left me."

"Gemma." I lifted my eyes from my hands, not liking the trepidation his voice held. His eyes were dark, shadowed again. "Hunter came back for you in the woods that night."

"Yes," I said with a tremble in my voice.

"Are you certain he wouldn't return to find you here?"

"He didn't. I was out there for days before you found me. He never returned."

"Do you have the stones?"

I shook my head, fear curling its way around my heart like a serpent's body. "No, he took them."

"There is no fire stone without the water stone. But you didn't have the water stone. You never made it to Iceliar."

"How do you know that?"

"I told you, I watched from afar. But so did Breck. He had his servant watching you both. Why were you in Laviak?"

"We were coming from Tronekrin, and it was the most direct route."

"A foolish route," he grumbled.

"I know that now, although it brought me to you, so perhaps it wasn't the most foolish."

He gave me a look that told me he thought otherwise. "Would you have continued to Iceliar?"

"Yes, but my horse got spooked and threw me. That's why I was out there for so many days."

"Days Hunter had to talk sense into himself."

"Days Hunter had to fuck me from his mind. I know him well enough to know he wasn't pining over me. He was shoving his cock in other women."

Ernan raised a brow.

"It's the truth. It's how Hunter works."

"A man who has loved you as long as he has won't find satisfaction in other women, no matter how many he takes. Trust me, I know."

The inhale I took was a sharp one that hurt my chest.

"And when he had his fill, he would have done exactly what he did that night," he continued.

"You think he returned to find me?"

"I think he went to Iceliar, expecting you'd be there by then."

"But I wasn't there."

"No. Did he know Breck hired you for the stones?"

"Of course, I told him everything." Almost everything, except the mistruth that had led to his leaving. But if Ernan was right, he'd returned to find me. All the cursing I'd done about Hunter, knowing what he was likely doing, I'd never once thought of what else he might do.

"What did Breck bargain with you? What did you stand to lose if you couldn't retrieve them?"

I swallowed, knowing his reaction would be just as bad, if not worse, than Hunter's. His eyes were penetrating, seeing right into my soul. "If I found them, he'd tell me what happened to Hunter."

"And if you didn't?"

"Then I'd stay with him. I'd be his...forever."

"Dammit," he grumbled, running his hands through his hair. "Why would you do something so foolish, Gemma?"

"Because I needed to know. I needed answers."

He calmed, but I could still see the tension in his jaw. "Did Hunter know any of that?"

"Yes." That fear coiled tighter around my chest.

"And if I were Hunter, I'd think the worst, but I'd hope the latter of the two worst options would be Breck. If he went to my brother to find you—"

"Gods, he would. He's foolish enough, pigheaded enough to do that. And he despises Breck for the same reasons you do."

"Oh, I doubt that very much. You know nothing of my brother, Gemma. He makes my mother look like she was throwing a tea party. Breck is everything your people fear in witches and sorcerers. If Hunter went seeking him out—"

My strangled cry interrupted him. Breck was powerful. I'd never feared him, but I'd seen him use his magic, and I was certain he'd never shown me his full strength. If Hunter went to confront him... My body shook as the fear twisted so tight within me I couldn't breathe. The beautiful moments I'd had with Ernan fled as my worry for Hunter tainted them. He stood no chance against Breck, and if he thought Breck had taken me, was using me against my will, he'd face death to save me. And death was all he'd find waiting there.

CHAPTER
FOURTEEN

HUNTER

I watched as the witch flew back to her master, her name still whispering in my mind. Mera. She had given it as she'd transformed, and somehow, I knew what she'd given me. Having a witch's name was power. The names of sorcerers, like Breck, did not hold power but a witch's did. It was likely the way Breck had captured her so many years ago.

I didn't know what to think of my witch. How to think of her yet. Gemma was who I wanted, but Mera would be who I'd settle for if Gemma was dead or didn't forgive me for leaving her. She would be the type of woman I needed. One I didn't need to commit to, to think of settling down with, to envision raising a family with...the things I'd imagined with Gemma. The same that had sent us spiraling out of control after my innocent question in the oasis.

Clearing my head, I thought about what I'd learned, my conflicted emotions about Mera erased with anger at Breck. Anger for all he'd put Gemma through. For everything he'd done.

My anger drove me, and I drove my horse, stopping only when necessary to ensure I didn't run him into the ground.

My ire grew with each day that passed as I neared the Endless Forest until it became a well of hatred and animosity. One that would remain unsatisfied until that spawn of the witch was dead. I envisioned locking him in that run-down cottage and burning it to the ground. Or running him through with a sword and plunging out his eyes. A myriad of vicious endings overran my mind about the bastard who had done nothing but use Gemma from the moment he'd let her run that night.

When I finally reached Spindara, I didn't stop to rest, to eat, to fuck. None of it mattered. I needed answers or I would rip out the tongue of that asshole and spear it to his heart with my dagger.

It was midday by the time I reached the clearing in the forest. I'd never questioned how I'd found it each time or how Gemma had found it, but now I knew. He had wanted it found. He'd been waiting for us, waiting for her. And now, he waited for me.

He stood at the doorway of the cottage, the candy remnants rotted with his presence. He looked to be in a mood, and I wondered if Mera had told him what I'd discovered.

Jumping from my horse, I threw the two stones to the ground at his feet. "Here are your fucking stones. Now find Gemma."

He glanced at the stones, then back at me, a scowl on his face. "You will find Gemma and bring me my last stone."

I rushed him, knocking him into the cabin so that we both went crashing to the floor.

"You set her up! This whole time. You manipulated her, brought her to you, groomed her, destroyed her and for what? Some stupid stones?" I was roaring, and he seemed taken aback by my sudden insight into his doings.

Recovering quickly, he threw me from him with his magic, the force of it sending me careening into the wall, which began crumbling behind me.

"You assume you can touch me?"

"I'll do more than that. I'll fucking kill you!" I yelled back. "You led her through every step, grooming her, taking her innocence—"

"She gave that over willingly," he snarled. "Besides, she wasn't that young. I've had younger."

My stomach turned, and I questioned how Gemma had never seen him for who he really was.

"I've never trusted you."

"Yet she did." He rolled his neck, his blue eyes becoming cloudy. "She trusted me enough to let me taste the pretty piece of candy she was and teach her how to please me. I believe you benefited from those lessons recently."

"Why you—" I lunged to strike him, but he sent me flying back into the wall.

"You're no match for me. She was a match." A devious grin formed on his lips. "Quite the match, and a quick learner. I enjoyed taking her purity and corrupting it. Shaping her, grooming her as you said."

"She loved you." The words hurt to say, but they were true. I may have been her first love, but he was the first to whom she'd confessed the words.

"Love. She was a child who wanted a man. One who wanted you and settled for me." He spat the words, his distaste clear.

"You never loved her," I said, seeing it now. "You drew her back here, lured her in, and used her."

"I enjoyed her flesh. She enjoyed my fucking her. I wouldn't say that I used her. If anything, we used each other."

"But you had another agenda."

He sneered, his lip curving to an ugly snarl. "I've always had an agenda. The day she walked into this forest, I saw her for who she was, and you for who you were. She was curious, brave, beautiful, even at such a young age. But you, you were a fool, a coward

205

who left her to wander the woods alone and so I took what you gave up that night. Her trust."

His words hit me like a punch to my gut. She'd lost her trust in me the minute I'd left her, even after I'd come back to get her. But he had let her go, saved her without hesitation.

"And with that trust, I led her back. Taught her to tap into her strength, her confidence. I made her who she is today. When she left me, I didn't stop her because I knew she'd be back. And so, I watched her, just as I did the day I let her go." He stooped down to where I was still sitting, winded, on the floor. "I've always watched her, led her, encouraged her. Every job, every falter, every setback, I was there to set it right until she could do it herself."

"You pushed her to become a mercenary...gods, you needed her to be that strong. To be that swift, that smart. All of it for the stones?"

"Exactly. I groomed her so she could retrieve the stones. Pushed her with every quest, sending every challenge her way, manipulating it so she received the tougher jobs. When she was strong enough, I went to her with the promise of the one thing she never let go."

"Me."

"You. Oh, the constant nagging for me to tell her what happened to you drove me mad when I was stuck playing house with her." He stood and stomped away. "Droning on and on about how she needed to know. I knew where you were, what you were doing, all the women you were fucking. And I must say, you put me to shame." I frowned at him, rising from the floor as he continued. "But even with all those women you took, I still got the prize candy first, didn't I? And she was a tasty one."

I moved to attack him, but he put his hand out to stop me. "Eh, eh. You want your Gemma back, to find out if she's still alive? Then *you* will find her."

"Me? You said to bring you the fucking water stone, and I did. Now you find her."

"I can't. I cannot see into Laviak with my sight or my bird... how did you like her, by the way? My little bird is quite the treat."

Crossing my arms, I stared him down, not about to give him any insight into how his witch had gotten to me.

"Oh, but you had a good time, didn't you? She knows how to enhance a climax with that magic of hers. It's intoxicating."

"Fuck you."

He laughed, the sound grating sharply in my ears. "Go to Laviak, take the water stone and find my Gemma and my fire stone."

"She's not your Gemma."

"And as I said before, she's no longer yours. How many times can you leave her before you completely destroy what little faith she has left in you? I don't think you have any chances left. I, however, have only guided her. She still trusts me, and she will until I have her for eternity."

My world spun, the room closing in on me. He wanted to keep her, but he would do what he'd done to Mera. He would enslave her, keeping her in another form and releasing her only when he needed her or wanted to use her body. The pressure on my heart made it almost impossible to breathe.

"Don't worry. I'll treat her well, and I'll pleasure her regularly, as long as she keeps me satisfied."

He walked away, leaving me stunned. For an instant, I wished she were dead. There was no way I could protect her from him. He had magic, something I couldn't fight. Even if I found her and somehow convinced her to run with me, he would hunt her down. He'd been watching her all these years, watching after she left the forest, watching every year after she returned. There was no escaping him.

"Take the water stone and head to Laviak. Do not return without my prizes."

The stones rose in the air, the water stone spinning toward

me. I caught it, seeing the other disappear into the pouch that contained the remaining stones.

In a cloud of fog, he disappeared, leaving me alone in the cottage of my nightmares, fighting the nightmare scenario I now found myself in and praying there was some way out.

THE ROAD from Spindara to Laviak was not as straight a path as the one from Tronekrin. I had to backtrack north in Carenth before I came upon the road into the fiery pits. Three more days passed, and I couldn't help but wonder what had happened to Gemma in the weeks that I'd been away from her. If she lived, then Breck's brother had her. She'd said Breck had told her he was far worse, terrifying even. He had killed his mother and would have returned to eat me. But that had all been Breck's words, words that I wasn't certain I could trust now. Words twisted in lies to mislead me and betray Gemma. The man was nothing like I'd thought, nothing like he'd led Gemma to believe. What did that make his brother?

I rested my horse before entering Laviak to ensure I could travel the expanse without stopping. Stopping in the pits was an invitation to the fire witches, the golems the gods had cursed them to be, and I didn't want any chance of waking them. As I traveled further in, I spotted the bones of what looked like a horse. They hadn't been there long; they were still recognizable, the heat and flame not turning them to ash yet. My heart stopped upon seeing the worn leather of the saddlebag that had fallen from its body before the golems had devoured it. Gemma.

I tightened my hands on my reins, afraid to admit what that sight told me. It couldn't be. Scouring the surroundings, I was relieved to find no human remains, but it wasn't enough to reassure me entirely. There was hope the horse had fled and left her, but as I remembered the heat and the golems, that hope faded quickly. She would have needed to stop. There would have been no way she could keep up in this heat without water or without resting. The guilt that sat upon my shoulders was heavy, weighing me down so that I felt as if I were carrying the horse and not the other way around.

I prayed the brother had found her. If she was his prisoner, at least she was alive. I could rescue her...if I could find him. Breck had told me nothing of his brother, nothing of where he would be. I could only hope the same strange draw Gemma and I had to the cottage in the Endless Forest would lead me to the brother. Ernan. I remembered Gemma saying his name when she'd told me about her quest, giving me the warped lies Breck had given her.

Time dragged on, my horse and my body getting weary, but just as I was about to give in and take a break, the heat lifted. The ground turned from red stone to black, the black of cooled lava. The surrounding air cooled once I passed into the new terrain. Before me stood a massive stone castle, the color of the ground below my feet. I looked with wide eyes at the structure, unsure of how I had missed it when I'd left Gemma here. The paths were so convoluted in Laviak that one wrong turn would take you into an endless maze of paths. I had remained on the eastern pathways, knowing they were a straight shot through Laviak. Gemma and I had followed one when we'd entered from Tronekrin, and I'd retraced our steps when I'd left her.

But never had I seen this castle. All I could attribute its appearance to was that strange connection the four of us had, the fated intertwining of our lives that kept leading us to each other. The same one that led me to Gemma the night I'd found her in the Governor's home.

I rode closer, passing through a stand of dead trees, their blackened husks standing eerily on guard. Leaving my horse just before the trees broke, believing he would be safe and remain out of sight, I slipped to the edge of the building. My hands ran along the bumpy stone that made up its consistency. I skirted the wall, finding nothing blocking my entrance to the front. The doors were wide open. Either he knew I was coming, or he had nothing to fear. Either option wasn't reassuring.

Pulling my knives out, I ventured in, hating the silence that greeted me. What I found further inside was something I hated more. In a room off the main corridor, a fire burned, framing two silhouettes. Gemma's strawberry hair looked dark in the firelight, but the hands that were threading through it were what made my heart screech to a halt. I dropped my hands, all strength fading while I watched her kiss the man she was with. There was no fight, no struggle as he held her in his arms.

"Gemma," I croaked.

She spun, her eyes large. Her lips, red from kissing, formed an *oh*. The man pulled her against him, his arm looping around her waist protectively. His eyes, one gray, the other blue, were narrowed and dark. The tussled gray hair with black streaks throughout it looked no different than it had the night I'd first met him.

"Hunter?" Gemma's voice sounded unsteady.

"All this time, I worried you were dead, that you were being held against your will or worse, being assaulted by him and I find you kissing him?"

She bristled, the shock in her eyes quickly turning to ire, their amber shifting to brown. "You left me," she hissed.

"He's the witch's son!"

"So what?"

"So what? I guess it shouldn't surprise me, since you seem to enjoy fucking them."

I threw the water stone to the ground, and Ernan released Gemma, walking closer to it.

"Find the fire stone yourself or let him figure out how to keep

Breck from fucking you for the rest of your life. If you're lucky, he'll turn you into a bird and only fuck you when he's not fucking his other servant."

I turned, feeling Gemma's eyes burn through me.

"You asshole! You have no right!"

"Gemma, he has the water stone." Ernan's voice scraped across my ears.

"So what? I'm so tired of these stupid stones."

"He went to Iceliar," I heard him say as I left the room, not caring what the two of them were saying. Not caring about any of this or Gemma or the pain that was wracking my chest.

I stormed from the castle, paying no heed to the sound of feet running after me as I made my way back to my horse.

As I passed into the dead trees, Gemma grabbed my arm. "Hunter, stop!"

I turned on her, not sure why I was being so hypocritical. I'd made my way through many women since I'd left her. But something about the way the two of them had been kissing, the softness of it that wasn't the unbridled passion that spoke of an unattached fuck bothered me.

She stepped back, bumping into a tree, the bitter burned bark shaking with the impact.

"Couldn't keep your legs closed for another witch's son, Gemma?" There was bitterness in my voice, a poison that I could see stung her. She flinched with each word.

"Don't you lecture me about who I fuck—"

"Dammit!" I punched the side of the tree close to her face, hating the fear I saw in her eyes. "You fucked him? You really fucked him? I thought you were dead! I thought I'd find you imprisoned by a homicidal sorcerer who was torturing you, not one making you come around his cock!"

"Seriously?" I could see the anger in her eyes, but there was something else behind them that told me I was right to be angry, that there had been more to that kiss. "How many women did you fuck after you left me?"

I reeled back. She knew. Of course she did.

"You're angry at me for sleeping with Ernan when you left me and fucked your way through the realms to assuage your conscience. Just like you did for the past fifteen years. How many, Hunter?"

"This isn't about me, Gemma."

"It's always about you, Hunter. You left me. You turned your back and rode off without looking back. Not enough whores for you to bury your cock in, so you had to come back to find me?"

"Fuck you. You're sleeping with a sorcerer. The brother to the one who used you and stole your virginity. You don't get to judge me."

"He saved me." That stopped me, cooling my anger like a wave of icy water. "He rescued me from the golems who were sucking the life from me, what life I had left after days in the heat with no water."

I didn't know what to say or how to respond. The story was not one I'd imagined. I'd only imagined the worst scenarios. "You were riding out of Laviak—"

"My horse threw me. I was walking out of Laviak."

The tension fled my body, the reality of what I'd done, the mistake I'd made hitting me with the force of a violent storm.

"Gem—"

"No, Hunter. You don't get to Gem me after what you did. Did you even think about me? Worry about me? Or did you bury your guilt up some woman's skirts?"

I thought of all the women I'd taken since that day.

"That's what I thought."

"They were nothing but a salve, a way to erase you from my mind."

She pushed away, but I moved closer, pinning her to the tree. "They were a way to erase your guilt, Hunter. That's all."

"I didn't fall in love with them, Gemma." I heard the vicious bite to my tone. Her mouth fell open, the flush of her cheeks the answer to my suspicions.

"I..."

"You fell in love with him. Fuck," I muttered, having hoped I was wrong. The truth of it tore through me like the claws of a rabid animal, making me feral. I pushed further into her, the nearness of her intoxicating. But she'd been with another man. A man she loved. It wasn't possible. I owned her heart, not some sorcerer from a night that had blanketed our lives. "Do you love him?" I growled, grabbing her waist and knowing the move was a mistake.

"Hunter, I—"

"Do you love him?" I squeezed and her mouth parted seductively, causing my body to react even with the betrayal I felt.

"Yes," she breathed, and I dropped my head to her neck. The words scalded their way through my skin and into my heart, further breaking it. But I'd been the one to do the initial damage. I'd been the one to turn from her, to leave her open for another man to take what was mine. Anger seeped from the depths of my soul at the thought.

"You're mine, Gemma," I snarled, licking her neck. "All of you is mine."

"You gave me up, Hunter. You left me to die."

I pressed further into her. "You will always be mine, pretty thing. No matter where you are or what has happened. No matter how many kingdoms separate us." I moved my hand to her breasts, ripping the front of her dress to access them, my hand squeezing her flesh. "Who owns you, pretty thing?"

"You gave me up," she mumbled, her voice hoarse.

I pinched her nipple, her moan reverberating through me. I should have walked away, left her, and never looked back. But I'd done that before, and I'd looked back every step, hating that she wasn't with me. I couldn't give her up. She was mine.

"Who owns you, Gem?" I asked again, my lips hovering just above hers. "Who will always own you?"

"You," she whispered, and it was the word I needed to hear. I smashed my lips to hers, kissing her with a greed only she could sate.

"You're mine, pretty thing," I mumbled between kisses, moving my hands to push her skirt up, "and I'm going to make it clear to that bastard that you belong to me."

"Hunter." Her plea was weak, her hands clutching my shirt as my finger broke through to the wetness that confirmed her desire for me. They sank into her, my hard-on pressing for freedom as she lurched forward, a cry tearing from her lips.

I silenced the cry, devouring it with a kiss that demanded her attention was only on me. Her hands threaded through my hair, pushing my lips closer as she broke. Her climax sent trembles through her, her body clamping down so tight that I couldn't remove my hand until she'd calmed.

"Gods, Hunt," she murmured.

"What, Gem? Don't you like it when I break you?"

She inhaled so sharply that it cut through my control. Bringing my fingers up, I licked her from me, savoring every bit of that sweetness before I pushed them to her. Her tongue reached out and swept over them. She pulled them into her mouth, her beautiful amber eyes never leaving mine. I ripped my hand away and weaved it into her hair, pulling roughly. Her gasp clawed at my desire, making me so hard I could barely stand.

"Does he make you come the way I do, pretty thing?"

Her groan was delicious, and I wanted to memorize the sound of it, to never have a time when that groan wasn't for me. I gripped the strands of her hair harder. "Does he?"

"Hunter, please."

My fingers clenched, her head pulling back. "Does he, Gem?"

"Gods, no."

"Good girl." Her words calmed my wrath, but not my craving

for her. "Did he fuck you today? Is his cum still inside of you?" I asked, biting her bottom lip.

"Yes."

The growl that rumbled through me was loud, and she shivered in response.

"But no."

I pulled away and narrowed my eyes.

"Did he fuck you or not?"

"Yes, but..."

"But what?"

She looked away, but I jerked her head, forcing her eyes back to me.

"We bathed."

My jaw clenched so tightly that I heard the grinding of my teeth. "You bathed...with him," I said, my teeth gritted so the words barely came out.

"Yes." Her voice was shaking, the fear behind it giving me mixed emotions. I hated that she was afraid of me, but the possessive monster in me thrived on it.

I ran my hand over her tits, squeezing hard enough to see her flinch before I wrapped it around her neck. Her eyes lit, calling to my body as if she had some magical hold over it.

"Well, I think it's time I remind you who fucks this body like it craves being fucked." Her bottom lip trembled, and I snagged it between my teeth, squeezing her neck as I dropped my hand from her hair and lifted her skirts again. "Does he fuck you like I do, Gem?"

I needed her to say no. I needed to know that I ruled her, that only I had the power over her body that made her submit. I steeled myself to her answer as I rubbed my thumb over her clit.

Her lips parted. "Gods, no. No one fucks me like you do, Hunter."

Shoving my fingers deep into her, I took that answer and let it fuel me. I was the only one who called to her, who broke her like this. I was the only one she submitted to, who owned her like I did. Stroking her clit as I continued to let my fingers drive her mad, I watched her fall apart again, her hands bunching under my shirt and pulling my mouth to hers. Within seconds, her kisses turned to a cry that I captured as I slid my fingers from her and freed my aching length. In one swift move, I lifted her, thrusting into her so hard that the tree shook.

Her legs clenched around me as I pounded into her, the tree fracturing. It exploded into a cloud of ash, our bodies falling. Protecting her from the fall, I kept her in my grasp, never slipping from her as we collapsed, the ash of the tree surrounding us like a snowstorm. She screamed as another climax hit her, her muscles spasming around me and calling to my need for release. I fought it, needing more of her, needing to re-claim her, to erase the touch of the witch's son from her. To erase the touches of the other women from me and bind us once again.

Shoving her legs up higher, I brought them around my neck and drove into her, my eyes on hers. Her breasts had fallen from her dress, and I dropped to suck on her nipple. I bit at it until she was clenching around my cock, another orgasm mounting.

"Hunter." My name fell from her lips like a call of ownership and I knew then that she was still mine, that she'd never stopped loving me, no matter how angry she'd been.

"Come for me again, pretty thing. I want to feel you coax my cum from me as you fall apart." Moving my hand to her neck, I held her tight, lifting my head and meeting her eyes. Her lips opened, a moan escaping, one I let caress my skin like the touch of her hands.

I dropped my lips to hers, saying, "Do you still love me, Gem?"

"Yes, always, Hunt."

"Good girl." Draping my lips across hers, I pushed deeper, sensing her climax rise, her body quivering as it sat on the cusp of release. "Now come for me, Gem. Show me I'm the only one who breaks you."

Her head fell back, her climax hitting so intensely that she destroyed my hold on my body. My orgasm swept through me like the wave of a storm, burying me in ecstasy so that I could barely breathe. I held her through it, our bodies convulsing against each other. And as she scratched at my back to bring me deeper, I knew she belonged to me. No matter what she had with him, I was the one who drove her over the edge the way no man did.

CHAPTER FIFTEEN

GEMMA

Dropping my head back, I released my grip on Hunter but didn't remove my hands from his back. I didn't want to let him go now that he was back, no matter how complicated this had become. No matter that Ernan had just made love to me hours before. The two were so different, both completing a separate part of me.

It had been days since Ernan had first taken me, making love to me. So many that I'd lost track. The softness of his touches, the gentleness that was hidden behind his stern exterior, claimed my heart piece by piece. And every day since then, I'd lost myself further to him, to the way he made me feel—delicate, fragile, like someone to be worshipped. It was so opposite to how Hunter made me feel, but I'd known, no matter how I was falling in love with Ernan, that I would always love Hunter. He completed the other part of me, the one Ernan couldn't touch.

I had decided to find Hunter, to leave Ernan's protection. He didn't like the idea, arguing against it, but I had made the decision, knowing I had to find Hunter. To know if Breck had hurt him, to give him a piece of my mind for leaving me, to touch him again. But Hunter had found me first, just as I was kissing Ernan, convincing myself to leave him but knowing somehow that I'd return. He owned a part of my heart now, and I didn't think I could give him up. I didn't know how I could return to him. Hunter was possessive and jealous. There was no way he'd let another man touch me again. But it was a problem I'd told myself I would deal with once I found him and knew he was safe.

And now he was here. He'd stormed off, but I'd followed, Ernan letting me go, not stopping me, not coming after me. Letting me go, just as his brother had.

I hadn't intended on doing anything more than talking to Hunter, but I couldn't deny the need I had for him when I saw him. Even if he'd taken his fill of women while he'd been gone, even if I'd been sleeping with another man. The draw we had to each other was one I couldn't explain. One I didn't think he could either. His touch, his demands to confess that he owned me, that he broke me like not even Ernan could do, were too much to resist. And gods, how he'd broken me again. My body was his, drawn to him like a bee to nectar. I needed him desperately because only he could calm the fire that raged in me when he was near.

Now he was in my arms, my legs slipping to wrap around his waist. His green eyes searched mine, but I didn't know what he was looking for. His expression was still hard. The softness I'd seen when we'd been in the oasis was absent. But I didn't mind. This was the Hunter I loved, the one I craved. He released my neck, his hand drifting over my breasts, taunting my nipples, which responded instinctively to him.

He slipped from me and pushed my legs down, rising. I watched as he silently buttoned his pants and tucked his shirt in. He never took his eyes off me.

"Close your legs, Gemma. I want my cum still filling you

when you return to him. I want him to know you belong to me, no matter how he fucks you."

He turned away, and I scrambled to my feet. "Hunter?"

He ignored me, acting as if he hadn't just taken me and reminded me I was his. By the time I'd adjusted my dress, he'd reached his horse, digging in his saddlebag. Grabbing his arm, I brought his attention back to me.

"Hunter, we need to talk about this. You just took me—"

He smirked. "I just fucked you, Gem." He stepped closer, that smirk growing. "The way you need to be fucked. Now start walking and remember, don't let a drop of my cum slip free. You're mine, and his weak ass attempts to claim what is mine will fail." He gripped my chin in his hand. "You will always belong to me."

"I know," I said.

His eyes widened with surprise before he frowned. Taking my elbow, he dragged me from the woods, leading his horse behind us.

"Hunter, let me go."

"I am," he said, but he continued to drag me with him. His words took root, and I glanced at him. He was letting me go.

"But Hunter—"

He shoved me ahead of him, and I stumbled to the ground. "You want what's mine, sorcerer?" he called.

Gods, if he was planning to fight Ernan, he'd lose. Ernan walked out of the castle, his arms crossed, the serious brooding expression lining his features. I brought myself from the ground, looking between the two.

Ernan stayed silent.

"You dare touch what's mine!" Hunter sneered.

Ernan didn't flinch. "I didn't dare touch anything that's yours. I touched what was mine. What you gave up and what's been mine since the night I first saw her."

My mouth fell with the power of that statement. Hunter's

hands clenched so tight that his knuckles were white. He rolled his neck, the veins in it protruding. He looked every bit as terrifying as Ernan, and my heart raced. Both men were so similar, yet so different.

A heavy silence sat between them, and I didn't know what to say or what to do. If I had to choose between them, I wouldn't. I loved them both, and both completed me in different ways. My heart was in my throat, and I swallowed back the fear of losing either of them.

Hunter turned from us.

"That's it?" Ernan asked. "Are you just going to leave her like you did before? Like you left her to die?"

Hunter's head shot up, the muscles in his back taut with tension, but he didn't turn back.

"Off to fuck more women so you don't have to face the consequences of loving her? So you don't have to think about what's happening to her?"

With the speed of the assassin he was, Hunter wheeled around. I'd never seen his eyes so dark. "Fuck you, asshole. You don't know me."

"Oh, I know you well enough, Hunter. Well enough to know exactly what you'll do when you leave her again. No matter how many women you fuck, it won't erase her. Run, and I'll stay here and protect her, just like I always have."

Hunter stormed over to him. "Always have? Where were you when your brother was manipulating her? Stealing her virginity? Using her, grooming her?"

I rolled my eyes, tired of the topic of my virginity. I had no idea it was such an important conquest, that so many men had lined up to claim it when I'd given it to Breck.

Ernan stepped closer, both men now almost chest to chest. Ernan was only about an inch taller than Hunter, but both were well over six feet. "I was there, trying to distract her, to keep her from him. While you were in Simeril fucking some whore's mouth."

Hunter swung, his fist meeting Ernan's hand, the magic behind it stopping his movement.

"I hate witches," Hunter muttered before tackling Ernan.

The two went down hard, Hunter throwing punches while Ernan punched back.

"Stop it!" I screamed, knowing this would get us nowhere. "Damn you both, stop it before I leave you both and never look back!"

They froze, turning to me. Ernan pushed Hunter from him and rose, wiping the soot from his clothes.

"I've always watched her when you couldn't," he mumbled as Hunter lifted himself from the ground. "But she's stubborn and pig-headed."

"Hey," I complained.

"You are. Walking into that damned forest and right into my brother's trap."

"Wait, you know about that?" Hunter asked, his voice calmer.

"Of course, I know. I can't go into the Endless Forest when Breck is present. It's his domain. I can only enter when he's somewhere else and when Gemma was with him, he shielded her from me, ensuring I couldn't reach her even when he wasn't there. Not that she would have trusted me."

"This isn't about me," I grumbled.

"Then you know he's using her to get the stones."

I glanced at Hunter, surprised that he was no longer trying to kill Ernan. His attention had shifted, the mercenary in him taking over.

"Yes. And you owe me a seeing stone," Ernan said, crossing his arms.

I watched, seeing the realization hit Hunter as he looked over at me. I shrugged, not really sure what to say but happy the two men I loved weren't still trying to kill one another.

"You're my buyer?" Hunter's voice was unsure, like he'd just had the ground ripped from under his feet.

"Yes."

Hunter glanced back at me, his green eyes large, before saying to Ernan, "You knew what he was doing, what he was having Gemma do?"

"Unfortunately." Ernan turned to me, giving me a parental look I didn't appreciate.

"Hey, don't turn this on me. I won't have you judging me for how I work."

"Working on your back makes you a whore, Gemma, not a mercenary," Hunter groused.

"Really? You who fucks your way through every town? Do you want to tell me how many women you had when you were away these last few weeks?"

"If you want to hear about them. There was this particularly sexy one I had a few days ago. Plump ass and tits like you wouldn't believe."

My hands went to my hips, and I knew if I could murder him with a look, he'd be dead.

"Do you think that's the right way to win her back?" Ernan asked, his tone suspicious.

"She's had your cock stuffing her while I was away. I don't think it's the wrong way."

"Can we just stop? I don't want to know, and you can't judge me."

"No?" Hunter moved closer to me. "I can't judge you? For falling in love when I turned my back on you?"

"When you left her to die. The golems had her when I found her, and she was on the edge of death. You lost your right to complain about her choices when you left her to die." The ferocity of Ernan's defense of me reached into my heart and stole another piece.

"I didn't leave her to die." Hunter's bravado disappeared, and he almost looked defeated. "I thought she'd find her way out. She's one of the strongest women I know, with a reputation of never giving up. I thought she'd be fine. If I'd known—"

"But you didn't because you didn't go back for her until you went to Iceliar, thinking she'd be there."

Hunter's head shot up. "How do you know I went to Iceliar?"

My heart soared. He had gone to find me. He'd realized his mistake and gone to Iceliar to meet me. The onslaught of emotion almost made me lose my footing. I'd turned to Ernan, letting him have me when all the while Hunter had been searching for me.

"Because Ernan thought you might do what you did that night in the forest," I explained. "That you'd return for me, thinking I'd already passed through Carenth and would be in Iceliar."

"And you did...but you didn't get the water stone then, did you?" Ernan asked, his expression becoming more serious.

"No, I went to your brother, who told me you might have her."

"Oh, I bet he did. Did he tell you I was torturing her? Raping her? Doing vile things to her?"

Hunter's jaw twitched. "Yes."

"I fucking hate my brother. The asshole turns every one of his kinks to me." He raked his hand through his hair.

"Wait, you're not like that?"

Ernan glared at him.

"Damn, Gem. I was right, wasn't I?" Hunter turned back to me, that devious gleam in his eye. The way he said my nickname sent the warmth rushing between my legs.

"You know you were right. Why do you have to hear me say it?"

He moved closer to me, like he'd forgotten Ernan was there, and I drowned in his mischievous look. "Because I like hearing you plead," he said, his fingers draping down my neck.

"Get your hands off her," Ernan said, the force of his voice calling to a completely different part of me, even more wetness soaking me.

Hunter's hand encased my neck, and my pulse pounded. "Oh, but she likes it this way, witch boy."

"I'm not a witch boy, and she doesn't like it that way. Get your fucking hand off her throat." Ernan was behind me now, and his hand wound around my waist to pull me back.

Hunter's sharp eyes evaluated me. "So I guess you didn't tell him how rough you like it with me, pretty thing?"

I shivered, and Ernan's muscles tensed in reaction.

"No," I squeaked out.

"Do you give it to her soft, sorcerer? Because my girl likes it dirty." His other hand gripped my hip, pulling it so that half my body was leaning against Ernan, the other pulling toward him. The move left me torn, not knowing which way to continue.

"She likes it soft," Ernan growled.

"Maybe from you, but she likes it rough from me." Hunter moved so that he pinned my body between them. Both their bulges were thick against me, and a shudder went through me at the thought. "Tell him what you like, pretty girl. Tell him."

"I..." His hand had worked my skirt up, and I was sure Ernan didn't notice. I couldn't see Ernan's face, but there was tension in his muscles and a twitch in his pants as Hunter's hand slid between my thighs, and I moaned.

"Me or him, Gem," he said.

"Don't make her choose," Ernan returned, his hold on my waist tightening at the same moment Hunter's two fingers penetrated me.

I cried out, letting my head fall against Ernan's shoulder.

"What the—" he started, but I gripped his thighs, holding on as Hunter brushed his thumb over my clit.

"Both," I cried out.

"Oh, Gem, I don't think it works that way," Hunter said, plunging into me deeper.

I lurched back into Ernan, whose length was so hard against my back that I wanted to rip his pants off and have it inside of me.

"You're not seriously—"

"Making my girl come?" Hunter said, interrupting Ernan. "Damned right I am."

The bulge in Ernan's pants jumped, and combined with the pressure of Hunter's fingers, it sent me careening over the edge. My climax ripped through me so that I couldn't stop the loud cry that fled my mouth as I lost all control of my body. Ernan's arm held me up as my knees gave out. Hunter's chest pounded deeply against me while my muscles gripped his fingers until the waves of my release calmed, and I could catch my breath again.

Hunter removed his fingers, backing from us as he licked the two that had just brought me to my knees. "Mmm, sweet like honeysuckle, Gem. But I believe that's my cum coating the inside of your pussy, isn't it?"

Ernan growled loudly, his chest quaking. His arm still encased my waist in a protective hold. He was so hard that my body pulsed with need for him.

"Keep her safe," Hunter said, adjusting himself as he backed away.

"What?" Ernan's shock was apparent in his tone, and I was certain his face reflected my own. All the pleasure Hunter had just brought me floated to the wind.

"I have an asshole to deal with who wants a fire stone and my girl. I don't know that I'll ever share her with you, but I certainly won't share her with that shithead. Keep her safe."

"Hunter, no," I pleaded, trying to move from Ernan's hold. His muscular arm kept me in place. "You can't go back there. He'll kill you."

He was on his horse by now. Taking the reins, he said, "Well then, you won't have to choose. I love you, Gemma. I won't give you up, and you belong to me. I'll deal with this situation later, but I won't let Breck touch you again."

He spurred his horse, riding off before I could say anything more.

"Shit," Ernan mumbled.

"Stop him," I begged, turning into his arms. "Please, you can't let him go. Breck will kill him."

"I can't stop him, Gemma. There's no stopping him. This is what he wants to do."

"But it's not what I want. I can't lose him again. He can't leave me again. My heart can't take it."

He pulled me to him, and the emotion of it all pounded through me, leaving me unhinged, my tears soaking into his shirt. The erotic pleasure that had overwhelmed me moments before was gone, fleeing with Hunter's exit and taking the last pieces of my heart along with it.

ERNAN HAD PICKED me up and brought me back into his castle, leaving me in the chair as he paced the room. I could feel his energy morphing, anger growing with each step, but I couldn't take my mind from Hunter. From what he'd done to me, from what he'd done with Ernan behind me, the two of them there driving the intensity of my climax. From the sight of him leaving again, turning from me and leaving me.

"Did you have to let him fuck you?" Ernan finally said, breaking the silence.

I raised my eyes to his, seeing the hurt there.

"I know you love him, but he left you to die. Why would you let him touch you?"

That fragile side of him was there again, breaking my heart.

"I can't resist him."

"No? You couldn't stop him? I didn't hear you screaming for

help, so I know he didn't force himself on you. Why, after what he did?"

"I don't know," I answered, running my hands over my face. "I can't help it. I love him too much. His touch destroys me each time, and I can't resist him because I like what he does to me."

"You like that? Him hurting you? He had his fucking hand around your throat."

The shiver that always happened at the thought of Hunter's hand around my throat went through me, and Ernan lifted his brow.

"Gods, you do, don't you? Why didn't you tell me? Or says something? I could have—"

I leaped to my feet, going to him. "No, don't ever. I don't want that from you. Hunter's the only one I've ever wanted it that rough with. I've always had aggressive men, but he takes it to another level with me. It's something between us that neither of us has with others."

"Aggressive, Gemma?"

I dropped my eyes as a guilt I didn't understand took hold.

"I could have taken you like that, but..."

"No, please don't. I only want you the way you are with me. Please, Ernan. I love the way you touch me, the way you treat me like I'm fragile, like your touch might hurt me. I need that from you."

He studied me, his thumb brushing my cheek.

"You can't love us both, Gemma. Especially when what we both have with you is so distinctly different."

The memory of them holding me as I came undone sent my heart racing, and his lip curved like he'd seen my thoughts.

"The way you fell apart for him..." He pressed against me, and I could feel how hard the thought had made him, "...was so wrong."

"But you liked it."

He sucked in a breath. "I did, gods did I ever."

"Hunter brings out a side of me I didn't know was there, a side that wants him to dominate me, to own me like he does. But you," I ran my fingers through his hair, enjoying how the black locks merged with the gray ones, "bring out another side of me I didn't realize I wanted to embrace. The one that wants to be pampered and worshipped. One that hides behind the strength I personify every day. I want both sides. I want both of you."

He laughed. "You can't have us both, Gemma. Hunter is possessive and demanding. He won't settle for sharing you and neither will I. I don't think I can watch him be rough with you without wanting to kill him, no matter how that turned me on. We're two very possessive men who won't settle for sharing." Sighing, I leaned into him. "It won't matter anyway if he goes and gets himself killed."

My head jerked up, remembering why Hunter had left, the pain in my chest returning. "I need to go after him."

"No, you need to go change." He flipped the torn top of my dress. "And wash his cum out of you."

I pursed my lips, backing from him.

"Don't give me that look. I'd forgotten for a moment that you let him take you out there when I thought you were just talking."

"I'm not washing him from me until I know he's alive."

His eyes darkened. "He's still alive. There's no way he would have made it there by now."

"Don't be a smartass. I'll change, but I'm not washing up, and I'm going after him."

"No." His roar was loud, bellowing through the room, the flames in the fireplace diminishing with it.

"You can't stop me from going."

"I can. You're safe here, and Hunter said to keep you safe. That's what I plan to do."

I hated that he'd thrown Hunter into it. "Why am I safe here? Just because you're here?"

"That's one reason. But this is my domain, just as the Endless

Forest is Breck's. He can't enter my domain if I'm here. And when I'm not here, I keep a protection spell over the castle just as he does over the clearing and the cottage. My domain spans the length of the castle, but not beyond into the dead forest or into the pits. He doesn't like it here, so the likelihood of him entering Laviak is slim, but I won't chance it. And once you cross from Laviak, he could strike, especially in Spindara."

"I need to go after Hunter. Breck will kill him."

"No. It was his choice to go. You stay within these walls and under my protection. I won't face my brother, and neither will you."

He shut down, his arms crossing, that broody persona shielding his emotions. I knew it wasn't worth arguing with him now. I wouldn't win. Irritated, I huffed away to change. I didn't like that he was caging me here, even if it had been Hunter's wish for him to do so.

I took a detour to the cavern springs first to rinse myself, as Ernan had suggested. The stickiness from Hunter still sat between my thighs. Part of me didn't want to remove it and wanted to leave it as a reminder of him in case...

I couldn't bring myself to think of anything happening to him. Removing my dress, I sank into the water, closing my eyes and letting the warmth take my worries away. I stayed that way, letting my head drift back and clearing my mind until I felt Ernan's presence. His hands embraced me, bringing me to his chest and holding me there. I gazed into his eyes, a myriad of emotions reflected between the two colors. He said nothing, guiding my lips to his and kissing me, his love brimming on the edge of the kiss and warming my soul. There was a distinction to the way he touched me that lit every part of me I tried to hide— the little girl in me who wanted to be protected and the woman in me who wanted to be held and saved by the man she loved. Everything the outer shell of me balked at. Ernan brought that side of me forth, protecting it, shielding it, adoring it.

He gently lifted me, guiding my legs around him as he entered me, filling me in such an exquisite way that a sigh surged forth from me. His hands caressed the length of me, cupping my breasts sweetly as my release built, each touch urging it forward but never rushing it. That was the difference. While Hunter fed on the power of controlling my body, of how many times he could demand my orgasms from me, Ernan let it build until it was so powerful that it met his own, the two of us jumping from the cliffs of ecstasy together in a long descent that left me riven.

His kisses deepened as he adjusted me, bringing his hands below my ass and tipping my hips so that he filled me completely. My climax teetered, ready to undo me, but he slowed his pace, bringing us to the edge of the pool where a ridge left room to sit. He urged my legs to loosen and sat, bringing me to my knees without ever leaving me. In that move, he yielded all power to me, but I didn't want power over him, just as he had never assumed power over me. We were equals, and as that realization hit me, I moved his hands to my hips, letting them follow the rhythm my body was taking. We remained like that, my arms tangled around his neck until his hands smoothed up my back, pushing me further into him, his kisses more desperate. With the touch of my chest to his, the pounding of his heart below in tandem with mine, my release flared through me. It left every cell in my body enraptured so that I thought I might lose consciousness. He tensed, his groan loud as he dropped his head to my shoulder and forced me down, shoving himself deeper into me with the burst of his climax. Passion dragged us both under, drowning us, our bodies and souls as connected as they could be.

Ernan held me to him, his breathing untethered, his arms so tight around me I thought I might suffocate.

"I love you, Gemma," he mumbled against my ear. "You will always have my heart. It has always been yours."

He kissed my hair and lifted me from him, setting my feet back down. His eyes were heavy and shadowed, and I couldn't tell what he was thinking. He rose, walking back to his clothes and dressing without saying another word to me.

"Ernan?" I said, hearing the tremble in my voice.

He turned back to me while he pulled his shirt on.

"There are fresh clothes in the room for you. Something you'll find more suitable. I'll be back."

He walked away as I climbed from the water and ran to him.

"Where are you going?" I asked, grabbing him and spinning him to me.

"I have an errand to run. I won't be long. Besides, we need fresh food and some wine. Lots of wine." His last words he muttered so low I could barely hear them.

"Ernan, I love you," I said, wishing he would tell me where he was really going and why he was distancing himself from me suddenly.

He moved a strand of my hair from my shoulder, letting his fingers linger on my neck. "I know."

He said no more, leaving me there. Leaving me, just as Hunter had, and I wondered if he would return or if he would leave me forever, needing to be away after making love to me for the last time. My heart cracked at the thought, the pieces that he'd repaired crumbling again. They'd been damaged so many times I didn't think they'd recover this time. Ernan had been the glue holding them in place, and now both he and Hunter were gone.

THE SOUND of footsteps woke me, and I rubbed the heavy hold of sleep from my eyes. After Ernan had left, I'd returned to our room finding my pants, shirt, and boots cleaned and left for me. My heart had stuck in my throat. He had been saying goodbye, knowing I couldn't let Hunter face Breck alone. That I had to finish the quest Breck had given me. Hunter had left me with the water stone, but I wouldn't go for the fire stone without assurance that Breck wouldn't hurt him...that he hadn't already hurt him. I'd lost track of time waiting for Ernan's return, having given up on leaving the castle, his spell blocking my attempts. I didn't know if hours had passed, but I suspected they had.

Rising from the chair where I'd dozed off, I found him across the room. His eyes remained guarded. The man who'd locked me in the cells below stared back at me, his heart locked away. Just as mine was.

"There's a horse tied to the trees beyond the castle. He's enchanted and will ensure you get to the Endless Forest quickly and safely. He won't throw you, he won't frighten."

Turning from me, he walked away, taking the last semblance of pain and raking it across my heart.

"Ernan, I—"

"I know, Gemma," he replied without turning. "You can't escape what you have with him. He's part of you, he always has been. There was never enough room for both of us. This is your journey, and this is as far as I can go with you."

He never turned back, and I watched him as he left me with agony in my heart, each step destroying the little of it that remained. He could have gone with me, but this was my journey. I'd taken the first step on the path by myself, ignoring his attempts to stop me, and now I had to take the final steps as he stood back and allowed me.

With a sigh, I left the confines of the castle, leaving a part of myself behind as I focused my emotion and used it to strengthen myself. Hardening the broken shell of my heart like I had all those years ago. I found the horse in the trees close to where Hunter's horse had been. It was a gorgeous steed of all black, a gray mist coming from its hide, its black eyes with magical streaks of red through them. Ernan hadn't bought me a steed. He'd made one from his power. That's why he'd been gone so long.

I rubbed its face, marveling at what Ernan had done and the

depth of meaning behind it. This was his show of love, that and letting me go. He hadn't left me. He'd returned so I could leave him and with my departure he had ensured as best he could that I would remain safe as I traveled through Laviak.

"My brother, always dramatic with his magic."

I whirled, finding Breck behind me.

"You failed me, my sweet candy." The sound of his voice had once seduced me, but after discovering the truth, it soured my stomach.

"I'm not your anything," I said, stepping back against the horse. I'd never liked that nickname, and the way he said it in that demeaning tone. When Hunter called me his pretty thing, it sent flutters through my body. Breck's nickname had never given me the same reaction.

"Oh, but you are."

The horse made a sound like a growl and moved beside me.

"So protective. That's cute. Did you fuck my brother, Gemma?"

The horse moved closer, going up on its hind legs, then dropping with a force that shook the ground.

"You did. You dirty little whore."

This time, the sound the horse made was a rabid growl, and he charged Breck, who threw his hand up to block the horse with his power. The horse broke through, although his speed had slowed severely.

"Asshole," Breck muttered.

I woke from my daze, from the sight of the horse protecting me, and ran, knowing I needed to get to the castle and back to Ernan. But Breck turned from the horse, his power coming out in a wave that knocked me to the ground, the horse screaming in pain before it collapsed. I cried out, reaching for the gift Ernan had given me, now so viciously taken from me.

"Gemma!" Ernan yelled, and I saw him running from the castle.

I scrambled up, trying to make it out of the trees where I knew Breck couldn't reach, but he caught me by the hair, yanking my head back so hard that I yelped.

"Leave her be!"

Breck twisted his fingers deeper into my hair. "No, she has something I need, and she will get the fire stone for me. You are the last one in my way, brother. There is no one left to stop me. What will you do?"

My chest heaved with the impact of his words. No one left to stop him? Hunter. He'd hurt Hunter. Maybe even killed him. The wail that cleaved from my body was shrill, echoing around us as Breck used his power to move us, taking me away while Ernan's screaming of my name echoed in my mind.

CHAPTER SIXTEEN

HUNTER

Although the ride to the Endless Forest encompassed only a few hours, it was torture. Gemma's betrayal of my heart had left it fractured, and no matter how I tried to shield myself from the pain, it continued to eat at me. In the weeks after I'd left her, she'd fallen in love, giving away what was mine. What I had given up the day I'd left her there. I'd thought the worst when I'd left to find her, imagining she was dead, injured, or even suffering abuse at the hands of Breck's brother. But I'd never imagined that I'd find her in his arms.

I don't know why I left her again, why I didn't stay and fight for her. She was mine, her body reacting to my touch in ways I knew he couldn't come close to. And I'd proven it after I'd ravaged her. Even in his arms, she still fell apart for me. And gods, how she had. It was almost like being with both of us had enhanced her climax. I'd almost taken her there—she'd been so wet, her body so needy—but I wasn't about to share her, no matter how badly I wanted her.

And so I'd done the only thing I could after wielding my

control over her. I'd left. She was safer with him. It hurt to admit, but he had magic, and I had only my fists and my knives, neither of which could defeat a sorcerer. There was no reason I should have headed back into the Endless Forest, no reason for me to find Breck. It was suicide. I didn't have what he wanted. But he'd betrayed Gemma worse than she'd betrayed me, and I needed to protect her in the only way I knew how. To stand up for her this time, to not run away or drown my love for her in other women. I would own it, no matter how much it hurt, and I would do what I could to stop what was coming. Whatever it was Breck wanted with those stones, whatever it was he planned, I would stop him or die trying. I no longer wanted Gemma under his influence and if it meant leaving her with Ernan, then so be it. At least she'd be safe and far from Breck.

I stopped my horse short of the clearing, leaving him to rest. He was barely standing I'd run him so hard. But I didn't think I'd need him again. I didn't think I'd leave the Endless Forest. It should have been my grave all those years ago, and now it would be. My fingers slid over a downed tree that had collapsed into the clearing. Movement caught my eye, and I looked up to see the white hawk. Mera. She shouldn't have been there, should have been far from this, but he was using her again, seeing me through her eyes. If I survived this, I would free her and let her drown the pain that was cleaving me in two, let her use her magic to unburden me of it.

"Witch's son!" I screamed, the anger at all this grove and that cottage had wreaked on me and Gemma surfacing. The complex web that had entangled the four of us since that night. A web neither Gemma nor I had ever escaped, one we never would.

"Where are my things?" Breck emerged from the cottage, storming toward me.

"I can't speak for the fire stone. You should ask the fire witches about that, if they don't eat you alive first in their golem form."

His gray hair seemed to rise from his head like a strike of lightning had hit him, his blue eyes sinister. "And my Gemma?"

"*My* Gemma is likely fucking your brother right now." Because that's what I would have been doing if I weren't facing this maniac. Fucking away the pain. And I knew she was in pain, that she loved me as much as I loved her. That twisted and wicked love we shared was one neither of us could hide from.

That set the witch's son off. He roared, the ground shaking in reaction. Damn, there was no way I could take someone that powerful. His magic ensnared me, pulling me closer and no matter how I fought, I couldn't free myself from it.

"You returned without my things?"

"They're not yours. And Gemma has never been yours, no matter how you manipulated her. I suppose you had her once, but her heart was still mine."

His hold on me faltered, and I took advantage of it, drawing my knife and barreling into him. He fell to the ground but wrenched the knife from my hand with his power.

"You dare try to kill me?" he bellowed, my body flying from him as he brought the force of his magic down on me. The air fled my lungs, my heart contracting. I brought myself to my knees, wheezing as the life painfully fled from me.

"No!"

I lifted my head to see Mera running toward Breck, her magic a black cloud around her. Breck's anger turned to her, his hold not releasing from me. I tried to reach out my hand in some attempt to stop her, but it was no use. I watched in horror as he grabbed her by the neck, a haze of magic around them both.

"You are my pet, you whore. Not his, and you have betrayed your master. Shame, I'll miss fucking you, but I'll have Gemma for that. She'll make an even prettier pet."

Mera's feet were kicking, her nails scratching at his hands.

"You were always weak, Mera. That's why you were so easy to capture. Weak and easy to manipulate. Thinking I'd marry you when you gave yourself to me, that you'd be anything to me but the whore you were."

"No," I croaked, fighting against his hold.

Her eyes glanced over at me, the fear in them disappearing.

"Leave her alone." My voice was barely a whisper, stuck in my chest like the breaths I could barely take.

"Did you fall for him, pet? Guess I'll take two things from him today."

"I hope you rot in the underworld," she hissed, her last word cut off as he tightened his grip.

"Oh, I will. I can guarantee that. I'll see you there, my pet, and I will use you the way I have since the day I imprisoned you."

He snapped her neck, throwing her body across the clearing. She landed, her lifeless eyes turned toward me. A muffled roar of agony came from me, stirring a surge of adrenaline, and I pushed against his magic. I made it to my feet, staggering toward him.

"You are a strong one, Hunter. It's been fun watching you waste your life on whores and alcohol. Running around the kingdoms with that bravado that you're untouchable, indestructible. I'll be sure to fuck Gemma extra hard for you, the way she likes it when you fuck her. Maybe I'll pull her hair harder or choke her. Of course, she'll be choking anyway with my cock shoved down her throat. I'll give her your regards and let her know your last thoughts were about her...choking on my cock."

Wind ripped at my skin, picking me up and hurling me backward, the downed tree stopping my movement as its gnarled uneven limbs impaled me. Pain raked through my body, the breath I'd gotten back for those brief moments, disappearing. I couldn't move, couldn't feel anything but the agonizing torture of my injuries.

"Ouch, that looks like it hurts. I think I'll leave you like that. Maybe you'll still be alive when I have my stones and my Gemma. How fun would it be to bend her over and force her to look at your dying face while I'm owning that tight body of hers?"

In a cloud of smoke, he disappeared. The tangy taste of blood filled my mouth. I was dying, but the only thing I could think of was Gemma and how he would hurt her, just as he had Mera. With what ability I had left, I prayed to the gods Ernan would keep her from Breck, that he would protect her in every way I'd failed.

A SHARP PAIN tore me from the hands of death, my body coming alive with the torture of my wounds. Something was pulling at my consciousness, driving me to wake. A resounding blood-curdling screech urged me to return to the world of the living and away from the torment of the underworld and the claws it had dug into my soul.

I coughed, choking on the metallic warmth of blood that was pouring from my mouth. Hands gripped my shoulder, keeping me on my side as it continued to exude from me in copious amounts. I tried to open my eyes, shutting them again against the pool of blood that was before them.

"That's it, get it all out. Your cells can't repair if they're drowning in your tainted blood."

That voice sounded familiar, and I struggled to control my choking long enough to shrug his hand from my shoulder and fall back. The moon was bright and full above me until Ernan's face blocked it. I tried to frown, but it hurt too much. Everything hurt.

"Try to sit up," he said, rising and taking my arm. I jerked away, regretting the action as pain flared through me. "And stop moving so fast. Your body is in shock and until it realizes it's not dead, everything will hurt."

I grimaced, slowly bringing myself up to a sitting position. It felt as if my insides were pushing out of me, and I looked down to see the rips in my shirt, the blood that saturated it.

"I was..." It was hard to say the word now that the truth was becoming clear.

"Dead?"

I gazed up at him. Blood caked his clothes and hands, running the length of his arms. My blood.

"Yes. How?" I glanced back, seeing the blood-stained tree limb where Breck had left me.

"In order to claim my place as the most terrifying sorcerer in Spindara, I had to master the most terrifying of spells. There's a reason the others fear me, a reason I'm the only one bold enough to claim Laviak as my home." He dropped to a crouch in front of me.

"You're not terrifying. You're a pussy who fucks like one."

He laughed. "And you know that because you fuck like a controlling asshole?"

"Yes," I gurgled, more blood filling my throat.

"Lean over and get that muck out of you. It's part of the spell. The underworld doesn't like giving up its hold on a soul."

I spat out the blood and wiped my mouth with the back of my hand. "You can bring people back to life?"

"I can, although you're the first human I've brought back. Stealing from the underworld has a price, one you only suffer if you steal a human soul."

Squinting my brows, I wondered what kind of price he'd paid. He didn't look like he wanted to share. "Why?" I asked instead.

"Because Gemma loves you, and I love Gemma. Your death would kill her in ways I wouldn't be able to fix."

"But with me dead, you win. She would be yours completely."

"Would she? She's never been mine completely. Your hold over her is too strong. It always has been. I would never hurt her, and leaving you dead would hurt her."

This guy was too good to be true. "How can you be such a fucking pussy yet have the power to bring someone back to life and bargain with the underworld?"

He stood, extending his hand out to me. I took it, hating that I owed Gemma's new lover my life. "Because no matter how gentle I am with Gemma, I'm still the most powerful sorcerer in the kingdoms. Even my brother knows that. It was part of the mantle I had to claim when the bastard killed our mother and blamed it on me. If you're going to kill the supreme witch in Spindara, you'd better be able to stand in her place. Breck thought I'd fail. What he didn't realize was that while he was out seducing young girls, I was learning everything I could from our mother and those in her circle. Enough to step into the role he handed me."

"And now you're the most feared sorcerer of your kind?"

"Damn right I am. All thanks to my brother's manipulations, the only ones I'm thankful for. He knows he can't beat me, knows the others follow my lead, and he wants that power. That's why he wants the stones."

"I thought the stones were to bring back the other witches?"

His jaw ticked, his strange eyes growing serious. "Lies he told Gemma. The stones hold the magic of all the lost covens. If ever brought together, fused to become one, the powers that were locked away by the gods will flow to the holder. That's why no witch or sorcerer can touch the stones, why they remained hidden all these centuries."

"He wants power? That's what this is about?"

"Not just any power. That kind of power is the kind that can destroy kingdoms, raise new lands, make him ruler over everyone in our world."

The thought was horrifying. Breck was an unstoppable madman with what power he had. Give him a hundred times that power, and he'd enslave or kill all of us. "Shit, and I thought you were the scary one." I scratched my stomach, amazed that the holes that had been there had healed completely. "Why should I trust you? You could be just like him. You're a sorcerer, the witch's son."

"And I just saved you."

"You might be tricking me, manipulating me like your brother manipulated Gemma."

"If I'd wanted to manipulate you, I wouldn't have hired you to find that stone. You double-crossed me, by the way, giving it to my brother."

I stepped back, still stunned that he'd been my buyer.

"Feel free to call that manipulation," he continued. "I needed you there."

I didn't like that I was seeing him in a different light, one that made him a good guy, the kind I would trust with my life or Gemma's. "You needed me there because Breck had Gemma there."

I doubled over as my insides twisted and he reached out, holding me up before guiding me to sit on the bloodied limb.

"You need to rest longer. Your insides are still healing. That part of the soul's return takes longer, especially with messier wounds. And yes, I knew you'd protect her when I couldn't."

As he poked around the place where my injuries had been, I studied him.

"Why should I trust anything you're saying? You were planning to eat me that night."

"My mother was planning to eat you."

"But you were helping her."

He looked up at me, his disturbing, two-toned eyes narrowing. "There was no disobeying my mother. The first time I tried, she stole the color from most of my hair, leaving some of my black strands as a reminder of her power. You'd think leeching the color from something would be painless. It's surprising how that's not the case. The second time, she stole the color from my eye, leaving the other as a reminder. I didn't try a third time."

He stood and walked away from me, leaving me to contemplate the horror of those words. She'd tortured her own children. Breck's hair was completely gray, and I questioned what he'd done to suffer that wrath, what either of them had done.

Ernan stooped next to Mera's body, the sight of it bringing a sting to my chest that wasn't an aftereffect of my healing.

"Breck leaves a path of destruction in his wake. It's too subtle for others to notice, but I've always seen it."

I pushed myself from the limb, dragging myself over to Mera's body without stumbling. With a grunt, I stooped on the other side of her, closing her lifeless eyes and only then seeing the hole in her chest, one her hair had been covering. I lifted my sight to Ernan.

"Stealing from the underworld comes at a price. One must always satisfy the gods. She was already gone, but she hadn't been dead long enough for her organs to be wasted. The gods of the underworld are greedy and, when given the right sacrifice, they will release their hold on a soul. A fresh heart and a few other parts were the offering." I swallowed back the bile as he continued. "Breck ensnared her when we were young, tricking her into his bed when she was just a child. She was no older than Gemma was when you stumbled into our world. Mera gave him everything, including her name, and he enslaved her for it. I warned her. She was sweet and innocent, too trusting, and he took advantage of it."

"You couldn't free her?" I snapped, suddenly tired of the cruelty of the witch world.

"No, the moment he used her name to trap her, the cage was upon her. A sorcerer who owns the true name of a witch owns her power and her life. There is no one who can free her but the one with the key, and Breck never frees his pets."

"He freed Gemma," I muttered.

"Only to use her to find the stones."

"He groomed her for it," I stated, his words validating everything I already knew.

"Yes. I tried to dissuade her from afar, but she surpassed every obstacle I put in her path. I suppose if anything, I'm as much to blame. In trying to deter her, I only strengthened her. I finally gave up and put you in her path."

His face had softened, and I could see the man below the façade, the one Gemma fell in love with. As much as I wanted to hate him, I couldn't. He'd watched over her in the years that I hadn't been there. He'd saved her in Laviak, and now he'd saved me.

"We need to go," he said, rising. "Do you have your strength back? I don't think you'll be fighting any battles, but if you can hold your own, I think we can save her."

"Save her?" The calm I'd had scattered, fear stepping in its place.

"My brother has Gemma."

"He what?" Rage overcame me like a furious storm. "You sat here, reminiscing about the past, talking as if there was no rush and he has her?"

"You needed time to heal, and Gemma needed to locate the stone. She's the only one who can. Breck has no idea where it is."

I was standing by now, my fists clenched so tightly I heard the knuckles cracking.

"Calm yourself. Believe me, I don't want Breck anywhere near her, but she's safe until she finds the stone. That's what he wants and until then, he will keep her free. Now, I'll ask you again, are you strong enough?"

"I've never been stronger, and when I'm done killing him, I'll kill you."

"Because you were so successful at killing him the last time?"

I glared at him. He stepped over Mera's body, saying, "Save your bravado for my brother. I'll need the distraction while I save my girl."

My jealousy scraped at the surface of my patience. He'd used my term, and I suspected he'd done so deliberately. "Your girl? I don't think so."

"We'll fight for her later. I need you alive for now."

I was about to respond when a cloud of smoke distorted my senses, and a weightlessness overcame me. When it cleared and my feet were on solid ground again, the heat of Laviak assaulted my senses. Ernan freed my arm, but he tensed, and I looked to where his sight had fallen. Golems surrounded Gemma, their charred limbs in distorted positions that were disturbing to the eye. The ground below was cracking, a crevice forming.

Ernan screamed just as I did. But Breck, who was standing outside the circle of golems, turned on him, his magic hitting him. Breck didn't see me, so I used that to my advantage, pulling my knife out and lunging for him. He roared as it sank into his back, and we fell to the ground. I looked up to see Ernan leap through the golems and catch Gemma, their bodies plunging through the ground that had opened below them. Gemma's eyes met mine, the amber of them diluted with terror and apologies before she disappeared, the pits taking her from me, and my heart along with her.

CHAPTER SEVENTEEN

GEMMA

Breck threw me to the ground, but I paid no heed to the pain it caused. Hunter was dead, leaving my heart twisted into mangled pieces that would never heal.

"Get up, my little piece of candy." His voice was like the sound of gravel below a broken wheel.

Resting my face on the hot ground, I pulled myself into a ball, sobs wrenching from me. I just wanted to be left alone to mourn Hunter, but Breck yanked me up by my hair.

"You will find me that stone!"

"And if I don't?" I asked, the words coming out in broken gulps of air. "Will you kill me like you did him?"

"No. You don't get to die, Gemma. You are mine, you will always be mine."

"But...but you said if I retrieve the stones—"

"Do you think me a fool? Once you were in my grasp, there was no escaping. You belong to me."

But I didn't. I never had. I'd always belonged to Hunter, and now, a part of me belonged to Ernan. The pieces that were

Hunter's had died with him, but Ernan's pieces were still alive. He would want me to fight. Hunter would want me to fight because I wasn't the submissive type. I was only that way for him. For everyone else, even Breck, I held my own.

I raised my eyes to him, straining against the grip he had on my hair, the fire in me returning. "I've never belonged to you. I've always been Hunter's."

"And he's dead." He jerked me toward him. "So that makes you mine."

"No, because Hunter isn't the only one who owns me."

His sneer morphed, his jaw clenching as the blue in his eyes grew violent. "Who do I need to kill next, little candy?"

"I always hated that nickname." I lifted my knee, making contact exactly where I'd intended. His grip slipped as he doubled over, and I made a break for it, running as fast as I could. I didn't know how I thought I'd flee him, but I wasn't going down without a fight. That wasn't who I was, and he should have known that.

"Gemma!" His roar berated my ears, the ground shaking below my feet.

Electrical currents penetrated my back, painfully coursing through my body. The magic was so intense I tumbled to the ground, my body convulsing uncontrollably. I couldn't breathe, couldn't think, could barely see. But I saw enough to notice the blackened, gnarled shapes emerging from the ground. The golems. Their distorted limbs moved in broken movements that sickened my stomach, dragging themselves from their prison in the underworld. These differed from the ones I'd seen before, ones that had been stationary, awaiting their next victim.

Breck grabbed my arm, wrenching me from the ground. "Now look what you've done. You've made me wake them early. Who the fuck dared claim you besides the man who lays impaled in my forest?"

The agony that slashed my heart gutted me, ripping away the shred of strength I had.

"Who?" he snarled, shaking me.

"Your brother," I hissed, anger surfacing at what he'd done to Hunter. My Hunter, who had been the holder of my heart all these years, the man I'd searched for in every man I'd taken, every man I'd ever let touch me. The anger burst through the pain, and I yanked my arm from him, punching him. The shock on his face from my words grew as he brought his hand to his jaw and rubbed it.

"You'll pay for that, and my brother will die. I'll string his lifeless body up next to your worthless Hunter and fuck you in front of them until you're begging me to make it stop."

He shoved me toward the golems, who were clamoring toward us in their grotesque movements. "Now get me my stone!"

"They'll kill me." And maybe that was better. If I were dead, this would end, and he would leave Ernan be.

"You die, and I will give my brother an excruciating death. Bring me my stone, and I will kill him quickly."

Gods, neither of those options was one I wanted. "How is that bargaining?" I asked, glancing back at him and making sure my scowl was noticeable.

"Just get me the fucking stone!"

I'd had enough of the damned witch stones. They'd done nothing but bring me pain and devastation. I took a step closer to the oncoming golems, thinking maybe that wasn't true. They had reunited me with Hunter, brought me months of time in his arms. Time spent in a bliss I'd never had. Perhaps I should have taken his offer in the oasis and stayed there with him. He'd be alive now if I had. But Breck would have hunted us down. And I would never have met Ernan again, never have realized that he'd held the other part of me all these years. The stones had been a curse, but they'd also been a blessing.

I fingered the water stone in my pocket, and, throwing one more glance back at Breck, moved toward the golems. With each step, I fought the terror that was brewing in my belly, the nerves that threatened to drop the stone with the trembles they were causing. I thought back to how the golems had descended upon me when Ernan had found me. How they fed on the weakness that had poured from me. Taking a deep breath, I let the hot air fill my lungs, exhaling in a long, thoughtful breath. Calming myself, I studied the golems. They were the remains of the fire witches, stuck in this form after the gods cursed them. Imprisoned in their charred bodies, a never-ending torture. I thought of the Laviak pits, their flame and lava riddled home, and the castle Ernan had claimed. Cooled lava. Cooled with their magic, a magic that was grounded in fire power.

I brought the water stone up to study and took another step. Retrieving the fire stone could only be done with the water stone. Two sides of the same power, one hot, one cold, one burning, one freezing. The golems stopped their path upon seeing the stone, freezing in disturbing positions, their limbs bent in ways that defied nature. Carefully, I approached, sure to remain calm, to not let any weakness, any fear, any emotion show, and slid between two golems. One small step at a time, holding my breath with each inch further, I came into the circle they had formed. When I stood in the center of them, I exhaled. Forcing myself to do what I doubted any other had done, I studied each one. Their eyes, the only recognizable part of them, darted back and forth behind their charred cages. The fire I'd seen burning within them had dimmed to reveal their actual color—some blue, some green, some brown, none terrifying.

The gods had punished them in the cruelest of ways. Imprisoning them in this form. Always to be feared, always to be the monsters. Never understood or seen for what they truly were.

"I see you," I said. "Show me and let me help you."

I didn't know how finding the stone would help, but the

shifters had thought it would. Perhaps the golems would as well. For what seemed an eternity, there was no movement, no sound but the flames that burned around us. But in time, the ground below my feet cracked. I remained where I was, knowing this was their doing and if I lost my faith in them now, I was dead. With each crack below my feet, I stayed as statuesque as they were. And as the ground gave out, I closed my eyes, praying I'd read the situation correctly.

"Gemma!" I heard both Hunter and Ernan cry. The sound of Hunter's voice, alive and strong, broke my concentration and I caught his eye just as Ernan tackled me, the ground giving way and pulling us both in. Hunter's very alive green eyes were terror-filled, and that terror seeped into me. But Ernan and I were falling, a pit of lava below us. The golems were looking down at us and I remembered what I'd been doing.

"Stay calm, Ernan!"

He started to argue, the lava growing closer and hotter.

"Trust me. No emotion, just trust. They won't hurt us."

I loosened my grip on the water stone, the cooling mist seeping from it. The golems were morphing, their charred remains spreading down the tunnel in which we were falling. It coated the heat as the water stone cooled the tunnel, steam billowing around us.

"Hold on!" Ernan screamed, pulling me further against him as the bottom neared, but we didn't land like I thought we would. Instead, a current of air pushed us back up, sending us floating for a brief time, the steam then breaking our fall. I pushed from Ernan's arms. As happy as I was to see him, I had a mission, and it was mine to complete. My feet hit the bottom of the cavern and I held my hand up to ensure he knew to keep quiet. I thought back to the golems, to the curse the gods had ravaged them with. Encasing them in lava until only charred forms remained. But inside that exterior burned the lava of Laviak.

I twirled the water stone in my hand. One stone paired with

the other. I dropped to the ground, running my hand over it and seeing the water stone glow a brighter blue when I hit a certain spot.

"That's where you are."

I looked up at Ernan, who was watching me with wonder in his eyes. Smiling, I said, "Once I have it, things are going to change quickly. Hold on to me and don't look back."

"Why would I look back with you in my arms?"

Gods, he was too good to be true. I wanted to kiss him, but I needed to get the stone. And I needed to see Hunter, to hold him, to touch him, to make sure he really was still alive. Calming my thoughts and the furious beating of my heart, I scraped at the cooled ground, peeling away the molten layers until the heat grew. I didn't want to do this, but I didn't think there was another way. Sacrifice had to be made, and I had to trust the golems, seeing past the ugliness, the shells, the horror they imbued. Just as I'd seen past the terrifying persona Ernan exuded.

Placing the water stone in my fist, I punched through the last layer, my hand plunging into the hot lava. I'd expected pain, I'd expected Ernan to yell out in fear, but he trusted me, and I had trusted the golems. The water stone was cool in my hand, fighting off the heat and the burning of the lava. Removing my hand, I watched the lava drip from my hand in frozen droplets. The stone had protected me. I opened my hand, my eyes going wide at seeing that both stones now sat in my palm.

"Gods, you did it," Ernan said in awe.

I leaped to him, instinct telling me that what I'd just done would have consequences.

"Hold on." The ground below us shook, lava boiling over through the hole my hand had made. Ernan held me tight, and I leaned into him, loving the strength I found there. The ground was rocking, the golems screeching, and I looked up at them. "I'll keep it safe, I promise," I said to them, hoping they heard me.

"We'll keep it safe," Ernan said, looking into my eyes.

The ground erupted below, the coating the golems had laid along the walls of the cavern coming undone and wrapping below our feet. It protected us as the cavern exploded, the lava pushing us out with a force that separated us. It sent me sprawling onto the ground, rolling to a stop at Hunter's feet, the stones slipping from my fingers and rolling to Breck.

Hunter pulled me from the ground, wrapping me in his arms. Even with the solidity of his body reassuring me he was really alive, I couldn't draw my eyes from Breck. He had dropped the remaining stones from a pouch, and they landed on the ground with the fire and water stone. Ernan ran to attack him but hit a barrier, flinging backward as the stones rose in the air around Breck. The ground quaked, thunder shattering the silence.

"We need to stop him," Hunter said. "Before he accesses the full power of those stones."

Ernan picked himself up and looked over at us, nodding at Hunter.

Hunter gave me a wicked smile before saying, "You've done your part, Gem. It's time to do what I've always wanted to do. Kill a witch's son."

He drew a knife from his belt and picked up the other bloodied one. Ernan was circling Breck, but there was no way for either of them to get through the stones. The power was breaking free from each stone, slithering out in a funnel that surrounded Breck. I looked back to see the golems, their charred bodies reformed, their angry eyes on me. I'd promised I would protect the fire stone, and I'd failed. Hunter and Ernan were still trying to break through the magic that now encased Breck. But there was no way they could.

No matter how much Hunter wanted to be the one to take Breck down, to be the one who prevailed, this was my fight. I'd found the stones, I'd fallen for his story, taken the bait, and let Breck lead me on this course. I was the one who needed to end it. A flash caught my eye, and I looked over to see the steed Ernan had made for me, darkness and fury streaking toward me. My heart pounded, my strength returning at his approach. I grabbed his mane and leaped on his back.

"Protect me," I told him as he pawed the ground. And I knew he would because Ernan had made him for just that purpose.

"Gemma, don't!" Ernan yelled, followed by a yell of dissent from Hunter.

But I ignored them, knowing this was my battle to finish. I nudged my steed, and he took off with a speed that had me leaning forward to avoid being thrown from him. He leaped into the air, barreling through the magic, the force of it wrapping around me as we broke the spell. Every line of cursed magic hit me at once, my body gripped with a pain that held me hostage. In the distance, I could hear the screams of Ernan and Hunter, the terror of Breck as the steed trampled his fallen body. But I could do nothing but scream as the magic of the stones wove its way through my body. My cells immediately rejected it, and a battle ensued. The magic ripped through me as it destroyed every part of me, and I closed my eyes, giving myself over to the agony that drowned me until there was nothing but silence.

CHAPTER EIGHTEEN

HUNTER

Horror dug its greedy talons into me, stealing my breath and locking my heart in an iron cage that squeezed like a vice, snatching the life from me as I watched Gemma fall from the steed.

Things had turned so quickly. I'd stood frozen, watching as she and Ernan had disappeared into the depths of Laviak. My lungs burned from the air I wouldn't release, my eyes barely blinking for fear I'd miss something. Breck had stood across from me, having separated my knife from his flesh and thrown it to the ground. His eyes remained riveted to the scene before us, just like mine were and, as if we'd forgotten we were mortal enemies, we stood in a forced peace awaiting the outcome. For what seemed like hours, I watched. The golems spread like melting statues down the hole. Steam rose from it, but nothing else emerged until Gemma and Ernan flew from it, clearing the funnel of lava that erupted behind them. My lungs exhaled the imprisoned breath as Gemma rolled to a stop.

But that had been the least of the terrors as Breck seized hold of the stones with his power and neither Ernan nor I could break through. I'd told Gemma to stay, that she'd done her part, and this was mine, but the stubborn, irritating woman I loved rebelled. She rode through the magic ring on a steed that looked as if he'd come from the depths of the underworld. My scream had ripped my throat raw and now, watching her lifeless body thump to the ground, sparkles of magic collapsing over her, my heart cleaved into tattered shreds I didn't think could keep it beating. I caught Ernan looking as horrified as I was, our eyes meeting over her body. He glanced at his brother, and I followed the path, seeing him now outside the stones, the steed having kicked him beyond their formation. A look of pure evil morphed what remained of his features so that they were twisted and ugly.

Rage burned through me, encapsulating every cell and taking over the shred of sanity I had left.

I bellowed his name. "Breck!"

"Hunter!" Ernan yelled as Breck turned on me. Breck's face was bloody on one side where the horse had trampled him, his arm broken and disfigured. "He needs to be alive to suffer punishment!"

"He needs to die!" I argued.

"And he will! But let my people deal with him!"

Breck teetered, drawing his hand up. What little magic he had left pooled in it. My knife left my grip before I could think, slicing through his hand. I ran, tackling him as he howled. If I couldn't kill him, I would ensure he suffered enough to experience everything he'd done to Gemma. I poured my anger into every blow I gave him until Ernan dragged me from his limp body.

"Leave him. He can do no more damage. Gemma still lives, and she needs you."

I stopped struggling, my ire fading. I looked down at my bloodied hands, then over at Gemma. The magic still hung in the sparkling light around her, the stones encircling her.

"I need to force the magic back to the stones, but I can't enter the circle. None of us can, except you."

Glancing up at him, I noticed the steed standing close to him. The golems with their strange, misshapen limbs stood in the distance, their almost human-like eyes on Gemma.

"She needs you, Hunter."

I stood, thinking of all the times I'd let her down, leaving her to fend for herself. This time would be different, or maybe it wouldn't. There were two of us vying for her heart now, both as willing to die for her as the other. Rising, I walked over to the circle, waving my hand through the magic that was pooling over her. It stung my skin, burning it, and I moved back.

"Only witches and sorcerers have the power to hold magic. It is foreign to your bodies. This magic is pure in its form, stolen from the witches and put in pure form by the gods themselves. It's killing her as her cells fight the invasion. It will continue to defeat them until we lose her. She's still fighting, but I need to harness the magic, separate it from each strand, and return it to the stones."

"Can you do that? I thought you couldn't touch the stones."

"I can't, but I might be able to harness the magic like Breck was trying to do. Instead of making myself a vessel like he wanted, I think I can direct it back into each stone. If you don't help her, she'll die while I'm trying."

"Tell me what I need to do." I didn't need to question him. I trusted him. He'd jumped into that pit to save her. He'd brought me back to life, knowing we were rivals, knowing she could easily choose me over him.

"Walk into the circle. It will hurt, but not as much as it's hurting her."

"Done." I turned from him, walking through the magic, the streams of it tearing into my skin, leeching the strength from me with every step I took closer to her. I had enough strength left to crumble over her, taking the brunt of the magic's force from her, shielding her from it as it dug further into me. The intensity was almost unbearable. Almost. But I kept Gemma on my mind, thinking of her, letting my love for her fill me and fight against the onslaught. Nothing outside of the feel of her in my arms and the torrent of magic against my skin existed. As the pain became so that my hold on Gemma was slipping, the magic began peeling away. First, the flames that scorched my insides, then the freezing cold that burned below the flames. Next, the sting of wind that flayed my skin, and the weight of earth that compressed my lungs and shortened my breaths. And finally, my sight returned, the storm around us fading.

After my body stopped convulsing, I lifted my head, seeing the stones, their magic sealed within again. Ernan had his hands on his knees, his eyes hopeful even through the exhaustion carved in lines on his face. He fell to his knees, his body giving out, but the hope remained. I turned Gemma into me, seeing the rise and fall of her chest, relief overtaking the emotions that had enveloped me.

"She's alive," I said, hoarseness coating my words. "She's alive."

GEMMA'S AMBER eyes blinked open, and with them, life returned to me. She tried sitting, but I kept her down.

"Not so fast, Gem. You'll get dizzy."

"Dizzy? I don't get dizzy. That's for those wimpy women in tight corsets and fancy dresses. I'm not one of those women."

"No, you're not," I said with a laugh.

"Why is my throat so dry?" she asked, reaching for the water next to the bed where we had her.

"Because you've been asleep for days." Days where worry had

drowned me and decisions had hounded me. Days spent getting to know Ernan and finding that I didn't despise him like I'd wanted to. Days spent realizing he'd risked his life twice that day. Once when he'd jumped into the ground with her, and the second attempting to harness the power of the stones. Power no witch dared harness, other than his brother. The gods had never meant that power for one witch to control and doing so risked death.

He had taken his brother before a council of witches to be dealt with, the punishment severe, his life taken in a gruesome way that turned even my stomach. Ernan didn't seem bothered by it, nor that his brother was dead. If anything, he seemed relieved.

"Days?" Gemma asked, choking on her water.

"That's attractive." I wiped a line of drool from her chin. "Sexy even, but don't turn me on. You're in no condition to fuck, and you won't be until your strength is back."

She pouted, but it wasn't a serious pout. I leaned over and took her bottom lip between my teeth, playfully nipping it before I kissed her.

"You may want to freshen that mouth up before you kiss Ernan with it. I can deal with your bad breath, but he's a bit of a pussy when it comes to that kind of stuff."

She pulled me back to her, kissing me again, and I lost myself, wishing I could keep her this way and savor this moment. But I couldn't. I'd done a lot of thinking while she'd been asleep, enough to know what needed to be done.

"You're leaving me again," she said, her eyes creased.

She knew me well enough to read my thoughts through just a kiss.

There was no need for lies, no need for deception. "Yes."

Sadness deepened the amber, turning her eyes a darker shade of brown. Her fingers wrapped in the material of my shirt, a desperate attempt to keep me there, one I would have given into if I hadn't made up my mind.

"You can't leave me again, Hunter. Every time you leave, it hurts. My heart can't take any more."

"Shhh. It won't have to. I won't return. This is where you need to stay. With Ernan, not me."

She sat up, her eyes wild, her grip tightening. "No, it's not. I'm a traveler. I live for being on the road, for the adventure."

"And that life is one you shouldn't have. Circumstances forced it on you through my father's actions, mine, and Breck's. You deserve someone who will pamper you, worship you, treat you the way Ernan treats you."

"I need someone who treats me the way you treat me. You own me, Hunter."

"Not all of you, Gem. I'm not sure I ever owned all of you. You went to him first in those woods that night. You trusted him before you trusted me because I betrayed you. He never has, he never did, and he never will. I've done nothing but hurt you. You're better off with him. You're safe with him. And your heart is safe with him. I'll only break it again, like I always do. I've never been good with fragile things."

"I'm not fragile," she said, tears behind her eyes.

"I know, but your heart is. I won't chance damaging it again. Let Ernan heal it. Let him be everything I can't."

I took her hand, removing it from my shirt, her grip slipping slowly. A tear fell from her eye, and I stopped it with my finger, leaning over and kissing her one last time. Saying my last goodbye.

"I love you, Gemma. I always will."

"Hunter," she whispered against my lips, "please don't leave me."

Her plea sent the shattered pieces of my heart breaking into even smaller slivers. "You no longer have to beg, Gem."

"But I like begging you."

I chuckled as I kissed her, dragging my lips from hers in a drawn out move as I memorized the feel of them. "Then never beg again. You're too powerful to beg, too beautiful when you do. So you save that. It's my one thing I get to keep."

I rose, letting her hand go and watching as she drew her legs to her chest, holding back the tears I could see welling. My fingers brushed her cheek, my eyes taking in her amber eyes, her strawberry locks, the beauty of her one last time. And as her lips trembled, I turned my back on her and left. Never looking back, for I knew if I did, I would falter and return to her.

LEAVING Gemma had been the hardest thing I'd ever done. Every time I left her had been hard, but this was the worst. I knew this was the end. She had Ernan, and he would replace me. As I'd left the room, her silence had been an enormous weight that followed me through the castle. I didn't turn back, and she didn't come after me. We both knew this was how it had to be. Fate had torn us apart time and again. We weren't ever going to live happily ever after together, and I had to accept that, as did she. She was in better hands with Ernan. Protected, safe, pampered, treated like the gem she was. All I could do was hurt her.

Mounting the gorgeous black steed I'd discovered wandering the dead forest, the same that had helped take down Breck, I turned from the castle and rode. I didn't care that the horse was Ernan's. He'd taken Gemma. I could take his horse.

I passed through Spindara, steering clear of the Endless Forest, and made my way to Simeril, indulging in ale and women on my way. The ale numbed the pain, the women not so much. No matter how many I took, I couldn't escape the hold Gemma had on me. By the time I made it to Simeril, it was only the ale I was indulging in. When I wasn't thinking of Gemma, imagining what Ernan was doing to her, my thoughts wandered to Mera. When

I'd left to face Breck, I'd thought if I could defeat him, I would free her and live my days with her. The two of us were the same, both needing to escape from something. She from the prison Breck had caged her in, me from the heart Gemma had caged. Neither of us could escape the bindings, only given that temporary moment of reprieve when our wounded bodies had been one.

But Breck had taken her from me. And his brother had taken Gemma.

I motioned for the barmaid to bring me another ale after downing the remains of my drink. She gave me a brazen smile, bending over the table she was cleaning far enough for me to get a clear idea of how well-endowed she was. For just a moment, I thought perhaps suffocating in those tits would be a pleasant release from the dull ache that sat in my chest.

"It won't help, no matter how nice her tits are."

A man sat down at my table, blocking my view. A man whose voice haunted my dreams. Dreams where Gemma turned to him each night and not me. He dropped his hood, his mismatched eyes evaluating me too easily. "More ale won't help you either."

I leaned forward, gritting my teeth. "And what will help? Because I've found nothing that does, and I've sucked on plenty of tits and ale since I left Laviak."

"Of course you have. Because you need a replacement for Gemma, and there is none." Her name was like a punch to my gut. I hadn't muttered it since I'd left her with him.

"I could have had a replacement," I groused, the ale talking. I'd lost count of how many mugs I'd had while waiting for my next hire to show. The note had come the day before that a man wanted my services to deal with a situation with his woman. She'd fallen for another man, and that man needed to be dealt with. I hadn't killed for hire in a few years, but given the circumstances, I was ready to gut the man no matter what the pay was.

"No, Mera wasn't a replacement."

I dropped my mug to the table, the echo of it loud. "How—"

"Mera knew the rules. She would never have stood up to Breck if she hadn't had a reason. She must have cared for you greatly if she risked her life."

"We found a common ground," I mumbled, looking down at my empty mug and wishing the barmaid would return.

He gave a chuckle. "Her ass wasn't too bad, either."

I couldn't help drawing my eyes back up. "You slept with Mera?"

"I've known Mera a very long time. She was an enchanting witch. There were times Breck had her follow me before I made Laviak my home. And during those times, I may have indulged the offering she made in exchange for information. It wasn't a hard bargain. She was alluring." He sat back, his eyes lighter. "But she wasn't Gemma."

"No, she wasn't." Crossing my arms, I leaned back, asking, "What are you doing here? Have you come to rub it in that you have my girl? That you won?"

"Ha, I didn't win. We both lost."

A rush of terror grabbed hold of me. "What's happened? Is it Breck again?"

He put his hand up, shaking his head. "No, no. She's safe."

Relief washed through me, and I let out the breath I'd been holding. "Then what is it?"

"She needs you."

"Too late for that. She made her choice."

"Did she? From what she told me, you made it for her. Chivalrous and unusual for you, but you did it all the same." I glared at him, my ire rising. "And now, she's miserable."

"Not fucking her correctly? I told you she likes it hard."

His lip curved to a snarl, his fist gripped so tight I wondered if he'd try to punch me. "She doesn't like it hard with me. That's you. And that's the point. She needs you—"

"So, you're giving her to me?"

"No."

I stood, my chair pushing back loudly. "Then leave me alone."

"You agreed to take the assignment. Now sit your proud ass down and listen to your payment."

"Fuck," I muttered, dropping back down. "You're my fucking buyer...again?"

"I know you better than you think, Hunter. If it wasn't women to lure you, it was money and a reason to kill."

"So I get to kill you?" I joked, liking the sound of it.

"I'd like to see you try. No, Gemma loves you, and I can't take that from her. I won't. But she loves me, too. And if you take me from her, she'll be just as miserable as she is now."

"What are you proposing if killing you isn't on the table?"

"A truce."

I eyed him, seeing the seriousness in his eyes. "A truce?"

"Yes. We both love her and neither of us wants her hurt. We need to accept that we're both part of her heart and to keep her from one of us will only destroy her."

I gaped at him, resting my arms on the table and leaning closer. In a hush I said, "You want to share her?"

He ran his hands through his two-toned hair, a defeated look on his face. "I don't. But I don't think either of us has a choice."

"I'm not sharing Gemma with you, witch boy." The snarl that accompanied my words was loud and timed just as the barmaid placed my ale on the table. She scrunched her eyes and looked between us, backing away slowly.

"I'm not a witch boy, asshole," he groused, moving so that his face was over the table and close to mine. Anyone watching would have thought we were about to wrestle, and I wasn't certain we weren't. "I'm a sorcerer who could snuff the life out of you in seconds. If it weren't for Gemma, I wouldn't waste my time on you and your stubborn, aggressive, sex-obsessed ass."

"I'm not stubborn."

"But you won't argue the rest?" he asked, sarcasm coating his words.

264

"No, I won't. If I didn't like sex so much, I wouldn't be able to make Gemma come as easily as I do."

He glowered at me. "You're not making her come anymore. I am." He stood and threw a pouch on the table. "Go buy yourself a whore or, better yet, fuck the barmaid and waste the money on ale. I don't know why I bothered."

He walked away abruptly, leaving the other patrons to stare at me. I grabbed the pouch, noting the full weight of the coins inside. Damn him for even coming to me, bringing Gemma back up when I'd been drowning images of her for weeks. Unsuccessfully. Not even remotely. His presence had awoken the pain, shaking away the dull numbness that had shielded me from it. I missed Gemma like I never had. I wanted to touch her again, to feel her kisses, to weave my fingers through her strawberry hair, to just hear her voice if that's all she allowed me. I didn't know how long I could last like this, how many months or years I could endure now that I'd had her. Before, I could live, never having touched her or known the sound of her cries as she fell apart for me. But now, those memories threatened to collapse the very man I was and leave nothing but a shell of him.

"If you ask me, you should take his offer. You're a mess, honey. Ravenous and hungry, never sated, no matter how many women like me you take," the barmaid said, giving me a warm smile. "I would have enjoyed letting you take that need out on me, but I don't think it would have helped you. She must be something to have the two of you so enchanted."

"She is," I answered slowly.

"Then go, before he leaves, and you never see her again. Sharing her is at least having her, and it's a lot better than what you have now."

I rolled the bag of coins around after she left the table, her words resounding through my mind. Could I share Gemma? Share her body and her heart, her cries, her climaxes, her laughter, her smile. I longed for any of those things and even having one of them would be satisfying, but all of them every night again, even if those things were only half mine?

Standing, I walked over to the barmaid, took her in my arms, and kissed her. I dropped the bag of coin in her shaking hands and ran from the tavern with only one thing on my mind. Gemma.

CHAPTER NINETEEN

HUNTER

Y ou're an asshole," I said as Ernan snatched my piece, winning the game yet again.

"No, I'm just smarter than you."

I grumbled, controlling my urge to stuff the board and pieces down his throat. Instead, I rose and paced, rolling my neck as I stretched out the kinks from sitting so long.

"Shouldn't she be here by now, so I don't have to deal with your angst?" Ernan complained, leaving his seat to reset the board.

"No," I answered, rubbing my neck. "It takes days to travel through each realm, and the stones needed to be replaced in just the right way to satisfy the gods and restore power. You were the one who told her that. Although I don't know why she had to go by herself and leave me with your broody ass."

"She had to go so I could sneak off and make love to her without having you riling her up." The daggers in my eyes should have killed him, but without magic like his, all they did was make him chuckle. "You can deal with me checking on her. I wanted to ensure she survived the shifters. I don't trust them, even if they gave their word that they wouldn't hurt her."

Ernan had gone to each witch family after the events and convinced them that the witch council had dealt with Breck. He further explained that the council wanted Gemma to return the stones or risk offending the gods further. I still didn't know how he'd done it, but the other witches all feared him enough that they'd agreed to give Gemma safe passage to restore the stones.

"You just wanted me out of the picture."

"That's what I want every day, but you're still here. Besides, you had your fill of women on your last job."

"While you had your fill of Gemma," I groused.

But what he'd said was the truth. Since I'd returned, Gemma had decided I should be free to take whomever I wanted while I worked, since she couldn't be entirely mine. It was a compromise I gladly accepted until I found myself imagining every woman was her and I didn't want to do the things I did to Gemma to any other woman. It didn't give me the same rush. So, I'd opted for my ale and my hand over the next few weeks, realizing she'd tamed me after all, and it wasn't worth resisting.

"Yeah, well, they weren't worth it."

He smiled, something that still unsettled me because it went against the terrifying persona he displayed most times. "No one's worth it."

"That's something we can agree on. Now, since you were such an ass and snuck off to fuck her while I was stuck here, I think I'll take her on my next job and leave you behind. It gets lonely on the road, and my hand gets sore from overuse."

"Then fuck a few women like she said you could. You're not taking her from me for weeks on end."

I wanted to hit him, but it wasn't worth it. Gemma would be angry, and he'd end up giving me a beating with his damned magic. He'd wounded my pride too many times to temp that fate again.

"What are you boys arguing about in here?" Gemma's voice broke our angry stare.

I turned to her, expecting to find her exhausted and dirty from being gone for so long, but she looked beautiful. She had piled her strawberry hair on her head, a few thick strands touching her cheeks and neck. She wore a snug pair of riding pants that emphasized her curves. Her long black boots hugged her calves as tight as her shirt was hugging her tits, which were bunched together magnificently under the cut of her shirt. A small part of her waist was bare, just enough to make me salivate. It had been too long since I'd had her, and I was ready to taste that skin again.

Ernan had her in his arms before I could move, and I cursed him under my breath.

"Just telling Hunter how I like his idea of taking you on his next job, because I plan to accompany you both."

"Are you kidding me?" I said, irked that he was kissing her already. The damned man had a way of making her melt with that romantic shit he pulled. I knew he had a rough side. He'd told me as much when we talked about our prior conquests. But with Gemma, he was gentle, and she loved it. "You sneak away and have her, yet I get to welcome her home after you?"

"I hold the power here, Hunter. Need I remind you of that?" He kissed her neck, his hands drawing down her curves.

"No, asshole. Did you return all the stones, Gem?" I asked, trying to calm the hard-on that was pounding against my pants.

"I did. Each one exactly how they wanted me to." She pushed Ernan away, but he didn't let her go. Instead, he moved behind her, his arm wrapping around her bare waist, his hand cupping her breast. I shot him an irritated look before I set my sight back on Gemma.

Her eyes were twinkling, the amber in them bright as she gestured me forward with the flick of a finger.

"My turn?" I asked.

She nodded, her lips curving deliciously.

"I heard you were a bad girl while you were gone, Gem," I said, yanking her closer to me and further from Ernan. He growled, her resulting shudder arousing me further.

"I haven't touched another man, Hunter. You heard wrong."

I nipped her bottom lip. "I heard a certain sorcerer visited you while you were away."

"Don't hold that against her. I kept her satisfied, so she didn't wander like you do when you're gone."

Gemma's lips pursed. She may have given me permission to play when I was from her, but it didn't mean she liked it. I rubbed along the waistband of her pants, my fingers dipping to linger on her hip. Her lips parted, and I kissed her, my other hand slipping into her shirt and encompassing her breast. She moaned in my mouth, and I dropped my fingers, spreading her legs with my thigh.

"Here we go," Ernan mumbled.

"Don't blame me if you can't get her worked up like I do." I threw him a sly smile, knowing that it irked him how easily she broke for me. I sank my fingers into her, another moan drowning out the complaints Ernan was mumbling. "Were you thinking about us, pretty thing? Or maybe just about me?"

"Gods, yes," she sighed as I twisted her nipple with my other hand. "Every night."

"That's a lie," I said, flicking her clit. She jumped, and Ernan gave me a deadly look. "Fuck off, witch's son. She enjoys the pain when I'm giving it to her, don't you, Gem?"

Her response was a beautiful, breathless one. "Yes." I sank both fingers back into her quickly, my thumb brushing her clit. Ernan pulled her back, and she groaned, telling me he was hard enough for her to feel him. "Please, Hunter."

"Please what, pretty thing?"

"Gods, do you have to make her beg each time?"

"Shut up, or I'll make you hold her while I fuck her. I had

planned to share her because she's wet enough to soak both of us, but you keep it up, and you can watch me."

I saw the flicker of desire pass through his eyes. As much of a softy as he was, he loved it when we were both filling her. Gemma twitched, her legs tightening around my hand. "I don't think so, Gem," I said, removing my fingers, her whine tearing at my raging hard-on. I licked one, savoring the essence that lingered, then brought the other to her mouth, wiping it over her lips. "Let Ernan have a taste. See if he doesn't come in his pants before you do."

He grumbled but pulled her head to the side, licking her lips clean before kissing her, his hand sliding over the breast I'd freed from her shirt. I was determined to bring out the rough side of him. The thought of us both taking her that way was titillating. Smoothing my hand up her neck, I plunged my fingers back down her pants and into her depths, her body quivering as Ernan continued to devour her lips. I squeezed her neck, her lips separating from his when her cry forced her head back.

"Damn you, Hunter," he mumbled, but he didn't let go of her breast. If it was one thing I'd learned since we'd made this arrangement, it was that the two of us brought Gemma to ecstasy in ways neither of us could alone. Her body was quivering, and I stroked my thumb up her neck as Ernan brought his other hand from her waist and tore her shirt from her, freeing both breasts. I sucked one into my mouth, her cry uninhibited as her climax hit. The way her body trembled clawed at my need for her, making it hard not to give up my game and just fuck her.

"That's it, Gem. Who makes you come best?" I asked, releasing her neck and stealing her lips from Ernan.

"You...you both do," she breathed, and Ernan laughed, pushing her pants down and removing her boots.

"Wrong answer, Gem," I growled. "I think you need some punishment for that."

Ernan groaned as I picked her up and laid her on the ground.

Her legs were weaved around my back, but I pushed them aside, spreading them wide and draping my tongue through the arousal that was soaking her. My reaction was uncontrollable, my dick jerking so hard it was painful.

"You punishing her or yourself? Because I'm definitely suffering," Ernan complained.

I looked up at him. His pants were bulging, and he looked about ready to kill me.

"Just take me," Gemma whined. "Please."

"Stop begging him." He hated it when she begged, and it only encouraged me to make her beg more.

I stood, looking down at her glorious body, and wiped my face. I glanced at Ernan, seeing his expression hooded, his broodiness hiding his true thoughts as per usual. The bastard was so hard to read. He removed his shirt and settled between her legs, his face disappearing before I could even react.

"Damn, that was my spot."

"Shut up and go back to making her beg," he mumbled.

Gemma's eyes lit up, her hand reaching for me. Her face contorted when Ernan hit that spot that broke her so easily. "Not yet, pretty thing. You need us to thoroughly punish you."

Her mouth fell open, and I dropped to my knees. Removing my shirt, I let her unbutton my pants, her hand grasping me as she licked her lips. I grabbed her wrist, pinning her hands over her head and kissed her. Our tongues danced playfully, her body wriggling as Ernan continued to pleasure her. Within minutes, her muffled cry filled my mouth, and I swallowed it down, refusing to stop kissing her, even after her body stilled.

Ernan hovered over her, stealing her mouth from me, and I growled at him. We didn't share well, and I suspected Gemma loved every minute of how we fought for her attention. She grabbed at his shirt, peeling it from him before working his pants free.

"You two are not about to cut me out of this," I said, watching as he did his thing, taking my aggressive girl and turning her soft. They sighed together as he entered her, the sound revolting it was so gentle. "Fuck, Ernan, you're getting her out of the mood."

Gemma pushed at his chest, and he rose, still impaling her. Grabbing a handful of my hair, she pulled me to her and kissed me, her hand reaching down to stroke me. I twitched at her touch, hating the control she had over me. "Don't think I'll let you own me like you do him, pretty thing," I said against her mouth, threading my fingers in her hair and pulling her lips from me.

She cried out, and I noticed the change in Ernan's thrusts, the way her cry tore at that darker part of him.

"You may own him, but I own you, Gem. Now ride him and let me use you like you want to be used."

Her moan clawed at my desire, lassoing around my erection, and making it lean toward her. Ernan shoved me out of the way and pulled her into his arms, thrusting hard before he rolled her over. Even he was looking forward to taking her the way we liked to take her. That dark side was coming out to play.

Gemma sat up and I watched her arch her back as she rode Ernan, his hands holding onto her hips in a tight grip. I removed my pants and walked behind her, yanking her hair back, her head hitting my dick. "Time for me to remind you which of us owns you, Gem."

I twisted her body sideways as Ernan held her still and I moved to her side, driving into her open mouth. The rumble in my chest went through my body as she took me deep. "That's it, Gem, get me nice and ready because I'm going to fuck you so hard, you'll soak Ernan's cock with cum."

She whimpered, and I heard Ernan chuckle. Twisting my hand in her hair, I held her still and used her mouth until she was gagging.

"Hunter," Ernan warned. I released her, letting her catch her breath as I watched the saliva dribble down her breasts.

I glanced down at him, giving him a wink before I climbed behind her and pushed her down on his chest. She was breathing hard, but the sensitive prick he was, he didn't take advantage of her. He wrapped his arm around her and softly picked her head up, wiping her chin before kissing her.

"You're a pussy, Ernan."

"And she loves me for it, you aggressive bastard."

"You love every gag she emits, so don't get snippy with me."

"He's right," Gemma said with a hoarse voice. "You were twitching inside of me while he was choking me."

"I told you, Gem," I said, rubbing her ass and easing my tip into her. Her body tensed, so I slapped her ass cheek. "Your sorcerer has a dark side that likes that kinky shit. Now relax and let me make you come again."

She relaxed, allowing me to drive into her ass. Rapture overcame me. The weeks without her sent my release climbing faster than I wanted. But as soon as we began moving inside of her, I knew I wasn't the only one who would topple over the edge quickly. This was my favorite position when I shared her. I'd never taken a woman with another man, and the tightness that greeted me the first time we'd both been in her had sent me reeling within minutes.

I tried not to think about how good she felt, how badly I'd missed being inside of her and how desperately I'd wanted her while she'd been gone. My climax was rising, pushing against the hold I had on it. Gemma shook, her muscles clenching down on us. Ernan's pace increased, forcing my own to match his, but as Gemma shattered, her release hitting her so strongly that she bore down on me, it summoned my body to heed her call. I exploded, Ernan's groan meeting mine, Gemma's scream of ecstasy overpowering us. My climax barreled through me as we both filled her, and only after there was nothing left of me to give did I slip free from her.

Gemma collapsed on Ernan, and I fell to their side. Sliding from his chest, she slipped between us, her hand caressing my face as she laid her head on his chest.

"Gods, I missed you two."

"You didn't miss him much since he was sneaking off to visit you," I groused.

She turned her head to me, giving me a dirty look.

"What? It's true. You owe me some alone time, and I plan to make you beg all night long."

"Keep that to your own room. I hate it when she begs."

"No, you don't. I keep telling you, you're going to emerge from that shell and show her your true side one of these days."

Gemma's laugh drifted through my ears like a soft caress. I took her hand in mine, letting my fingers slide across her skin.

"So, no more solo adventures?" she asked, changing the subject.

"I didn't say that. I don't want him tagging along."

"You're not taking her with you if I'm not going."

I rolled my eyes, thinking of all the ways I could kill him in his sleep and wondering if any would leave Gemma less heartbroken.

"Good," she said, rolling to her stomach and resting on her elbows. She folded her ankles over one another and looked between us.

"I don't think I like that look," Ernan said, eyeing me.

"Me neither. And trust me, I'm always up for a new adventure. What are you up to, Gem?" I asked, suspicious of how cute she was being.

"The witches in Tronekrin have a task for us."

"The wind witches? Those blasted sand demons?" Ernan said, disgust in his voice.

"Yes. They have a pest that keeps slinking through their sand and disturbing their sleep."

I glanced over at Ernan. "Do I want to know how she suddenly knows how to speak to wind wraiths?"

His lips curved into a sly grin, and I shot him a look. I was due some serious alone time with my girl, and I wasn't planning to lose it to his smooth ways.

I turned back to Gemma. "What kind of pest? Like a rat?"

She jumped up, her tits bouncing so that they mesmerized me.

"Stop staring at her tits," Ernan said, punching me.

"I'll stare at them, touch them, and bite them any time I want. Now what kind of pest, Gem?"

I sat up, grabbing her wrist and pulling her to my lap, her giggle music to my ears.

"A little bigger than a rat."

"Gemma," Ernan's voice was stern, commanding even.

"Damned darkness in there, Ernan, and I plan to free that."

"Well, don't do it until we're in Tronekrin." She wiggled from my grasp and was on her feet again. "They have an infestation of rock trolls that have burrowed under their sand, fleeing from the dragons in the far western mountains."

"Rock trolls and dragons?" Ernan asked, his color turning a little paler.

"Yes, we set out in two days, and since you're both coming with me, I'd suggest you get your fill of cozy beds and warm baths." She backed away another step with each word. Ernan's mouth was hanging open, and I was rubbing my head, knowing there was nothing misleading about what she'd said. The dragons had been disturbing the rock trolls for years, hoarding the mountains, determined to make them their own. "I'm going to wash up. If you'd care to join me, I'm not yet satisfied. If not, I'll satisfy myself." She ran off with a laugh, leaving us both in shock.

"Dragons?" Ernan said again.

"They're not the ones you should worry about. The rock trolls shit boulders and if you're under them at the time they let loose...let's just say it's not a pretty sight." I offered my hand out to help him up. "You sure you want to join two mercenaries on their adventures?"

He swatted my hand away and brought himself from the floor. "I'm sure. It can't be as bad as dealing with my brother."

I turned to follow Gemma. "Your brother was easy. It's the rest of this godsforsaken world that's the challenge."

I glanced back at him. He was deep in thought, creases around his eyes. He may have tracked Gemma and me with his enchanted ravens all those years, but seeing our lifestyle from afar was nothing to being immersed in it.

"Come on, our girl needs pleasing, and I'm not about to let her do that herself."

"Dragons?" he muttered, catching up to me.

Shaking my head, I wondered how he'd fare. He had power, which would be useful. Gemma and I had the skills; he had the magic. Between the three of us, it could work. As I entered the bathing cavern, Gemma gave us a sexy smile. We'd make it work, just as we had this strangely twisted and sometimes wicked life we'd settled into. It was worth it for both of us because it came with Gemma, and for the two of us, Gemma was an everlasting candy that neither of us could live without.

ABOUT THE AUTHOR

J. L. Jackola is a writer of love stories with fantasy, darkness, feisty women, and morally gray men. She's an admitted sugar addict with a penchant for anything with salted caramel. When she's not weaving tales, snacking on sweets, or downing her morning cup of tea, you can find her logging miles in her running shoes, watching movies with her family, or curled up with a book.

She resides in Delaware with her husband and three children.

To learn more, visit her website at
www.jljackola.com

Made in the USA
Las Vegas, NV
18 June 2024

91207220R00173